I0760675

I'VE BLED TO BE
Worthy
OF HER.

Own

BEAUTIFUL SINNER SERIES

ELENA M. REYES

SUMMARY

The De Leons are a criminal dynasty.
No one makes a single move in South Florida without our knowledge, and yet, it's not enough.

Not as a man. Not as a boss.

Not when I've vowed to lay an entire country at my little Mermaid's feet.

Every man has a path to walk, and Ivan De Leon's is set in stone. The price to pay for my decisions has been steep, but the gains are mine to claim, and I will. I've killed to be where I am—walked away from the most important person in my life—and now, one phone call changes everything.
Success comes with casualties. Hunger and desperation.
I've bled to be worthy of her.

I broke her heart, but I'll also put it back together again.
My little sirenita. My Amberlyn.

This is a Mafia Romance and as such, you will encounter descriptive scenes of violence and sex. It contains dark elements that some readers might find triggering. These men are brutal and unapologetic, please read at your own discretion.

OWN (BEAUTIFUL SINNER #6)
was written by Elena M. Reyes

Cover Design: T.E. Black

Editor: Marti Lynch

Publication Date: June 9th 2022
Genre: FICTION/Romantic Suspense/Erotica Suspense/Thriller

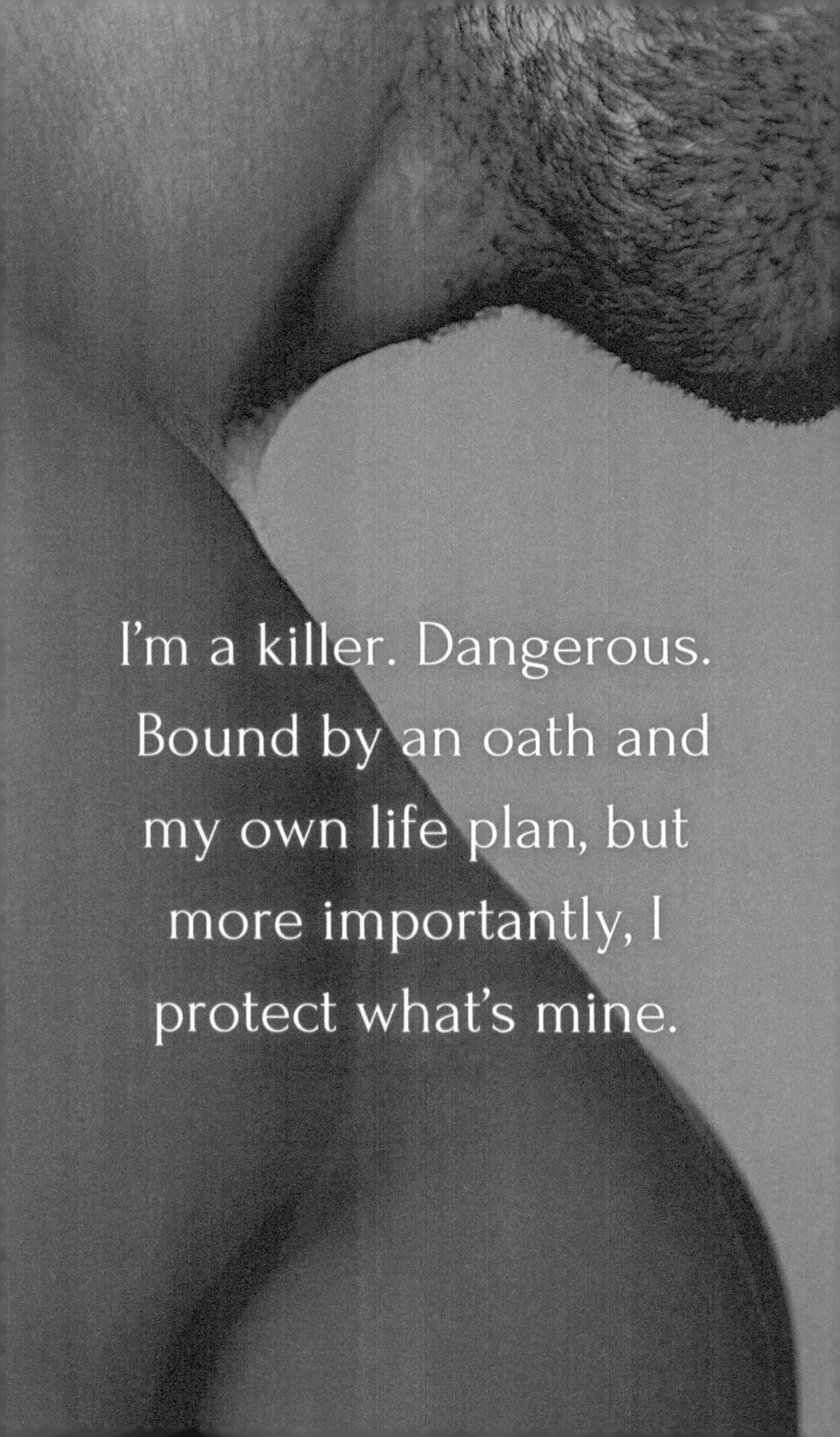

I'm a killer. Dangerous.
Bound by an oath and
my own life plan, but
more importantly, I
protect what's mine.

Beautiful
SINNER

ACKNOWLEDGMENTS

HAPPY READING, MY BEAUTIFUL BABES!!!

Before you get to the crazy/sexy fun; I want to give a huge THANK YOU to my team.
Seriously, I couldn't do this without you.

Emina Ros, Ana Rita, C.M. Steele, Marti Lynch, & Tonya Fox Summerlin; I couldn't have finished this book without you guys. You push me and don't let me doubt myself. You keep me going on days when the writing isn't flowing, and always believe in me when it's hard to believe in myself.

I love you all so much and I'm thankful to have you in my life.

Also, another HUGE thanks to Lyra Parish and her kick-ass sprints. Those things are heaven-sent and so much fun!!!

GLOSSARY FOR SPANISH & CUBAN SLANG:

Sirena/Sirenita: Mermaid

Viejo/Vieja = Old Man/Woman

Mierda = Shit

Chivato = Rat/Snitch

Coño = Fuck or Damn

Bebe = Baby

Cabron = Fucker

Mamajuana =
This Comes From The Dominican Republic And Is Made By Combining Rum, Red Wine, And Honey And Soaking The Mixture With A Special Tree Bark & Herbs. The Color Is A Deep Red, And Some Say It Tastes Similar To A Port.

Singao = Fucker or Asshole

Hijo de Puta = Son of a Bitch

Que Vola = What's Up

Acere or Asere = Friend

Tio/Tia = Uncle or Aunt

Salsa Rueda or Salsa Casino =
This style of salsa dancing originated in Cuba. Here, the couples form a large circle or rueda, and they execute turns, steps, and patterns in unison to the calls of the singer or leader.

NOTE FROM AUTHOR

When I started this series in 2019, I pictured the De Leon brothers as Cuban males with a Latino family dynamic; the crazy cousins and funny parents and the get-togethers that never ended. Because no one parties like we do; what starts as a barbecue never fails to end like a block party. LOL

Writing these books hit me with a bit of nostalgia I wasn't expecting. I was born and grew up in Miami, and the places and people within these pages are me and my stomping grounds. My friends and family. And sure, the whole crazy-mafia aspect is fiction and for fun—an escape—but the longing to see where your family comes from is real.

So, I dedicate this to the people that were never able to visit the places your grandparents talked about while reminiscing. To the countries our parents left behind to give us a better life.

And lastly, to my Abuelos—my Mima and Pipo—may you always rest in peace. We never got to make our trip to Cuba, to the city you were born in, but I plan to do it with Mom someday.

Elena XoXo

Chapter 1
IVAN

THE CUBAN MALECON is beautiful at night.

Havana is nothing short of paradise.

And more so as its citizens come alive beneath the stars. The area from one end to the other is full—people young and old are dancing and singing, sharing with each other what they have even though it's illegal to do so by the government's standards.

They decide what you eat and when.

They decide what kind of business you are allowed to own.

You can be arrested for something as simple as speaking your mind.

There are no liberties here, because freedom means *they* lose power.

Those bastards sit comfortably inside the national palace and hold court surrounding a ridiculous round table, giving nightly discourses on a nonexistent threat that's dangerous to only one percent of the island's population. They fear everyone outside this country, and projecting that same emotion is how an abuser stays in control of a situation.

I'm the real threat within their midst.

And while I understand the notion that I hold no moral high ground, there are limits you don't cross. My family doesn't take kindly to abuse, not of innocent people, and their day of reckoning is coming.

In my grandfather's name.

In my grandmother's memory.

On the series of digits that grace our family's wrists in honor of a man who fought against oppression and demanded freedom.

Patria y Vida. Country and Life.

Their day is coming. The people here can taste it.

Smiles spread across those socializing near me, a few catching my eyes here and there while pretending it's just another hot summer night. The stone-built embankment runs for five miles and is an attraction that pulls in tourists and citizens alike; they come to relax and enjoy the cooling cocoon of never-ending sea mist while making deals.

The legal kind. The ones solved in alleyways and away from the military police who seems to be absent tonight.

This evening, though, those visiting the island have been warned to stay inside the National Hotel just a short walk from here. And while they watch from the windows and lobby, I stand right within the sight of the large fountain of said establishment in my black jeans and shirt with an old pair of combat boots on my feet. The tattoos on my arms and neck should be enough to pick me out of a crowd.

I'm not hiding.

The president knows I'm here and waiting.

A few feet from me, people begin to clap in key, keeping in tune with the salsa playing on someone's old-school stereo. It's loud and full of life, even catching the attention of a few vintage cars. The taxis are empty except for one driver, who passes and honks while a group of twenty-somethings begins to dance in a rueda formation.

They move in sync, turning to face their partners while staying in step. The count is the same as your standard salsa, but quickly changes when the couples begin to execute choreographed moves that are interconnected with each person—turns and dips and the occasional trick where the men lock arms in a circular pattern and the ladies sit atop their forearms.

The circle breaks when the song's chorus does, and those near us cheer.

Moreover, I find myself nodding along to the beat, humming low, when I see him. The man isn't wearing his normal military uniform, choosing instead to blend in—his guayabera and dress pants combined with a pair of dark aviator glasses are meant to make him seem harmless. It fails.

He's anything but.

A killer can sense another.

Those around me also take him in. They know who he is and what he's capable of.

General Ortega smiles at a woman not far from him, trying to seem nonchalant before moving closer. And to keep up his charade, I bring the bottle of Cristal beer to my lips and take a deep pull while looking at those still having a dance-off.

Ortega doesn't disappoint when he stops beside me, facing the same way. "You're playing a dangerous game, De Leon. One might say you're overstaying your welcome."

"Am I?" After another sip, I tip over the rest over his feet and soak what I'm sure are expensive moccasins. "I had no clue."

His face reddens, hands clenching at his sides. "What do you think all this will achieve? You're no one's hero, asshole. Instead, you're putting marks on innocent people."

"And you care about these people?" We both know he doesn't, and I snort, waving at an older man that I consider to be family sitting on the embankment's edge. He's my mermaid's uncle and one of the many eyes and ears here. "My, General, you're as corrupt as he is."

"And you're not?" I'm not blind to the way his right hand slowly reaches his hip—to the tight grip he now has on a small pistol. "The De Leon family has more blood on its hands than I do. A criminal should never point fingers, kid. That's something your family should've taught you by now."

"Is that so?" Turning my head, I meet his beady eyes and smile. Fucking idiot has fallen right into my hands. "Do tell me how to run my business. How should I bow to you?"

Two of my men give me a nod from over his shoulder, coming a little closer while those watching do the opposite. They make more noise, celebrating, while Junior brings out a syringe from his pocket and stands at the ready.

There's enough sedative in the small dose to knock him out and transport him without issue.

"Scum like you always ends up on his knees with a mouth full of steel, tears rolling down your cheeks. President Rodriguez won't be gentle either; he wants to see you choke and beg for mercy."

"What else?" His vitriol is unimaginative at best. Pathetic. "Will I be forced to kiss his feet?"

"No, but your puta will."

"You're wasting my time, Ortega. Say your piece," I say, and while on the outside I'm calm—my smirk in place—the ire within is barely contained. This is something every man in my position deals with at one point or another: the threat to a loved one.

My girl. My mermaid.

It's a test. Not my first either.

It also gives me a sick sense of pleasure to watch his composure slip a little at my nonchalance. He's expecting yelling and curses, for me to react with violence while I'm sure his men are nearby. Another mistake, and at this point, I'm going to tally them up and deliver my reprimand before I snap his neck.

"You're egotistical now, Ivan," he spits out through clenched teeth, voice low as to not attract attention. Ortega's not entirely stupid; he knows I have people here, but he just doesn't know who is who.

Is it the old man clapping?

The mom holding a rum bottle tightly in her grasp?

Or the young man kissing his girlfriend?

Any one of them is a possibility, but not the case this time.

"Will you ever finish explaining yourself?"

"I'm going to personally shove my gun against Amberlyn Ibarra's head, cabron. I know her schedule, where she sleeps, and who her family is here on the island. Working in that bail bonds office near the police station won't protect her from us." With two fingers, he taps his temple and smirks. "Our reach is just as deep as yours."

"So that means your wife and son in Curacao are fair game? What about the whore you keep here…Barbara, is it?" Tilting my face a bit, I give him an innocent shrug. "I'll bleed them both dry and then make you drink it, Ortega. Don't get cocky with me. That mouth of yours is already going to cost you dearly."

"Listen here, hijo de puta—"

"No one calls my mother a whore."

"Fuck you and your..." A snap of my finger and Junior stabs the needle into his neck before he can finish, injecting the concoction into the great general's system and then stepping back. "What the hell was that?" He brings a hand up to the pricked area, cupping it while frantically looking around. Eyes wide, he stumbles within a few seconds and mumbles something. It's unintelligible, but I'm sure a few curses were insinuated.

His hands dig at his side, but they're more than likely asleep and just keep dusting his sides.

I take his gun and phone, dropping the latter and stomping on it. The screen shatters, and he tries to say something but fails. Words come out, but they're garbled and my men shrug, not understanding the idiot either.

I'm sure it's some insult either way.

"What was that? Did you say something?" I grab Ortega's arm when he stumbles again, while my other guard, Israel, takes the opposite side to steady him. "Inebriated and while on duty. So irresponsible, General. Such a grave mistake, too."

There's anger in his eyes, so much hate, but both roll back and he slumps completely against Israel. The entire ordeal lasts but three minutes at the most. Those around us clap when he loses consciousness, still pretending, and I tilt my head toward the newly restored Ford Fairlane parked a few feet from us. The driver is my personal one while on the island and has his orders:

No stops until on the family compound.

And as they move toward it with the passed-out general, the crowd follows. Covering. They block the view and most of the street, the party growing while all traces of them being here is erased within a blink or two.

I'm left behind to stroll off at a leisure pace with a smile on my face.

President Rodriguez made a huge mistake today.

Never show your hand ahead of time.

Never leave your messenger without proper protection—men who can't be paid off.

Never threaten a De Leon or his girl.

Chapter 2
IVAN

"WHAT THE FUCK!" General Ortega sputters, coughing up the old water from the hog pen Israel threw at him. He's alert at once, eyes screwed shut as I'm sure something nasty fell in there. "What's going on?"

I don't answer him. Instead, I sit back and get a little more comfortable.

We've been inside the family compound for a few hours now. The drive here didn't take long; our estate is located west of Havana on a private stretch of land not far from the Mariel port and with the gulf as our backyard. My abuelo made the first move to own property here, more for vacation purposes, but my father transformed the land into a fully functioning colonial monstrosity with a twenty-four-hour staff, a small airstrip—and a private jail at the back end away from the family communal areas.

No neighbors for miles.

No questions asked.

Only one way in and out of the premises.

We also have access on and off the port without bypassing security, something that worked perfectly fine—smoothly—until my guest's master became greedy. That doesn't sit well with me or Thiago; their fear, while attractive, can lead to stupid decisions made by the heads of this country.

I'll kill every one of them first.

Another rancid-smelling bucket of water is thrown on the near-naked man, the rivulets dripping over the side of his gurney and onto the floor. The noise isn't loud, but just enough to rouse the attention of the other residents of this land.

I've always been an animal lover, just like my viejo and his father. Working the land and tending to them is relaxing, a decompression from our day-to-day operations. It's also one of the reasons I've decided to move here permanently in a few weeks.

There's a freedom here you don't have in the city.

My brother can rule the 305 while I overthrow a government.

The Mariel port will continue to be our gateway to Miami. Our products enter and disperse from there, while I receive and account for everything here. It's how I pay back what I owe him while also following my own path.

Two bosses.

A few partners.

One familia.

To be worthy of her.

Moreover, we have plenty of livestock here, from cows to chickens, a few goats, horses, and lastly, hogs. Large ones. Hungry ones. The kind that always stay near the rear of the building and I moved their pen closer because of it, with a back door that lets them in and out.

The noises alone haunt those staying here as our personal guests; the shivers and soiling of themselves is quite disgusting. I'm used to the fact but do bite back a grin at the look that overtakes Israel's face.

Junior isn't fazed, though. Not when Miguel, his father, has worked for the family for years and is trusted. The kid's come into his own in the last few months working with me. Steadier—sure of himself—and has earned the right to move up in rank.

However, the newer of the two soldiers, Israel, a recommendation from Luna's uncle from his time with the Miami Police Department—his rookie partner before making the mistake of trusting another officer—is a different beast. That man took a small bribe from a celebrity needing to make the evidence against him—the drugs and guns confiscated in his possession—disappear.

Israel did a favor and caught the false charge.

He's been out now for a few months, and I offered him a position. His knowledge comes in handy.

"Hose him down." At my voice, Ortega turns his head in my direction and blinks. The wild hogs know my voice and a bit of screeching follows, causing the general to pale, body thrashing against the restraints. *Idiot.* "Calm down before I bring them in."

"Done."

"Cabron, let me go." Israel and Ortega speak in unison, but it's the general I'm focusing on.

"One second." Bringing two fingers to my lips, I whistle and the noise travels through the large space. It's sharp enough for my pets to quiet down, and I tilt my head to the side. My eyes never waver from him. "Now explain. Why would I do that?"

From my periphery, I see Israel walk toward the cell next to the hose spigot and step inside. He's in and out within seconds, dragging a piece of machinery behind him.

Smart man.

Ortega's tries to shift his face, to see what's happening, but

Junior is quick to yank on the hospital bed's lever and force a half-sitting position. There's a grimace on his face right after, uncomfortable as the action stretches his arms back with how they're bound. It reminds me a bit of the way my hands were tied down before my gallbladder surgery a few years back.

Strap on each wrist. One across his waist.

He's unable to move much. In pain.

You have no idea what real pain is yet.

He swallows nervously, wrists trying to yank free. "You have no idea what you've done."

"I do."

"My president will never…*fuck*!" His scream reverberates through the large space; it's loud and full of pain. A small yet hard jet of ice-cold water smacks him in the face and he splutters, choking as the strength digs into his flesh.

Torturous. Painful. Such a thing of beauty to watch how something as simple as a pressure washer with enough PSI can be wielded as a weapon. Like butter, it will slice through every layer until reaching bone, and even that can be cut through with ease.

Israel is taking it easy on him.

I look over and give him a nod. "Increase it."

"Yes, boss." My guard fiddles with a button at the front of the machine and the fine-tip nozzle, shifting it a little to the right. In the background, I can make out the whine of my hogs; they dislike being kept out, but for now, remain calm.

They've been taught to be patient. They'll be fed soon enough.

"I'm going to kill every member of your family! Hijo de puta!" Ortega screams, trying to shift away, but Junior grips the back of his head. With strands of hair between his fingers, he holds the general still while I simply watch. From the right corner of his lip to his cheekbone, the skin gives way and the blubbering that follows is truly pleasing.

Makes me smile.

Blood pours from the wound and drips onto the plastic mattress, pooling a bit before his life's essence adds to the stained floor. It mixes with grime and filth and the more direct the hit digs into his cheek, I begin to see bone.

I raise a hand, and Israel pauses. "Rinse the rest of him."

"They'll be here any second now to rescue me. You're fucked, cabron."

"I'm shaking in my seat." My monotone grates on him. There's still plenty of fight in him, and yet it dies the moment Israel opens the water again. Pain fills his expression while rivulets of red run down his body, limbs shaking in their confined seat.

There's no true direction to my soldier's cleaning method. From the soles of the general's feet to his chest, there are quick and semi-deep slashes now littering his frame. He's been reduced to nothing in a matter of minutes—from a high-ranking member of the Cuban military to a whimpering pussy.

How fast the mighty fall.

Once deemed as clean as can be, Israel shuts the machine off and retakes his place a few steps back. Junior does the same, but not before bringing a rolling cart I have behind the bed to within my guest's line of sight.

Nothing covers the top, and the two items ready for me make him pale a little further.

"Talk." And while he swallows hard, his red teeth chattering a bit, I remove my shirt and lay it behind my chair. While he mutters under his breath what I know is a prayer for help to whatever deity he believes in, I shake out my arms and crack my neck.

I've been docile.

Keeping a tight leash on the monster within I've come to accept.

Because everyone has one. This evil that lurks beneath the surface, fighting to overthrow rationality, and I embrace mine.

It's been a part of me since my childhood. From the first time I witnessed my father slit a man's throat after catching him trying to sell us out, I knew we were different. That our norm isn't for everyone, but I learned quickly to thrive in it.

To protect what's mine. Just like every member of the De Leon family, we bleed for each other.

"Fuck you." That's his response, the open wound on his face gushing a bit with each word. Funny.

"Not my type, old man." Next, I remove the bracelet and Cartier watch on my wrist but leave the family ring. It's a thick gold band with our last name branded over the top, and right over the letter "D" there's a yellow topaz representing my mother's birthday. A bit eccentric from the rest of the family's; I consider my design to be a little more brutal when meeting a direct hit. My letters are 3D and with specific points meant to embed in the skin, tearing through flesh with each sharp edge. I flex my hand and then close my fist. "But you did mention someone I will kill for. Who's watching her?"

"I'd never betray my boss."

"You will." My steps are loud, the soles of my boots sloshing on the wet floor as I stop at the foot of his bed. He's following my every movement, fighting back the urge to cringe when I raise a hand and scratch my jaw. "Last chance."

"I'm not afraid." Yet his bottom lip quivers.

"Let it be known, you made me do this." Without another word, I walk to the tray and pick up a metal meat tenderizer. It's a little heavy in my hand, a very old kitchen tool my grandmother used and now I possess. She had a purpose for it, and I've eaten many meals where the meat melted in my mouth after a good pounding.

Now, though, it'll break down a different kind of flesh.

I make my way around him, from his head to his feet, pausing right beside his bare feet. These we did not strap, but he won't have much movement soon.

The first strike is right over his ankle, fast and hard, and Ortega disappoints me greatly.

His cries fill the space, and my animals outside once again get rowdy. Now, they thrash against the door, banging their bodies on the metal, and the sound nearly overthrows the general's pain-filled yells. I hit the same spot again, and then again, taking in how quickly the skin cracks and a fragment of bone slips through the opening.

He's also quick to pee himself once again, and I crinkle my nose. *Disgusting.*

My hard eyes meet his and still, his cracked lips remain quiet. I nod and trail the red-stained metal up his shin and pause at the knee. Waiting. Being hospitable enough to let him talk, but nothing comes out.

Nothing but whimpers of pain.

So be it.

The tap against his knee is a caress, very light, but I do enjoy the way he jumps in place right as I drop the mallet.

Holding a hand toward Junior, I wait for the next tool. This one, much like the previous, is meant to hurt, but the cross between hammer and sledgehammer is still comfortable in my grip. Easy to swing—same weight—yet the handle is smaller, fits better in my palm.

My fingers close around the sturdy base, and I arch a brow.

"He's the brother of a detective in the Miami P.D." Ortega licks his lips, shivering a little harder than a few minutes ago. "That's all I know."

"Liars never make it to the kingdom of heaven." The saying is funny coming from a man like me, but my mother drilled that into our heads while we were young. Be an asshole, a murderer, but your words should never be questioned.

A real man always keeps his promises.

Always admits to his wrongs.

Sins shouldn't be hidden under a veil of bullshit.

It's why the people here accept us so freely and without blinders. We give, provide, and protect, but discretion is the cost. Never bite the hands that feed unless you're willing to pay with your life.

De Leons value loyalty, not ass kissers.

They want to rise against and demand their freedom.

A mutual agreement that both sides respect.

"I swear it on my daughter's life. He lives in Hialeah."

"Hmmm." That's all I give him right before swinging the large steel hammer at his right, then left knee. One blow shatters both and he vomits, the sight of it slipping out of the facial wound quite disgusting. "Give him some water."

Ortega blanches, and the shivering increases. "Please stop."

This time, I don't hold my snort in. "Thought you said you weren't afraid of me?" Flicking my eyes to Israel, I shake my head when he goes for the power washer. "A bottle for the man, por favor."

Israel rushes over to a stack of room-temperature twenty-four packs and pulls one water out. He's back within seconds and untwisting the cap before placing it against Ortega's lips. And while the asshole rinses his mouth, spilling more than anything, I take my place near his opposite hand.

I'll give him points for having somewhat of a high pain tolerance. Laying the head of the hammer over his knuckles, I clear my throat and Israel retakes the bottle and dumps what's left on the floor. Ortega opens his mouth to say something, too, but I shake my head.

"I've given you every opportunity to come clean. To die with dignity and not as food for my pets, but you failed time and time again. So I'll do what you didn't and share with the class what I know."

"Ivan, I—"

One hard smack to the face shuts him up; Junior's hand is poised for a second hit. "He's Mr. De Leon to you." Nothing else is said, and I bite back a smirk. His father would be so proud of him right now, of how far he's risen in my ranks since starting at the bottom. "My apologies, boss."

"None needed." And when the guard retakes his place a few steps back, I refocus on a pathetic Ortega who looks nothing like the man threatening me earlier. How quickly that changed; he's a bloody, beat up, and scared man now. "From now on, all I want from you is a *si* or *no*. Do you understand?"

"Si."

"Good boy." Ortega doesn't like the praise, and his eyes narrow a bit; I remedy that by breaking the middle knuckle of his hand. Once again he screams, a sob catching in his chest, and I wait for the man to find his composure before continuing. "Now, tell me if I'm wrong." His nods are quick, as is the low *yes*. "Detective Jaime Uriel and his brother, Dalian, are related to President Placido Rodriguez through his current wife. They're her nephews from a dead older sister and have been in trouble a few times in the past. The only reason Jaime is on the force, and a detective, is through a heavy donation and favor called in by your boss to the now-deceased Miami mayor."

"Si." There's no hiding the surprise on his face.

Did he really think us to be so stupid? "Dalian is watching my mermaid."

"Si."

"They focused on her since she's not publicly claimed yet."

"Si."

That burns me with guilt; I put a marker on her head due to circumstances created out of duty. *This one's on me, and I'll right the wrong no matter what it takes. My sirenita will be safe.*

"Dalian and Jaime have asked for Amberlyn and control of Miami through us, as payment." Ortega hesitates and I break two fingers this time, my blows consecutive until the pressure of each direct hit makes the digits burst. "Did President Rodriguez offer those two singaos my girl on a silver platter to be at their service, if I was brought to my knees? If Rodriguez got control of the De Leon operations in Cuba?"

The pain is getting to him, and his eyes roll back. The blood loss from each injury is substantial.

"Bring the pigs in."

At those words Ortega perks up, eyes wide and full of tears. "I'll tell you everything. Just please...end this."

"Answer the question."

"Yes. He offered them the girl and a cut of your Miami profit while he controlled Cuba's."

"Why?" Below him, there's a lever that'll lower the bed and I kick it, bringing him closer to the floor. At just the right height, while Israel heads toward the only other exit. And when he does, the squeals become deafening. Animals are intelligent, can sense things we don't, and know what's coming. "Explain why a man like him would make such an ignorant move."

"Rodriguez is afraid." Ortega voice is low, and spit dribbles over his lips. He's slipping, but not as fast as he'd like. "People are talking, and the citizens are beginning to organize. He blames your family for this."

"So control the head of the beast, and the body follows."

"Si."

"Thank you, General Ortega. Your wife will be compensated for your brave contribution." No sooner has the last word left my lips than the sound of hooves fills the space. They rush to where I stand but don't touch me; instead, they focus on the bloody body atop the hospital bed with no way of getting out.

Not that he fights it. Instead, his limp body heaves in breaths while his eyes close.

The animals surround him, fighting for a bite, and I walk out when the bed topples over and every piece of him is covered by a hungry mouth. Nothing will be left behind, and once I cross the main entrance and step out into the warm night sky, those horror-filled screams of his disappear.

Tonight confirmed what we already knew.

It also cements my worry for Amberlyn and the life she'll have with me.

I can't allow her to be hurt.

"Placido Rodriguez has no idea how dangerous a man like me can truly be."

Chapter 3
IVAN

"STAYING AWAY is an impossibility."

Using my copy of her house key, I walk in and only pause long enough inside the entryway to remove my clothing. Every single article is tossed aside like the nuisance it is, my boxer briefs holding the proof of my need for her in the few drops of pre-come that have slipped from the angry tip.

I'm hard for her. Always am.

I've been away for too long.

Cock in hand, I walk to her room at the end of the hall like the asshole I've become. Her door is open, a habit of hers from my late-night visits, and I kick it closed as gently as possible in my state. It's been four days since I've seen her. Too many, and I know this sensation—the feigning crawling under my skin—will only get worse when I move to Cuba.

Our expiration date is close, and she'll hate me soon enough.

I have no other choice, but first, I'll rid Miami of every cabron who's a threat to her safety, moves I've already put into motion.

After yesterday's incident with Ortega and then leaving instructions with the crew there, I flew right back onto American soil. Then made one small stop. Some people need motivation, and the proof of our talk is more than likely on my shirt or pants; a single punch broke his nose, and the idiot was a bleeder.

However, all other thoughts die when my eyes find her lithe body atop the bed, face down and with a strewn sheet across her ass and upper thighs. She's bare underneath that sheet; I know this just as I know she's already slick between her thighs.

"Motherfuck," I groan, voice low, yet she sighs in her sleep as if she's heard me. There's also the way she lifts one knee, further opening herself to me. Gifting me access to what I need to satiate our hunger—that primal fucking need for each other.

Amberlyn can't fall asleep without coming first, and I suffer when it's not around my cock.

She's a restless nymph with an appetite that rivals my own, and I live to see those light brown eyes roll back and her lips part in a seductive gasp—the feel of those thighs trembling around my hips and the sweet way she digs her fingernails into my back, leaving her mark behind.

Then, there are her toys for the days I'm not around. They range from the simple to light bondage—from intense to hours of teasing—and yet her favorite is the replica of my cock we made together two years ago. What started off as a joke, a teasing birthday gift, became a badge of pride for me.

Her desire for me makes me feel like a god.

Her need gives my life a purpose I didn't know had been missing.

Leaving you here is going to be so hard, sweetheart. My eyes adjust to the dark, the only source of light coming from the half-closed blinds. They give me just enough illumination to find her wand a few inches from her sleeping form, and I bite my lip. There's no doubt her pussy is wet and wanting. My favorite dessert. *Fuck, she's perfect.*

Taking the few short steps between us, I pause beside her nightstand and turn the bedside lamp on to the lowest setting. It's just bright enough for me to appreciate her beauty without waking her, and I walk back to the end of the bed and place a knee on it, and then the other. The mattress dips under my weight and then settles, slightly shifting as I crawl over her soft skin while removing the thin sheet. I'm careful and keep every touch lingering, maintaining most of my weight off while I enjoy the view beneath me.

She's soft, tan skin and long dark hair with bright scarlet highlights. Red has always been her signature style, from the fire-engine tones she used in her teens, to the now jet-black strands with delicate pieces in a lighter devilish shade that frame her delicate face.

The contrast suits her, even if I miss the way it looked in high school.

At least she keeps it long and wears it loose just the way I like it.

I reach out and grab the end of one loose curl and twirl it around a finger. "One day, I'll make everything up to you." It's my endless vow each time I come to her in the dead of night, the blood of an enemy still fresh on my skin. Not that she'll push me away. Instead, she loves me harder and then helps me wash away my sins. "My beautiful little sirenita."

I've kept my little mermaid a secret all these years.

The first time I kissed her was a week before Thiago turned himself in to the authorities, and I used her crush to our advantage. The first time I made her mine was on the anniversary of his imprisonment when she came to me, tried to make me feel better when my own guilt threatened to drown me, and I've never been able to put a stop to this affair.

Amberlyn has become my only. I won't touch another woman.

But I also know what this life does to people, and I owe her more than this. Than being selfish.

"You'll bear my last name one day. Take over the world with me." Lowering my body against hers, I keep her face down while positioning my cock at her entrance. Her skin is soft, and I shiver at the first contact; she's my heaven. There's also a hint of awareness in her, a small arch to her back and a pucker of those plump lips, but she's not fully awake and resettles. Nevertheless, when she's like this, all warm and vulnerable—this is when I lower my own guard. Love her the way I'll fight to make our future. "But not yet, sweetheart. Just give me a little time."

"Time?" Voice low and groggy.

Ignoring her question, I rub the engorged head of my dick against her opening, just letting her feel me. Letting her wetness coat, kiss my flesh. "You're so wet, bebe."

"Always for you." There's a hint of a whine when I slip the head inside and pull out. Once. Twice. Three times. "You're mean."

"And you love it."

Amberlyn smiles at that, eyes shifting toward the alarm clock, but stops when I nip her shoulder. *She doesn't deny it. Me.* "What time is it, papi?"

"Too early for you to be awake."

"But I need you." Those four words and her pout destroy any self-control I have left. Her body shivers beneath me when I grip her hips, pinning her against the mattress, but it's her face I focus on when I thrust inside. One smooth stroke and I'm nestled deep within her warmth while a peaceful smile graces her mouth. *Beautiful.* "I've missed you."

"*Fuck.*"

"I know." That curl of her lips stretches right before she bites down on the plump flesh and I watch the shift, memorize each sigh and whimper as if it were a slow reel—a private movie just for me. Time slows down as I take her body, never pausing the pump of my hips, fucking her hard and rough, yet all I can focus on is her pleasure.

On making sure she can feel me for days after. Craves me when I'm not here.

I'll never accept her loving someone else. *Wait for me.*

"You're my perfection, bebe," I hiss out after she clenches, her walls gripping me so fucking tight. Her wetness coats me, the sweet nectar grazing my balls and upper thighs and spreading more with each piston of my hips, the drops making a mess of her too. Amberlyn tries to move, to meet my thrusts, but my weight doesn't allow it. I'm in control of her pleasure. "So wet and tight just for me."

"Papi, I—"

"Tell me, Sirenita." I slam in deep and hold still, just giving her small flexes of my cock. "Tell your papi what you need."

But I know what she's missing. What she always craves.

"You. Always you."

Three words now sit on the tip of my tongue. Everything within me demands that I tell her, but I bite them back. The day I say them, I'll be hers. Can't have it any other way, and that can't happen until I settle my responsibility to our family.

Thiago gave up so much for us, and now it's my turn.

I need to eradicate any threat to her happiness.

One day, baby girl. I promise. "Good girl," I say instead and pull out slowly, dragging my thickness against her pulsing walls. The cool air of the room greets my slick cock. My balls feel heavy, but I'm focused on the way she trembles in anticipation.

And I let her while kneeling behind her. For a few minutes we stay like this.

No contact. No relief.

But it doesn't last long; I can't help myself and unconsciously start running my fingertips up the back of her legs, taking my time while following the path to her asscheeks. Her hips gyrate against the bed, a sweet offering, but still once I grip them tightly again.

With both hands I pull her up and onto all fours, her holes clenching—searching for my dick. *Motherfuck, she's a work of art. So mine.* My hand comes down over her right cheek and then left, a little harder than I intend, but she responds with a moan and a wiggle of her hips. I smirk at the sight. At the pink highlight of my palm on her flesh before slamming back in.

I don't pause or slow down or so much as breathe while fucking in deep and pulling out, riding her hard and fast like she craves. Because this is what we live for. What we both need.

It's a clawing need that tears us apart and then rebuilds the pieces into one being. One heart.

The slap of our skin is loud inside her room, obscene, but not enough.

I need more.

So does she.

A growl rips from my throat as I bring a hand to her neck and bring her up with me into an almost sitting position. My cock is nestled deep, her back to my chest, and the sharp breath she lets out at the change in angle brings a smile to my face.

Still not enough.

For a second my eyes shift to the wand not far from us, but jealousy licks at my blood. Toys can be fun when we play together, but not this time. Right now, there's an overwhelming urgency to imprint my touch into her every pore. Her soul. So I cup her with my other hand, fingers against her clit while pumping in and out.

Almost punishing as I take what will always be mine.

No rabbit or dildo or wand could ever replace what only I can make her feel.

Three deep strokes and she trembles.

Two rough circles over her trembling bundle of nerves and she tenses.

"Come, bebe. Give me what's mine," I hiss out, the sound primal and hungry. Her walls tighten at the demand and her back arches. It's near difficult to move, but I refuse to stop. Instead, I keep a rough pace while rubbing her clit. While watching the tantalizing way her bigger-than-a-handful tits, dusky-pink nipples hard, bounce for me.

"Papi, I'm so—"

I cut her off by tightening my hand on her neck, my lips now at her ear. Nip the shell. "Motherfucking come, love."

Amberlyn's mouth opens, but no words come out; she always comes so prettily.

She spasms, pussy so tight I bottom out and let her massage the come from me. And she does. These small gyrations and the feel of her juices coating—bathing my length—rob me of my senses. Everything within me throbs. So painfully sweet.

"Oh God," she moans, and brings one of her own hands down to cover mine cupping her. Amberlyn presses it harder, moving my fingers over her while pleasure rips me in two, and I empty every drop inside her warmth. We're a mess. Satiated and tired, but I refuse to pull out and slowly lower us down to the bed again and turn us so I'm curled around her much smaller frame.

No words are exchanged.

No declarations.

I know this always makes her sad, but I can't offer more until I make things right.

Soon. I mouth against the back of her head once I know she's asleep and pull her closer. Let my touch soothe her for now. Let it calm down my own urge to forget my commitments and drag us to Vegas to tie us together.

My phone beeps then from down her hall and I exhale roughly, closing my eyes for a few minutes. It pings again, Thiago's tone this time, and it's a reminder of what happened yesterday and the mess left behind by our livestock.

I should've reported to him the moment I stepped back on American soil.

I should've told him I'm okay and my crew is safe after visiting my forced-to-snitch friend, but I didn't. Couldn't. Not when the only thing that mattered was seeing—being with my sirenita and making sure she's safe and taken care of. Knowing someone has been watching isn't the issue, because as Dalian follows her, I have a tail on him. He'd never get close enough to touch, much less savor the sweet scent of sugar cookies that surrounds her.

It's that someone dared covet what's mine.

That's an insult to me as a man.

I'm a killer. Dangerous.

Bound by an oath and my own life plan, but more importantly, I protect what's mine.

I give myself another few seconds to soak up her sweet scent and warmth before slipping from the bed. Quietly, I fix the sheet and cover her before leaning over and kissing the corner of her mouth. Amberlyn doesn't stir but sighs, and it pains me to walk away once again.

One day I'll openly love and cherish this beautiful woman and lay the world at her feet.

I just need time.

"Be patient with me."

Chapter 4
IVAN

SHE'S CLOSE.

I can feel her warmth from across the near-full room at my brother's rehearsal dinner two days later, and it's an indulgence I've imbibed in when I know it's wrong of me to do so. That I'm going to hurt her in the end, at least for a while.

Our timing is off. Our paths have a different timeline, no matter how much I want her.

Wish it were different.

Not when I'll be leaving the country without a return date after my brother comes home from his honeymoon. When after tomorrow

I'll be in the shadows—out of sight— and life past those stolen moments is an impossibility until I remove all threats. But then again, that's always been the problem when it comes to Amberlyn. *My little sirenita.*

I can't say no. I let our relationship remain hidden for so long, and now, when I'm ready to settle down, I'll become that asshole once again.

She is my weakness. Always holds me captive with a mere look or the sinful curve of her plump lips.

I'm powerless against her. Can't fight the ever-present need for a taste.

Like every time I sneak into her bed, and all the ones before that. Because she's mine.

And because I'm also the man who adores her, yet leaves her just as fast when responsibility calls.

"If it's the last thing I do, I'll make us right. But first, I'm going to break your heart again."

The moment I crossed her threshold, front door closing behind me, I pulled my phone out and pressed number two. It rang twice before an audible click and then the rustle of wind met my ears. "You okay?"

"Yeah. I'm good." I look down at my shirt and there's a few specks of blood on it, not much since all it took for a friend of a friend to talk was a single punch to his nose and a warning: speak now or never do so again. *"Just had two stops to make before checking in. Everything good on your end?"*

"Jaime moved near the old courthouse in one of the new high-rises. Close enough to discourage and get around on foot if need be. Couple of precinct buddies also in that building."

"Coincidence?" Tucking the phone between my ear and shoulder, I make sure her lock is engaged and check the position of my camera there.

"Nothing in life ever is."

"Agreed." I walk down her corridor and toward the stairs, fore-

going the elevator. Amberlyn lives on the eighth floor of a posh building with good security, but it's easily hacked. I've done so a few times, and I refuse to leave a single trace of my visit behind. Only we know. "One in Hialeah and the other in Downtown."

"Good source?"

"Ortega was very cooperative near the end, and the chivato confirmed."

My brother's snort is loud. "I bet. Heard you fed the masses."

"I did, but there's more to this. Their moves are either overconfident or—"

"You think there's a third location?" Thiago interrupts, voicing my thoughts. Then there's what sounds like a lighter sparking from his end. He pulls in deep and exhales just as quick before repeating the process a few times, the action telling me it's a cigar. More than likely one I brought back from Havana on a prior trip. "It'd make sense."

"My money is on Homestead. Enough land and farming to hide."

"Hmmm." For a few beats he's silent, but I know my brother. He's thinking. Planning. "I'll send someone out tomorrow to have a look."

"There's also the matter of the fake money to take care of. That purchase was to test us."

"You think?"

"Yes." This one's personal. He knows Dalian...went to school with the brothers. "I think he's involved to some degree and also runs out of Hialeah."

"How soon?"

"Three nights."

"You think he'll bounce?" Another exhale, this time slowly.

"It'd be difficult to move his printing equipment. The machines are old and the local he's using is free. Owned by a friend who likes free weed and uses the fake currency to remain high."

"The connection to the brothers must be deep." Not a question.

"Henry's nothing more than a nuisance hiding behind false

protection, brother. The man is a low-level criminal with the stupid penchant for paying for his purchases with his homemade cash." His mistakes are something I'll make him pay for before his last breath. Just like I'll be seizing his operation and assets—real money and the counterfeit as payment to the De Leons.

"Okay. Get some rest." On his end, the sound of a woman comes through the line asking if everything's okay, and a pang of jealousy hits. It doesn't happen often, but I also can't stop it. I want what he and Luna have. How simple it is. The comfort in having someone on your side. "My wife says to behave and make the right choices in life."

A bark of laughter escapes me, yet that tightness in my chest intensifies. "I'm a model citizen. Honest and honorable."

"Sure, you are." Her voice comes through clear, and I know he's placed me on speaker phone. "Should I ask around and take a poll?"

"Be my guest, sis."

"Dork."

"Takes one to know one," Thiago grumbles something on their end that's too low to hear, something she giggles at, and I know it's time to get off the line. "All right, children. I'm done for the night."

"Three nights." Not a command. He wants confirmation.

"Yes."

"Brother, you look like a man about to commit a grave sin," Thiago says from beside me and I look over, then follow his gaze. I'm not surprised in the least to find his focus on his soon-to-be wife; she's his world. "Regret looks good on no one. Remember that."

"Never said it did." Luna's standing beside my own obsession, the women laughing at something another member of their group said, and I can't help but watch *her*. From her short stature to the sexy little black dress and stilettos from a designer she loves. The latter are in the same color, a gift from me on her last birthday—she rewarded me by wearing them and nothing else while escaping for a weekend trip to a private beach in the Gulf of Mexico.

I'm also aware of the way my hand rubs across my chest; I'm

hurting us both. Moreover, I can't help but to be drawn in. There's something so pure about Amberlyn's carefree expression right now, the hint of pink on her cheeks tugging at my own lips. "But I have my own redemption to navigate when the time comes."

"Amberlyn's a sweet girl, Ivan." A waiter stops to Thiago's right, extending a tray with two drinks on it and a note. My brother picks up the small paper first and chuckles before pocketing it. "That woman will be the death of me."

No need to ask who he's speaking about. There's only one person in this world that can make him bend the knee. "How much is this going to cost?"

"Depends on how much we piss her off in the future." At my raised brow, he sends a wink in her direction. She's watching him too. "Luna wants us drunk. Says she needs new blackmail material for later."

"Jesus." The women in this family are insane. *But then again, I'm the same for Amberlyn.* A sobering thought because the truth is, I can't. Not yet. Taking her with me would be irresponsible, and while my men are loyal, until I have complete control over the island—more importantly, its government—I'd never put her in that position. "Then so be it." Taking both drinks, I knock them back while he raises a brow. "I'm sure she'll have plenty against me soon enough."

"Two more." He tells the waiter while grabbing the glasses in my hands and placing them back atop his tray. "And she's already pissed at you."

A rough exhale leaves me, and I scrub a tired hand down my face. "How many people know?"

"Those that matter." Thiago shrugs. "We also don't agree. Never have."

"I don't need you to." It comes out much harsher than I intended it to, my jaw clenching. The phone in my pocket also vibrates then, and it reminds me of each text I've ignored in the last forty-eight hours. All hers. All make the guilt worse.

How's your day going? ~Mermaid

I'm all sore and achy today. ;) ~Mermaid

Is everything okay? ~Mermaid

You know where to find me when you're ready. ~Mermaid

"True, but we care enough to warn you that there's an unnecessary huge wall you're about to slam into." Thiago's hand on my shoulder gives a squeeze, while his head tilts in my mermaid's direction. "What you do with the warning is your problem, but don't complain afterward. You crash and burn, and I don't know if she'll ever forgive you."

"Luna forgave you."

"She also knows I love her more than my own life." His eyes meet mine, his expression deadpan. "Can Amberlyn say the same?"

The answer is no, and that burns like acid in my chest.

I've kept her in the background for different reasons, possibilities that change depending on the scenario, but they're all the same. With Thiago in jail over a bullshit setup, I took over and as such, the threats toward me were large enough to crumble a weaker man.

She's seen the evidence of my car being shot at.

She's been there for Luna during Thiago's incarceration.

She agreed for the time being to silently stand by my side until normality returned to our family.

And maybe it's been selfish of me to keep us private and without the attention that comes from dating a De Leon, but not once have I given her a reason to question my loyalty to her. I'm also man enough to admit we can't continue like this.

I just need a little more time. "Cuba isn't Miami, Thiago. We both know what I'm walking into." While South Florida has always been great for business, the product we move through the island is vast and fast, two things others covet. Things are ever changing, the demand for the black-market weapons procured overseas and the perico Casper provides has quickly become a large percentage of our last quarter's earnings, and this has brought unwanted attention our way.

The US government is sniffing.

The Cuban regime wants to fuck us in the ass.

Many here want to make a name for themselves.

More so, I won't allow anyone else to pay for my sins. She won't become a casualty.

I'm here to bend both countries over and discipline them as one would a child.

The De Leon hand feeds and takes and will fuck you over without a second of remorse.

"It's a mess and won't be easy, Ivan, I'll give you that. But, keep in mind that the women in our lives are resilient and have bigger balls than we do at times."

"And stubborn," I mutter, but he hears. Fucker chuckles, too. "That woman is going to make me pay."

"Agreed." My brother shrugs. "They know who we are and accept it."

"I'm not doing this to be an asshole. They threatened her because of me, and keeping her close will only feed their ammunition—they'll know how important she is to me. All I want is her safety—just that."

"What if she walks, Ivan? That's always a possibility."

"Her feelings for me are what I'm holding on to." Have to. "Besides, between political greed and civil unrest—the kind of anarchy that will burn the country to the ground using the accelerant I provide—it's unsafe either way. I won't take the chance. Not until our family has complete control over the island."

"What about the threat here? Are you going to tell her?"

"No." My eyes narrow, the warning clear. He might be slightly older, but I've never been one to take his shit or be afraid. Respect is one thing, but betray me and I would kill my own blood. "That's not up for discussion. I want her free and happy and untouched by this. They'll also be dead before I go."

I'd never forgive myself if she spent a single moment of her life afraid or watching over her shoulder. That's my job.

"You forget just how much of a grudge she can hold." The waiter returns then with our drinks, and we each take a tumbler. He takes a sip and grins. "Remember when I crashed her car?"

This time I snort over the rim. "Is she still giving you the stink eye for that?"

"You know it's more than that." And I do know because every once in a while, my mermaid gives me the same hard look. What we asked of her all those years ago, to make Luna believe that Thiago cheated, still grates on her. More so, because I'm the one that talked her into it, knowing and using what was a crush back then. "Don't lose her. Don't repeat my mistake."

Without another word, my brother walks away and toward his fiancée, taking Luna's hand before pulling her out of the room. The reception fills with chuckles and his not-so-subtle flip off from over his shoulder is typical, but I'm more riveted by the quick look of longing that flits across Amberlyn's face.

It's there. So much sadness.

But then it's gone just as fast, and she says something to those around her that makes them laugh before excusing herself. I follow her every move; she's heading toward the bar when my father intercepts and then points toward the dance floor.

"Old fucker," I say, shaking my head as he twirls her three times fast before those around them join. There's an old-school merengue playing, and people begin to sing, moving their hips to the beat while my viejo begins a series of fancy turns. The faster he goes, the louder my mermaid's giggle get before passing her over to one of Luna's family members from the Dominican Republic.

My smile drops and body tenses. The hold I have on my glass is close to cracking it, even if they're doing nothing more than dancing. Even if the distance between their bodies is respectful.

Yet I hate it. Any male close to her.

I know him. He's an okay guy, a few years older than my twenty-six and with good hacking skills. He's related to the bride's mother somehow—I think a stepbrother—as Luna's grandfather continued having kids very late into his life.

They're a total of twenty-four kids with only sixteen alive.

They're also not the closest, something my sister-in-law wants to remedy by making him a part of the wedding party.

For the next two tracks, I don't move from my spot. Can't. Not when every single part of my DNA demands I pull her away from him and show the world she's mine.

And almost as if she senses my reproach, Amberlyn's smart enough to take a step back after the next song ends, and with a smile and turns to walk away. His eyes stay on her, though. I see the interest, but I'd never allow it.

Not in this lifetime. Not ever.

"Long time no see, primo." Mirabel slides in beside me, pulling my attention away from my girl. There's a sassy grin on my cousin's face, a tell of her amusement. "Did she finally kick you to the curb?"

"Your shoes are hideous." I have no clue if they are, but the woman is in the fashion industry and takes that shit seriously. And at the moment, if pissing her off gets her to shut up, so be it. The last thing I want or need is more meddling. "Dress is last season, too."

"Asshole." Not annoyed—there's too much mirth in her tone.

"Everyone has one." Bringing the glass to my lips, I knock back what's left and wave the empty tumbler toward a waiter who nods. "Speaking of...where's your husband?"

"No argument there, and at the bar talking shop with all the old men in attendance."

"What is he selling now?"

"A '56 Chevrolet Bel Air."

"Nice."

"But enough about cars and husbands..." she trails off and I look over, catching an arched brow and a smirk on her lips. "When are you going to make it right?"

"You're fishing for something that doesn't exist."

"Or am I calling it as I see it?"

"No clue what you're talking about." It's then I sense my sirenita close. The heat of her stare is coming from my back. There's this rush of something I can't quite explain whenever she's near, this electrical wave that settles on the tip of my cock and it flexes—fucking throbs against the zipper of my dress pants. My entire body, every muscle, tenses, and I exhale deeply. "Quit trying to annoy me."

"Sure I am." Mirabel's eyes scan the room, searching for something, and then she flicks them back to me. She knows. As Thiago said, they all do. "Where's red hiding now? I thought she'd be over after her spin on the floor. She asked me for information on this trip—"

"No clue. Don't care."

"Stop that. You love it."

"She's nothing more than an obligation." My voice is loud enough that it carries, and the low gasp from behind me makes my chest ache. *Please forgive me, little Sirenita. Trust me.*

Chapter 5
AMBERLYN

"S*HE'S NOTHING more than an obligation.*"

Heat flames my face, and it's from shame.

Embarrassment.

The way my heart breaks as I watch the man I've loved since my youth talk about me as if I were a nuisance and not the woman he slept with a few nights ago. But then again, I've always been an idiot—weak—when it comes to Ivan De Leon.

I've given him my first kiss.

My virginity.

My heart.

What has he given me in return?

I should leave. Move or curse at him for the pain currently building inside my chest—for how hard breathing is—but instead, my high-heeled feet are rooted to the marble floor beneath me a few feet from him. I'm unable to do anything but lean against the large pillar and watch as he laughs at my expense. The sound feels like the cut of a sharp blade, and not one of the usual butterflies he brings present.

Always from the fringes. It's what I've always done.

Since we met as teenagers and every time he's asked something of me, I've been there but kept at arm's length. Unless he wants to warm my bed, and then and only then, am I given affection.

A glimpse of what could be.

At first, that was okay. We agreed that the timing was off and with his brother in jail, it was best to wait. I stood by his side through numerous attempts on his life, rough nights, and dangerous meetings —I never questioned my place with him until recently.

Our relationship should've been celebrated once Thiago came out, yet I'm still waiting months later.

I've been a constant. I've been a fool.

"Don't be an ass, primo," Mirabel chastises, lips thinning as she cuts him a glare. "But then again, men are always this stupid. You'll be just like the rest, crying when Amberlyn walks away."

"She'd never." Not a single ounce of doubt, his voice hard. Almost angry at her audacity. "Her love keeps her here."

"But I'm learning to hate you just as much." The words leave me in a whisper, not that he can hear inside of the large ballroom where the rehearsal dinner with the entire De Leon family is taking place. Well, more party than dinner for Luna and Thiago's big day. The wedding is tomorrow at their home. The family is full of happiness and laughter is all around me, yet I feel as though someone died.

Suddenly, sweat dots across my forehead, and the room feels too small.

Too many people.

My shame feels as though it's on full display and they all know.

Fuck, I need to get out.

"You look like you're in need of an escape."

There's no need to look over; I've known this woman just as long as anyone else here. "I do, but I'll be fine. This is your day and..." my head tilts and eyebrows furrow "...didn't I watch Thiago nearly drag you out a few minutes ago?"

"He just needed a little sugar."

"Sugar?" Voice low. It's hard to get the words out with the huge lump in my throat.

"What can I say? I'm so sweet." Luna snorts, her arm slipping through mine as she begins to pull me away from Ivan. Each step is painful, yet my lungs expand with a much-needed breath, and I don't look back no matter how much my heart demands that I do.

No one stops us as we make it outside and onto a large balcony overlooking the warm South Florida waters. And even though the daytime hit a high of ninety-five, the cool seventies gracing our skin now feels suffocating.

Maybe it's what happened. The harsh truth that's been smacking me in the face for years and I've been ignoring, hoping, and praying they were false. That he did feel for me and not that I'd played a game and lost; a mere puppet to be moved as he pleased.

"Talk to us." I've been so lost inside my head that I never heard Natasha follow us. I also have no idea how we ended up near the far left and sitting on a large stone bench a few feet from a set of stairs that leads to a small garden and then the beach. "What did Ivan do?"

"I'm not sure what you're talking—"

"Cut that out, chick. You two aren't as careful as you think you are."

"I'm pathetic." *How long have they known?* A self-deprecating laugh slips before I can school my expression, and my best friends each grab a hand. It hasn't always been this way for us; at first Luna thought Thiago cheated—another place where my feelings for Ivan made me stupid—but meeting them has been the biggest blessing.

They're the sisters I never had. "And nothing that should surprise me. I should know better by now."

"Love makes us do and accept crazy things," Luna says, and when I turn my head in her direction, I find the striking brunette looking out into the late evening sky. The smile on her face is one I've seen before and holds a tinge of anger, but it's pushed back just as soon and replaced by understanding. "The men in this family are nothing more than stubborn idiots, I swear."

She's been where I am. Hurt by one of the brothers.

Yet, Thiago did what he did out of love. Out of the need, barbaric and stupid as it may have been, to protect her even if it meant pushing Luna away. His idiocy came from loyalty, while Ivan's is fake.

Obligation: I'm nothing more than an easy lay and someone he has no choice but to put up with.

"Or maybe I've been too blinded to see and accept my reality." The first tear rolls down my cheek, and they squeeze my hands in solidarity. For a few minutes we stay in silence, enjoying the clear evening sky, but it doesn't last long as I fight to swallow a sob. Hurt is churning and turning and is quickly becoming ire. At me. At him. At fate for putting him in my path. "I can't do this anymore," I say after a while and close my eyes, fighting to control my emotions. My voice is low. Breaking. "Can't keep putting myself in a vulnerable position when who I wish would catch me, always lets me fall. I'm worth more than that. Deserve more than late-night visits and empty words."

"You do," they say in unison, but then they give me the silence I need.

For the most part, I'm not the most emotional person. I'm more of a suffer-in-silence type of person, and yet, he's my exception. Ivan is a weakness I need to shake off, but in the past have failed to do so time and time again.

So while the clock sounds in the distance letting us know we're at the top of the next hour, I make up my mind.

I'm done.

Fuck him.

The sigh that leaves me is heavy. "Please don't hate me, Luna."

"I'd never, Lynnie. Just tell me what you need me to do."

Turning my face toward hers, I open my eyes and meet her stare. Luna's giving me a smirk that says she'll get her fiancé to punch Ivan if I ask, and all I can offer back is trembling lips and more than likely ruined makeup. "You want me to have his—"

"I say we slash his tires." Nat cuts her off, and I shift my attention. She releases my hand before clapping once, then stands and paces—muttering under her breath while shaking her arms out like fighters do. "What if I add eyedrops to his coffee? Get his mom to serve him liver and onions for a month straight...she'd do it, too. That woman is brutal, and I love her."

I'm nodding, wiping my tears. They don't stop but have slowed. "Maritza is my shero."

"So payback it is? We choose violence?" Nat asks, and Luna laughs a bit. Crazy women.

No whining. No complaints. No hesitation.

It's why I love these two and would do anything for them. Their friendship is honest and giving. Never selfish.

"I don't want to walk down the aisle with him." Even as the words leave me, I can't help but cringe at them. My emotions are all over the place, and between the guilt and selfishness I feel for asking this of Luna, there's also so much relief. Distance is the only way I'll survive the next twenty-four hours. It's how I start getting over him. "I'll do it if there's no choice—"

"Done."

"That easy?"

"Yes." Luna didn't pause. Not one second of hesitation or analyzing. She gives a short, low whistle and Nat quits her pacing, pausing to meet her cousin's stare, head tilted to the side. "Ivan's your new partner, prima. You okay with that?"

"More than. I'll make sure to jam my heels into his toes the first chance I get."

Even with a little bit of smudged liner on my fingertips, I can't help but giggle. "I love you two so much. Needed this."

"You better." An older man I recognize as one of the family's most trusted guards pokes his head out, gets a headcount, but at the glares sent his way, leaves just as fast. Less than fifteen seconds. "That has my Thiago written all over it." The bride rolls her eyes, and we don't argue the truth. The man's the textbook definition of obsessed. I'm jealous of it in the best way: happy for her, but wishing I'd find someone as committed. "Now, Alvin will be your new partner. You know him."

My face scrunches up. "I actually don't. Who's that?"

"Do you trust me?"

"I do."

"Then don't worry, and let's get a few drinks in our system. The night is hella fucking young." Standing, Luna pulls me with her and loops her arm with mine while Nat takes up the opposite side. "Besides, I'm going to enjoy his reaction tomorrow. Ivan is going to be livid."

They walk me down the stairs and to a side door that says *Employees Only* that's unlocked and we step inside, following a short corridor that leads to a bathroom not far from the private party in her honor.

They're quick to help me fix my face and gather myself.

They're by my side when we eventually make it back inside, and I immediately catch his eyes. The honey color seems darker as he takes me in, and it feels like a dirty caress. Everything in me heats; no matter how much I fight the reaction, it's beyond me. Uncontrollable; a need that breaks me a little more as those words replay again.

And again.

Nothing more than an obligation.

"Goodbye, love," I mouth the words, and as if he understands,

Ivan takes a step toward me. One step. That's all I get before once again, I'm given something I've come to expect.

Nada. Nothing. Emptiness.

He'll never be with me in the way I need. Love me with every fiber of his being as I do him.

Instead, the man I yearn for accepts another drink while his unoccupied hand goes inside his pant pocket. It's there for a minute at the most when my cellphone vibrates inside my wristlet, and I know it's him.

The same things he's done when around others; I'm number "1" on speed dial, and it's another means to control me. Keeps me thinking that I mean something—anything—more than what I am:

I'm his duty. Work.

I don't acknowledge it and give him my back, focusing instead on those around me and the drunken group dance taking place. They're laughing and off-rhythm while those who are still sober enough to not join egg them on. It's loud and full of happiness, and I don't want to be here.

"Here, take this and breathe," Nat says from my left, passing me a glass of red wine. "Knock it back, and I have the next one on its way."

"Thank you." Taking her advice, I sip it quickly but not fast enough to draw attention. The robust red is drier than I like, but the warmth that follows gives me something else to focus on, and I close my eyes for a second. It spreads, soothing my nerves a little while the empty glass is replaced. The first sip is a blind one. I just bring the glass to my lips and then snap my eyes to Nat when the sweeter spirit greets my tastebuds. Much lighter, the berry notes in this one is stronger, and I take another light sip. No rush.

The last thing I need is to end up drunk and in bed with him *again*.

That's also when I notice that Luna is now missing.

"Where did Lulu—?" A whooping chorus comes from the dancing group and when I shift my gaze over again, I find the bride and groom are busy showing the older people how to do the Macarena. Well, more her than him. Thiago just watches Luna with amusement while following her lead. “Never mind.”

“I say we teach them how it’s really done.”

“Do you, now?” If she can tell my laugh is flat, Natasha doesn’t mention it.

“I do, chica.” Grabbing my arm, she begins to tug me along and I don’t fight her. “Let’s drink and dance and forget the bad shit for now. Don’t let him steal your happiness, mami.”

“You’re right,” I say and place my wine on a passing waiter’s tray before joining the dancing to-be newlyweds. She turns her head in my direction, never missing a step with a raised brow, and I shrug. “You looked lonely.”

“She’s mine,” Thiago grumbles, placing both hands on his hips but doesn’t gyrate. More like hungrily watches Luna shake hers. “I don’t share.”

His bride blows him a kiss. “Cool it, Romeo.”

Their playful banter reminds me of Ivan. Of that side of him that I see when it’s just us, no work or family, and distractions are limited to our moans and teasing.

So I do what any friend would do in that instance and bury my jealousy deep—shake it off until this is all over. Taking up a spot on the dance floor, I finish this dance and three more after without searching for him. While ignoring the intensity of his gaze that slowly burns me alive. From one song to the next, I keep my pace and swallow down the hurt inside my chest that makes it hard to breathe.

I’m one of the maids of honor and will do my duty.

I will party. I will be supportive. I will live.

And even surrounded, I feel like an outsider now more than ever.

This is the final nail in my love for him.

I’m done.

He’s lost me without ever appreciating how devotedly his I was.

Chapter 6

AMBERLYN

I FEEL RUN over the next morning, and it's not from a hangover.

No. This comes from heartache and self-reproach—from hours of over-analyzing everything we've been through while acknowledging the ever-present truths I've ignored. I'm at fault for not accepting them sooner, for thinking *he will come around* when Ivan's never given me any indication that I'd ever existed outside of the shadows.

I drank but kept it to a low buzz while Luna and Nat subtly watched over me. Their concern is sweet, but at the moment it's unhelpful as it unfurls along with my guilt, and the concoction isn't pleasant. No fuss from me and while they checked on me in between dances, I kept up the charade of being angry—not hurt—into the early morning hours. Instead of crying and venting, I put my feelings aside and did what a good best friend does when her girl is hours from getting married to the man of her dreams:

I smiled.

Laughed.

Hid my emotions.

Were they totally convinced? No.

Did Luna demand I let it out once we were back from the hotel? Yes.

However, I chose to hug her instead and then retreat into the guest room for a night of restless tossing and turning. Because when you're alone at night and without distractions, you can't escape reality and it's a vicious punch to the gut that knocks the air from your lungs.

I've gone from angry to hurt, and then consider taking a leave of absence from work.

Maybe being out of Miami for a few weeks would do me some good. The distance will help me with the ever-present clench in my chest.

Flicking my eyes to the bedside clock, I watch the numbers turn and the bright white lights announce that it's a little after eleven in the morning. Somehow, I managed to catch four hours of sleep and know it's going to be a long day. Luna and Thiago decided on a late-evening wedding, anticipating the all-out party the reception would turn out to be.

Hair and makeup will be here in another two hours, and I sit up against the headboard, try to get comfortable while breathing in deep and exhaling slowly. Right now, I need to get control of myself and my emotions.

The silence today is everything I want to avoid and I grab my phone, opening the Spotify app. Working in the bail bond industry has its up and downs like any job, but what drains me is finding those who skip and put unnecessary financial hardship on their families. It breaks a piece of my heart each time, and it's why I take those cases on personally.

The De Leon family is in business with my family as backers.

It's a mutually beneficial agreement that I've never questioned before. They get easy access to bail out anyone in the organization if needed, and we don't use outside insurance companies or local government programs, which makes it dangerous for those who choose to wrong our clients.

I'm loyal to those paying the bail, and our private backing guarantees the casualties are minor.

It doesn't stop many from trying, but the chase is never long.

Maybe that's the catch. Keep me complacent and easy to agree to just about anything as long as he's touching me. "Is that why?" No. It can't be. Won't accept it, because if I do, I'll hate people I've come to love as if they were family. "Please let there be any other reason. Don't let me be just another pawn."

Exhaling roughly, I choose my work playlist after the app loads and let a soothing classical composition run through me. There's something calming in the low cadence, how each chosen song in this list doesn't have large crescendos in their peak, but more of a soft melody meant to lull.

And it works. I can feel my muscles begin to loosen up and by the third song, I'm running through the day's plans while shutting off my emotions. The stylist will be coming here soon to the couple's home, and they'll set up in the main living room that's been emptied for that purpose. No fuss. No muss.

To be honest, it's kind of cute how Thiago's taken care of her every whim. Flowers, food, and location were all inconsequential when all he demanded is that she slept with him every night. No exception or night before separation as tradition dictates. No overnight planning sessions either; Luna has been by his side every day.

It's also one of the reasons she chose to have it at home.

The woman is as addicted and obsessed as he is.

"I'm never going to find a love like that if I stay here." My whisper travels through the room, echoing back the grief residing within my heart, yet there's also determination building within. It solidifies and almost feels as though it were a real entity—this being that pushes me to breathe in again and exhale my tension.

It's time I accept that Ivan isn't for me.

I need a man who wants to be by my side out in the open and with no stipulations.

Free. Honest. Raw.

My calm lasts as long as my solitude. Until the padding of feet comes closer, and I turn my head in the direction of the closed door. Then I put on my office smile.

The one that greets customers and makes them feel at ease in my presence. *I won't ruin her day.*

My best friends are anything but subtle on the other side, and their muffled exchange would be funny any other day.

"You open it." That's Nat.

"It's my day. You do it," Luna hisses.

"I can hear you," I call out.

Not a few seconds later, the door opens and Nat pokes her head in. "How's it hanging, chica?"

My lips twitch at that, and I can't help myself. "To the left and soft."

"Dork." Luna snorts, pushing her cousin out of the way before padding over to the bed and climbing in beside me. She's glowing. So happy. *I want that, too.* "By the way, Alvin's all set to be your new partner."

"Are you sure? What about the girl—"

"I have a back-up plan for everyone." Mrs. De Leon to-be winks and then lays her head on my shoulder. "Besides, it's a three-person switch and no hassle at all."

"Thank you." This leaves me on a long exhale.

"My pleasure, babes." I'm so blessed to have them in my life. How many women would do something like that, on the day of their wedding no less? But then there's my guilt for creating this problem to begin with.

Another reason to get away; I don't want to burden anyone. "I'm sorry."

"Stop that." She smacks my thigh hard and lifts her face toward mine, eyes narrowed. "I love you, and breakfast is ready. The others are starting to arrive. Just the women, by the way. Thiago kicked out anyone with a penis."

Remorse flares again. Did she ask him on my behalf?

"He doesn't need to do that."

"It was for me," Luna reassures, but I don't believe it. *Does he know? Do they all?* If they do, I know it wasn't because of Nat or Luna. This is all on me. My fault. I've spent years chasing after Ivan like a lost puppy. "The decorators are outside with the planner and with the ladies getting ready downstairs, it would've been too many people. My anxiety was high just thinking about it and Thiago reacted, almost shot Ivan—" At his name, I cringe but they don't call me out on it.

"Anyways..." Nat drags out the word, and I also don't miss the pointed look she gives her cousin. "Everyone's gone but the bridal party and Mami De Leon. They're downstairs and waiting, babes. We're going to eat, drink some mimosas, and get dolled up within an inch of our lives. You in?"

Not a question. More like testing how I feel.

"I am. I'm in need of a lot of coffee, not booze."

"How much are we talking about here?" Luna lifts her head and bumps her shoulder with mine. "Because I have the good stuff straight from Colombia; Alejandro sent it as part of his wedding present. Coffee and money. Can't ever go wrong with the two."

"Like an obscene amount, ladies."

"Obscene sounds good." Nat walks to the bathroom and comes back with a silk robe. My initials are over the right side and *Main*

Bitch 2 is embroidered on the back. I also notice it's just like hers, except she's number *1* by default as her cousin. "There's also pastries and tostadas and churros."

"You had me at pastries."

"I know." She tosses the robe at me, and I catch it before slipping from the bed. "Now let's go. We have a lot to do, and the bride needs to be ready early. We both know Thiago isn't staying away for long."

Closing the wrap and looping the belt, I walk toward the door and then look back from over my shoulder. "My money's on him barging in mid hair and demanding we get out."

"I don't think he'll make it that long."

"Hundred bucks?"

Nat winks, getting that I don't want to talk about me today. "Five hundred and you're on."

"Deal."

"You two suck." Luna's smiling, though. She scrambles off the bed and rushes to the door, smacking Natasha on the arm as she does. In a few strides, she's beside me and wraps her arm around my waist. Our eyes meet and I see concern in them, the last thing I want for her wedding day. "Tell me you're okay, and I'll make sure you win."

"I am."

"And you won't let him get to you?"

"He won't. Promise." *My heart can't take him being close again.* "So let's get you married."

"Yeah." Her smile widens. The kind of look she gets when she's about to be a smartass. "Let's go make an honest man out of Thiago De Leon."

"Are you hiding from me, Sirenita?" Ivan says from behind me fifteen minutes before the ceremony starts. I've been avoiding him, keeping myself upstairs while everyone else mingled or had a pre-wedding drink. I know he's been looking. The constant text updates from Natasha saying he'd grown irritated the longer I took.

And not just from her. His own mother told me as much.

> He's going to crack, mi niña. The De Leon men are all hard-headed, but they have one weakness. You're his. Trust. ~Momma Leon

That came in forty minutes ago, and it still eats at me. Because one thing is speculation, while another is having the proof that they all know.

My shame threatens to consume me once again, but I exhale slowly. *Just a few hours. Luna only needs me for a few hours.* "Not at all, Ivan." Not papi. No sentiment. The words spill from my mouth and they're dry—empty while I continue to stare straight ahead. "Just been busy."

"Hmmm." His deep hum dances across my skin, and it takes everything in me not to shiver. "Is that so? Are we lying to each other now?"

"Isn't that what you've always done?" I couldn't swallow back my bitter response, no matter how much I should've. The shrug that follows is meant to look unbothered, but I think I failed that too. "But that's not important. I've learned my place."

"Turn around." Tone heated. A hint of anger.

"I'm heading toward—"

"Turn around, Amberlyn. I need to see your face, beautiful." And, I do. My feet—body—move without my permission and on my next blink, it's his hazel eyes I meet. "Much better."

"I'm busy, Ivan." Slipping a hand into my dress pocket, I dig my nails into my palm. *Get a grip.* I don't want to be swayed by his good looks and height; at over six feet, Ivan makes me feel petite—like his doll. But then there's the tan skin, low fade, and hazel eyes while the tattoos marking his flesh tell a story I'm all too familiar with. "Can I go?"

"No." Expression calm, he stares at me with a heated intensity that makes my thighs clench. Can't help it. Can't stop it. Not when his masculine scent, this whiskey and woodsy panty-destroying weakness, surrounds me. Not when his eyes darken while roaming over me from head to toe and his tongue slides across his bottom lip. "You look delicious, bebe."

"Now isn't the time."

"The fuck is that supposed to mean?"

"Just that. We're here for your brother's wedding, not to mess around." Ivan swallows hard while his chest expands on a deep breath, but before he can give me some *line* meant to seduce—because I'm weak and want nothing more than to get closer—I turn to leave.

One step. That's all he allows.

Warm fingers curl around my elbow, grip tight, but before Ivan can turn me around again, two people arrive. And because I'm an *obligation* and nothing more, he steps back like I knew he would.

This time, I swallow hard. The act stings. "Exactly."

"We'll talk about this tonight, Amberlyn."

"No. We won't." Looking at him from over my shoulder, I give the man I love a rueful grin. "Now, go find your partner. She's up first."

"You're walking with me." His brows furrow and lips thin. Also don't miss the way his hands clench at his sides. "That's not up for discussion."

"Incorrect." That's when the man I danced with last night approaches. Nat is beside him, and they share the same sly look. *So he's Alvin.* Turning to face them, I widen my smile. "My new partner just arrived."

"Hello again, Miss Ibarra." Alvin's tone is deep and smooth and immediately puts me at ease. He's not interested in me romantically. If anything, he'd be checking out the mother of the groom. The man likes them older, told me as much last night after I caught him checking out Maritza, Ivan's mom.

I also warned him to never do that again. The De Leon men are protective of their women.

He'll never be like that with me. Not like Thiago is with Luna. Like Orlando is with Maritza.

"Hola, Alvin. Natasha." Immediately I lean forward and kiss Natasha's cheek, and when I pull back, she's biting her lips to keep from laughing. *You are so bad,* she mouths while I give a subtle shrug. I'm not doing anything. I'm clear on where I stand for once.

He's not mine.

I am not his.

"So, you ready to strut it down the aisle?" Alvin moves to greet me as I did Natasha, something common for any Latino, when I'm pulled back and into a warm chest.

"She walks with me."

Chapter 7
IVAN

I SHOULD BE happy she's trying to keep her distance.

At ease knowing it'll make the separation easier, but I'm not.

Instead, I'm burning from the inside and have been since last night. *Goodbye, love.* I read her lips, saw the truth behind those expressively warm eyes, and it was a punch to the gut.

My resolve is weak. My need is too strong to contain.

And more so after watching my little sirenita walking down the stairs in a sea-glass, floor-length chiffon dress that complements her naturally tan skin. It's sleek and sophisticated with just the right amount of sex appeal—the halter neckline with the keyhole opening —that draws my eyes to the perky swell of each tit. No bra. Just a thin layer of fabric draping carefully over each, highlighting the way her nipples tighten under my attention.

But then again, they always has.

Amberlyn embraces her femininity and is open sexually without fear of judgement. As she should be. My mermaid isn't promiscuous, but comfortable inside her skin with the right partner…me.

Hungry and sweet. Motherfucking mine.

My eyes travel lower again, and I bite my lip at the high split in her dress, the way the material shifts and caresses her right leg. Smooth skin. So soft. "So beautiful," I say low, unable to stop myself. Even angry—burning with jealousy—I can't help but follow the tease of each curve when she leans over and kisses Natasha on the cheek. There's a look exchanged, a smirk from Luna's cousin at my girl, but then *he* makes an unforgivable mistake.

Alvin tried to put his lips near her cheek.

Over my dead body.

Their conversation is inconsequential to me. Her attempt to walk with someone else, to push me toward an amused Nat, and even the audacity to think I'd go for it, is insulting.

If she wanted me to feel the lash of this strike, Amberlyn won.

Before they can greet each other, my arm is around her waist, her back against my front. No hesitation. That primal part of me—the man who recognizes her as mine—nearly bares his teeth like an animal would.

"She walks with me," I spit out, and they each take a step back.

No one says a word, and I also don't miss the way Amberlyn shivers, how unconsciously she moves in a little closer. Even mad at me she seeks my touch, and it's something I treasure.

One day I'll make it all up to her.

One day it'll be her walking down the aisle toward me.

But then she freezes and tries to step away: a silent rejection. It stings. Her body language says everything she won't verbalize, and I hate it.

Abhor the most minuscule separation between us.

I've hurt her. Again. *There's no other choice. Not until they're all dead.*

Until I can bring their heads to her on a silver platter and then worship at her feet without restraint.

Maybe I should let her walk with him. Every cell in my DNA burns bitter at that thought.

Even now, her cold shoulder is more than I can take.

I've also accepted that living in Cuba while she's here will destroy me little by little. Many will bleed because of it.

"Let go, Ivan." Voice low, Amberlyn elbows me in the stomach, but I don't flinch. She stomps her foot over mine, the six-inch heel digging into the leather, and I smile. I like her a little violent.

Accept it like the gift it is. Means she cares.

"You walk with me, Sirenita. No one else."

"That's not up to you, De Leon," Natasha answers, yet I don't pull my eyes away from the woman in my arms. Can't stop focusing on how good her petite stature fits against my much harsher planes. "Luna decided last night that you'd be better off partnered with me. Alvin will—"

"Will be smart enough to not interfere. End of."

"Not your wedding," my girl hisses from between clenched teeth, the blunt end of her fingernails trying to find purchase on my arm, but the tuxedo prevents that. "Quit being difficult."

"Enough." Lowering my lips to her ear, I let out a rough exhale. We stay like that for a second or two, with me inhaling her sweet scent before speaking loud enough so only she hears. "Do you want me to show you what real stubbornness is, bebe? How crazy you make me?"

"No." A whisper, yet she still tries to move away. That won't do. While the other two watch, surprise on their faces, I turn and move us away.

There's a door that leads to a private weapons room on this level that only the to-be newlyweds and I know about. It's behind a bookcase and opens with the press of a button beneath the third shelf. There's an audible click and then a shift while Amberlyn gasps.

Grabbing the side, I pull it open just enough for us to fit. "Go on."

"What the hell is this?"

"Do you trust me?"

"With my safety? Yes..." those warm brown eyes meet mine and inside them, there's her love, but it's also tinged by the smallest hint of hate "...everything else, though? Not so much."

Fuck, that cuts, but nothing less than what I deserve. *One day she'll know the truth.*

"Please."

"Two minutes." I find it adorable when she tries to take charge.

Amberlyn walks inside and I close the door behind us, adding the extra lock to make sure she doesn't escape. Before I came to look for her, my brother went in search of his bride, smirk in place, and I'm more than sure they'll be busy for a little bit.

It's why I brought her here. Why I don't pause and take the few steps separating us before slamming my mouth down on hers like I've wanted to do since yesterday.

The kiss is possessive and urgent. It holds my apology and her denial.

And more importantly, this time she clings to me.

Her hands grip the lapels of my jacket while nipping my bottom lip before sliding her tongue against the flesh. And while she whimpers and fights me for control, I grip her hips and lift her off the ground, careful to not rip her dress.

Four steps and I'm across the room where a small table is nestled against the back wall. I place her atop it, not once removing my lips—breaking what I know will be the last kiss for a while.

This is a mistake.

I shouldn't.

"Papi," my sirenita moans into my mouth, and it's my breaking point. Between her rejection outside, her anger, and now that moan —*motherfuck.* I'm feigning, my cock aches, but there's a bigger hunger I need to satiate.

No matter how much I want to bury myself deep inside her tight cunt, it's the taste—memory—of her pussy I'll survive on. What I'll fuck my hand to until we reunite.

Because she won't see me after today.

The hold I have on the skirt of her dress is tight, pushing it up and out of my way before Amberlyn's next intake of breath, but it's the way her legs part that I focus on. They spread of their own volition, her warm skin trembling beneath my fingertips as I drag them up her skin at a torturous pace.

Goose bumps appear and she shivers, her fingers never releasing my jacket. "What are you—"

"I need to make you come, sweetheart." It's a barely contained growl, my entire body thrumming with yearning.

"But the wedding." No real strength behind it. Also don't miss how her hips shift a little closer.

Gripping a thigh in each hand, I squeeze and bring my mouth to hers. Just press them, savor her every exhale. "Please."

"I should say no to you."

"Please." One word. My plea.

"*Fuck,*" she moans, nodding once and I drop to my knees, lips against her right knee. The thin fabric is so breakable, delicate like my mermaid, and I carefully push it up to her hips with a gentleness that betrays the demonic thirst inside me.

I want her juices on my tongue. Drying on my skin.

Slowly, I nip her knee and then higher, sliding my tongue over the soft skin of her thigh. She's heat and temptation, and I inhale deep the sweet scent of her arousal, let it calm me.

It's a natural decadence that makes my mouth water and cock harden, throb behind the zipper of my pants. I can feel each bead of pre-come as it beads at the tip and then rolls down the underside while making a mess of the fabric.

I'm not wearing any underwear.

I want this torture. Deserve it.

"Spread your thighs, sweetheart. Let me taste you." She does so, careful with her shoe not to dirty my jacket. I could give less than a fuck if the heel tear the expensive garment. "Wider."

"I'm trying not to…oh God!" Amberlyn yelps when I pull her closer to the edge and throw both legs over my shoulder. *Beautiful.*

She's wearing white silk, the gusset clinging to soft lips, and right at the center is proof of her desire for me. The wetness pools there, soaking through and I don't hesitate, pressing my nose against the nearly translucent fabric.

Inhaling deep. Reveling in her need.

"Fuck, Amberlyn." A groan. A plea for mercy.

My mermaid's always bare and pink. The edge of labia peeking from the edge of her panties is fucking mouthwatering—so soft as they rub over my lips while I shake my head from right to left.

Her body trembles. Thighs squeeze me.

I can't live without her. Refuse to.

"Please." That one word sends a shiver down my spine.

"Move it to the side." Small fingers slide down her front while the other folds the front of the dress so it's out of the way and not scrunched up. Flowy material out of the way, she looks up and catches my raised brow, lips hovering over her cunt.

"What?" Breathy. Nipples hard. "You'll ruin it."

"Show me your cunt, Sirenita." Another hiss, this time as I watch two fingers slip beneath the edge. "Feed your papi."

"They'll be looking for us." Even as the words leave her lips, she does as I ask, exposing her slick flesh to me. "We shouldn't."

"Yes, I should." *Owe you this.* Not that I give her a chance to take in my words, my mouth lowers onto her wetness and I drag my tongue through her folds, groaning as her sweetness overtakes my senses.

I'm ravenous. Starved.

My patience is nonexistent, and I trace my tongue from slit to clit, nearly snarling as a sweetness uniquely hers caresses my senses. I'm lost to this ardor—a crippling thirst that dominates me.

Without Amberlyn knowing, I'm her puppet.

Tied to her.

The next pass of my tongue is rough, and so is the one that follows as I lose myself. All I understand is her softness and heat, the near painful throbbing of my cock. I eat her like the demon she's created: licking and nipping—lapping up every single drop.

There's no pausing to breathe or giving her a chance to catch her breath; I suck her bundle of nerves between my lips and flick the tip, watching how her chest rises and falls.

My mermaid is breathing hard.

Eyes on mine.

Teeth embedded into her bottom lip.

"Gorgeous," I growl against her heat, slickness coating my lips and chin as another rush warms my tongue.

"Papi, I'm—"

"Come for me." A command she fights, thighs trembling on either side of my head, and that's unacceptable. Bringing a hand to her pussy, I circle that tight little clenching hole.

"No."

"No?" I ask, sliding in one finger and then the other to the knuckle and stop. "Is that a challenge?"

"I'm angry at you." Out of all the things she could've said, that's the last I expected. Anything but that.

It makes me pause, but I don't remove my fingers. Instead, I pull back just enough to fully meet her eyes and let her see a little of what she's always been blind to.

I'm not perfect.

I'm an asshole.

But more importantly, this woman is my world.

"I know, and you have every right to be." That catches her off guard, head tilting a bit while the walls squeezing my fingers tighten a little more. Not that she says anything, but the doubts and hurt are plain as day to see. My girl might think she's unreadable, but I see what others don't. "I'm sorry, Amberlyn. It's never been my intention, but out of necessity, I'm the devil incarnate." Pulling my digits out, I circle her opening with the tips and then slam them in deep, immediately finding that one spot that I've tattooed with my name. "Just remember everything I said to you late at night. That you know a part of me no one else does."

Lips opening, she licks the bottom one and takes in a deep breath, ready to ask me questions, but I don't give her the chance.

"Ivan, what...oh *God*!" There's my sirenita. The gorgeous girl with the bright hair and love for the ocean that looks at me with nothing but love. Even if it's for a second, I saw it. With me, she's an open book.

But as the first wave of pleasure crests, she throws her head back and arches—legs widening a little more to accommodate me. So I can take what's mine and freely given, and I love her clit through each ripple while stroking my fingers deep. She's swollen and flushed, juices dripping down into my palm while her bundle of nerves throbs against my tongue.

Fuck, this is my heaven.

I can't live without her for long.

"So perfect," I groan deep before scraping my teeth over her sensitive flesh, reveling in the way that heated stare meets mine again. How those supple thighs tremble yet try to hold me in place. "Thank you, bebe."

Gentler now, I bring her down with slow licks and kisses after removing my fingers. With each, her breathing slows and body relaxes while that beautifully satiated grin gives me all the satisfaction I need. I've ignored my cock's throbs and the beads of pre-come that now stain my pants, how each flex against the zipper—the way she moans low in her throat—brings me closer to my own release.

Instead, I grit my teeth and bear this as punishment.

The next time I have her, she will be mine in every way a man can claim a woman.

Placing a final kiss on her clit and then wet hole, I pull back and stand. Then we're eye to eye, my still-wet lips a hair's breadth from hers, and I just watch.

Take into memory how sweet she looks a little disheveled. *Mine.*

We don't talk as I help her down and then fix her dress, both of us ignoring the slight wrinkles in her garment. We're lucky that the cut is made in a way that it hides them since the bodice is tight.

"I think we should head outside," Amberlyn says after a while and I nod, but when she makes to move past me, I halt her with a hand out. "Ivan, we really need to head out. We've been gone long enough."

Still, I don't budge and grin down at her. "Say you'll walk with me."

"Listen, I need—"

"Please." I bring the hand halting her exit up to her face and cup it. Relish in the way she nuzzles my palm unconsciously. *I know, baby. I know.* "Please walk with me, Mermaid."

Her entire body melts, and all anger evaporates for now. "Yes."

"Thank you."

Chapter 8

AMBERLYN

THE REST OF the wedding party is there when we arrive. They're laughing and smiling while he walks a step or two behind me, a warm hand on the small of my back. Not that they pay us any mind. Instead, they talk among themselves while the planner keeps watching the clock.

Most of these people are family members of the De Leons. A few are friends of the bride.

But they're all smart enough to avoid being nosy.

It also helps that Alvin and Natasha are keeping them busy with an impromptu toast while my heart feels as though it'll beat out of my chest. I'm sensitive and in shock. I'm a little lost, too.

He seemed almost desperate. More possessive than he's ever been.

What the hell is going on?

I thought he'd be happy with my decision to walk with Alvin. That he'd appreciate the distance—to not have to placate the lost puppy always following him around.

Was I wrong? Does he care?

Not that I'm given more time to dissect as a flushed Luna walks in with an apologetic look. "Sorry for the small delay, guys."

"We'll blame the groom," Nat calls out and I flick my gaze in her direction, catching her eyes for a moment. She's pulling Alvin behind her as she walks over to her cousin, but the quick glance my way warns me we'll be talking later. As does the bride, so many questions in the quick wrinkle of her nose and raised brow, but I'm not going to make today about me. They each share a quick kiss on the cheek and whisper something low so no one else hears, and then they nod. "All right, folks. Let's get me hitched and calm Thiago down. He's not a patient man…something that runs in the family."

The dig is clear, but other than Ivan clearing his throat, nothing happens.

"Yes, please. Let's line up and be ready to walk in five." Mercedes, the wedding planner, claps once and then lifts her tablet, pointing at pairs to come over. "Same placement as last night."

One by one, the matched partners move into place, and I follow, coming over to Luna first for a quick hug. "You ready to become the chain to his balls?"

"I was born to be." Her sassy response earns a chuckle from her brother-in-law who also gives her a small hug after I pull back. They don't exchange words, but the quick glare she sends his way makes the man nod once and then retake his place beside me, hand on my lower back.

The heat sears me. Feels so good.

But I fight the shivers back—how much I want to kiss him.

Because I heard him today. Those words while hovering over my core, they're something that I can't ignore, forget, or even begin to comprehend. They make no sense.

One minute I'm an obligation. Reduced to a nuisance.

And now…?

Truth is, I still don't know. There's also this hint of betrayal that looms at the edge of my mind: what game is he playing? *What do you want from me?*

Our stares meet then as if pulled by an inexplicable force, and time once again stops for me. I love this man, always have, but those doubts, that for years I've buried deep, can't be contained. My mind and heart are at war, fighting for domination now that the lull of my orgasm has faded, and I feel as though I'm being split in two.

"We're up next, Mermaid." My heart stutters at that, and the two low gasps from my girls mean they heard this too. That in my confused state, I didn't make this up. "You ready?"

"Yeah." Because what else can I say? Not at this moment. So instead, I take the bridal bouquet of white calla lilies he's holding out for me, no clue when or who gave this to him, and then shift forward.

Those behind me are staring. I can feel it.

I'm just as lost as they are.

"…your hand," Ivan whispers, bending a bit to my level and his warm breath caresses my cheek. This time, I can't control the shiver. "Amberlyn?"

"Huh?"

"Your hand, sweetheart. We're up."

A throat clears, and it's like I snap back into place on autopilot. My hand wraps around his elbow and in a few steps, we're over the threshold, the warm ocean breeze flowing all around us. He leads me toward the beautifully decorated arch, our movements in sync while his brother stands upfront by himself and anxious.

You and me both, buddy.

At that moment—heck, since he handed over the flower—it's

like my mind has disconnected from my body and I move without conscious thought. Something's wrong here. I know it, but can't seem to shake it off.

Not that anyone can tell.

I'm smiling and greet the groom while my hand lingers with Ivan's for just a moment or two longer than they should. I also shrug when his brows furrow at Alvin walking with Natasha, not understanding why someone he met recently is walking with one of the maids of honor.

Yet the moment his beauty walks through the doors, he's done for.

You can see it on his face. This feeling of peace and completion comes from being close to the one you love.

Nevertheless, I can't help the way my eyes water at the sight. I'm crying in joy for them and sorrow for myself, a contradicting set of emotions that I hide behind a watery smile for the happy couple.

Ivan's also watching, but not them. It doesn't help my nerves, this anxiousness that creeps in when his words from last night and today mix. Confusion leads to weakness en route to heartbreak, and he's the one holding the guillotine.

Nothing more than an obligation.

It's never been my intention, but out of necessity, I'm the devil incarnate.

"I now pronounce you husband and wife." That snaps me back to the present, and I wipe at my damp cheek with the fingers not gripping my bouquet. "Mr. De Leon, you may now kiss you…never mind."

Laughter fills the large backyard, his mother's being the loudest. There are hoots and hollers, clapping as they continue to kiss without a care in the world.

A shoulder bumps into mine, and I turn my head. "You won the bet, by the way."

"Never a doubt."

"So cocky."

"No. Just smart." With everything but *him.*

"Tomorrow, late lunch?" In other words, we'll be dissecting what happened in the last twenty-four hours. Fine with me. At this point, I need someone to help me make sense of this.

"It's a date."

"Never a doubt," she parrots my same words, dipping her hand into the pocket of my dress and slipping something inside that feels like money. Nat also nudges me forward a second before someone grabs my hand, a touch I'd know anywhere, and winks. "You'll be paying, too."

My head aches a bit and my legs will be sore tomorrow, but it's worth it to see how happy my best friend is. The couple is dancing to a slow bolero being played by the band, an old romantic song that reminds some of us of where we come from, or a love lost.

This was a favorite of the De Leon abuelos, and it's touching to see their mother sing it to them. Her watery eyes shift from the couple to her husband, and lastly, to the man a few feet from me.

His presence is overwhelming. Hasn't given me the space I need to clear my head.

I chose this empty table near the back to relax after hours of nonstop running around because the actual ceremony was just a small part of today. You have pictures and toasts and avoiding questions while jumping in to help at the slightest infraction to help things move along smoothly.

If a vase fell because someone's tipsy aunt second removed bumped into a table? I got the person out of the way while the clean-up crew made it disappear.

If Luna needed a change of shoes? I ran upstairs in my death traps and grabbed her flip-flops.

But now that the night is almost done and people watch the final dance before they leave, I'm without a compass.

Lost. Exhausted.

He's also a lot closer than he was an hour ago, and I inhale deep, taking in that liquor and man scent that all women find attractive in men. *Not all men, though.* There's something about that combination on who you lay claim to that's near controlling in its pull.

It's woodsy and strong with just the right note of spice that makes my thighs clench underneath the table.

"Get ahold of yourself, dammit," I mutter under my breath and pick up my glass of wine, taking a sip. Then another, the crisp white flowing through me—warming me after my fourth glass. "You're not that girl. I'm not this weak."

The couple stops their swaying, turning to look over at the family matriarch while the rest of the guests begin to applaud. And I tag along, throwing back the last bit of chilled wine before pushing my chair back.

Yet before I can stand, a strong hand with a tattoo of a lion's head greets my line of sight. The fingers are extended in my direction before turning over, offering me his help to stand. My eyes quickly shift around the room and notice people glance away, his mother and father being two of them.

"You're bringing attention our way, Ivan." It comes out breathy and not the uninterested I'd been hoping to go for. Too much has happened, and my defenses are down—my anger at bay.

"You've always taken my breath away, Sirenita." That's his response. No hesitation and I narrow my eyes a bit, feigning annoyance to mask my anxiousness. This, his attitude and need to be close, is everything I've ever wanted, yet he's never given it to me before.

Why now?

Why after I heard him say that to Mirabel?

Is he trying to control me again? Straightening my back, I exhale deeply. "What's this? What are you hoping to accomplish by—"

"All I want is a dance, bebe. Just one."

"You're confusing me, Ivan. I want to hate you so much..." Trailing off, I try to step back and bump into my seat. For a second, I teeter on my heels, but then strong fingers curl around my wrist and with a gentle tug, I'm against his chest.

After the pictures, he'd removed his jacket and dress shirt, donning instead an off-white guayabera similar to his brother's tailored fit to be destructive for my ovaries. I'm sure this request came from his mother, a woman I'm currently cursing in my head as my hand lands on his pec and Ivan gives the muscle there a flex.

Bastard.

That cocky grin also tells me he knows what he's doing. "Come on, bebe. I won't bite tonight."

"That's a lie, and we both know it."

"Guilty when given the chance." The younger De Leon's imposing figure blocks any attempt of escape, not letting me move an inch while wrapping the other arm around my waist. "But I swear, all I want is to dance right now. I'll behave."

"What do you want? You're confusing me."

"To forget the world and my duty for one night."

"Okay." There's gratitude in his expression before he walks me to the edge of the dance floor where the lighting is dim. Not close enough to join the others, but our bodies are only a few inches apart and his soft exhales skim over my temple. *This is just a dance. No need to make a big deal out of it.* "This will either be a blessing or a curse."

"What was that?"

"Nothing." Thank God he didn't hear me; I've made myself a fool for this man enough times in the past. Moreover, I'm not looking for a repeat even if love makes you do stupid things, and there's no doubt in my heart that this is one of those times.

Ivan turns me twice and then pulls me closer. Not an inch of space separates us now.

My heart races and goose bumps rise across my skin. My core clenches violently.

I let him talk me into walking with him as my partner, stood by his side in every photo, and now I'm swaying to a slow song the band is playing. We're almost chest to chest, though my heels still don't make me tall enough, but being nestled like this feels right.

His strong arm is wrapped around me, and his scent lulls me into a cocoon of affection and safety I never want to leave. And yet, something is off.

It bothers me. This large elephant that's overtaken the room, yet neither of us calls out.

"Ivan, I can't do this anymore."

"I know."

Chapter 9
IVAN

"IVAN, I CAN'T do this anymore."

"I know." Lowering my mouth to her forehead, I place three quick kisses there and then pull back. Every muscle in my body is tense, yet my arm around her is gentle, keeping her close these last few moments like the precious treasure she is. "Do you remember the time back in high school when I asked you to skip class and go kayaking with me?"

Her expression is perplexed, yet she nods. There's even a small curl on her lips. "You've always been weird and asked for more of me than you should."

"You were scared of the mangroves and thought a gator was hiding beneath us."

Sirenita smacks my shoulder hard but doesn't miss a step. "And you laughed at me and asked me to trust you."

"That day was the beginning of our adventures, wouldn't you say? We've skydived, raced bikes, and got our first tattoos together." My finger slides across her hip where there's a bundle of white mariposas, Cuba's national flower. Amberlyn shivers and bites down on her bottom lip. "Every time, I've been there. Never far, Sirenita."

Maybe I've been chauvinistic—it's been easier to keep her at bay—but this is the most I can offer. The hostile environment and bloodshed are unavoidable outside these walls; one goes with the other in a world dominated by greed, but keeping a clear head is what wins wars.

I'll remove the threat to her life.

I'll kill Rodriguez and his men for this.

And then I'll lay an entire country at my little mermaid's feet.

"What are you trying to say, Ivan?" If there's one thing my girl is, it's perceptive. Especially in her line of work: criminals are the best kind of liars.

"Things are moving in the background that need my attention."

Sliding my other hand down her arm, I skim her wrist before using it to turn her twice, stopping with her back to my chest. The last song ended and gave way to bachata, the melody a little bit faster, and we fall right into step. We gyrate, keeping to the basic three counts while I lower my face to her neck.

I inhale deep, and my groan isn't quiet. It's full of the hunger only she can create. "Yes."

"Okay." No more questions, and I leave it at that too. She's aware of who I am and what I do.

We stay in this bubble for a while, ignoring those around us who continuously shift their attention our way, while everything from merengue to salsa to house music plays well into the night.

I have no idea how much time passes, but the vibrating on my phone stops me.

Pulling it out with my unoccupied hand, I bring it up and let facial recognition open the screen. The message is from someone running surveillance on a building deep in the heart of Hialeah, a city neighboring Miami and whose population is heavily loyal to my family.

The eighties and nineties were great decades for business.

> Dalian Uriel is with your mark at a bar in Hialeah.
> They mentioned Mariposa Bail Bonds. ~ Cisco

They're dead men walking.

I'm not far from my exit on the Palmetto thirty minutes after the newlyweds departed, fingers twitching against the steering wheel while some club banger plays on a popular station. The dashboard's lit screen tells me I'm going well over eighty, yet the two cops I've passed have been smart enough to not stop me.

My mind, though, is on the look Amberlyn gave me right before I walked away after the first text came in. I knew exactly who Cisco was speaking about. They live in the same building, and my informant owes me a few favors.

And like the saying goes: *one hand washes the other.*

Mermaid picked up on the shift in mood at once and didn't ask questions. Instead, I was given a nod, a quick squeeze to the arm, and the space to leave while defeat mixed with exhaustion flashed across her expression.

There was also doubt. Worry.

She has every right to feel that way, and it burns me.

I've never regretted the life I was born into, not once, but tonight, a part of me wishes it'd be easier for us. But that's on me. My selfishness to keep us private and enjoy everything that came without the interference of our families has come back to bite me.

"Our day will come, Mermaid. I'll be back for you." Taking the exit with a sharp turn, I get off on Red Road in Hialeah and make the first left. I need this. The kind of release that comes from revenge, wearing the blood of an enemy on my hands.

Because this is more than anger.

I'm shaking as a deep-rooted rage—hatred—scorches my veins while driving down the deserted-at-this-time avenue. This area is a great mixture of new and old, from homes to businesses and everything in between while the east side of the city is known for its small factories and cafeterias.

My destination, though, is a small apartment complex near 49th Street and behind a shopping plaza.

That's where I find my informant, cigarette in his mouth while a pistol is tucked into the waistband of his pants. The tank top he's wearing barely conceals it.

"Acere," he calls out the second I step out after grabbing what I'll need, coming to my side of the vehicle. Cisco keeps his distance, eyeing my Glock and holster while extending a hand out toward me, which I take, giving it a hard squeeze. "Good to see you, bro."

"You been good?" I ask after releasing his hand, knowing he had a kidney stone issue in the past. Had to be operated on because of it. "Your family?"

"All good, thanks to you." A few years back, he saw himself in debt with a loan shark over a few default parlays and I paid them, with the agreement he do odd jobs for me here and there. Like this one: follow and report.

"Glad to hear it."

Cisco's phone pings then and he takes it out, showing me the message on the screen. It's from his older brother.

> The asshole just left. He's drunk and on his way to you. ~ Tito

Three dots appear right away indicating he's typing a second message, and it comes through before I can ask if Dalian is with him.

> Solo. Uriel is here and not alone. A woman came to see him. ~Tito

An image follows of a blonde woman no older than her late twenties with an arm sleeve of roses and thorns. She's sitting in his lap, whispering in his ear, while his hand is under the table. He's touching her, it's obvious, even if the empty beer bottles littering the wooden top block a bit of the view.

"He doesn't leave them until they're behind closed doors. I want a location."

"Understood." Cisco's already typing this before I'm done, pocketing the device before digging into the opposite pocket. There's nothing left of his cigarette but the butt now, and after smashing it onto the asphalt with the sole of his sneakers, he hands me something shiny.

"A key?"

"An apartment key, to be exact."

A grin tugs at my lips; I don't care how he got it. Instead, my body welcomes the rush of excitement that fills my limbs. It's heady. This lick of fire snaps at my heels and brings forth a different kind of pleasure.

Because every human has a beast inside—a vengeful demon that I accept—and mine demands payment in blood.

Never threaten what's mine. A lesson to be learned tonight.

"Gracias, Cisco. I owe you for this." His head shakes at that, but I pay my debts. This goes beyond what I asked of him, a man who made a mistake but isn't a criminal. This show of loyalty made him a friend. "Text me with an address when your brother gets it and pull back."

"If you need me—"

"I know. Appreciate it, too." With that, I walk away and toward the building with him coming up slightly behind me. There's a small click to the door after he swipes a card, the lock shifting, and then I'm inside after pushing a signal scrambler given to me by Casper's IT guy.

That British fucker is full of surprises, and this one has come in handy more than once.

With no record of my being here, I enter the elevator and wait for Cisco to push the floor's number. I'm going to eight while he exits on the seventh, leaving me with a piece of paper that reads: *number 808 and no neighbors.*

Cisco's response to my raised brow? *One just moved out and the other is still at the bar.*

I plan to leave a lovely present for Dalian and Jaime. They'll know I'm coming.

The door in question is at the end of the small hall where there's a circular ending and three separate entrances, and I slip inside the middle one without the worry of being seen. I find the entire unit in the dark, except for a small table lamp that illuminates a lonely grey armchair in the corner. It's made of corduroy from the looks of it; I find that it suits my purpose when it faces the entrance, and the bar cart is slightly to the right of it.

Funny thing is, for being a dipshit, this asshole has decent taste in liquor. There's an unopened bottle of expensive tequila, a few rums, and a whiskey that's got a good age on it.

Opening the latter, I take a sip straight from the bottle while removing my gun from the holster and placing it atop my lap. I also straighten the bracelet on my wrist, a gift from my brother, and undo the safety clip on it.

This could go two ways:

Quick and clean.

Or messy and agonizingly slow.

On my fourth sip, there's a rattle at the doorknob and I watch in silence as the man in question stumbles in, sloppy and drunk, singing to himself. He's unaware of his environment, the danger that lurks, and I almost snort when he manages to hit his toe on the entry table while tossing off his shoes.

Fucking moron.

"Buenas noches," I say, causing him to jump/fall against the door while I place the bottle atop the cart. Poor judgment on his behalf as I'd given him a slim window to run out the door and into the humid night, but to his surprise, the fucker managed to close it instead. "It's rude to not greet someone back. I expected more from someone with such fine taste."

The apartment is full of nice furniture, some paintings, and a gaudy coffee table that screams new money.

"H-how did you get in?" In response, I toss the key at his feet and raise a brow. He reaches for it while his body turns toward the door; the click of the gun safety being removed makes him pause, a pathetic whimper slipping past his lips.

"Get up and go to the rooftop terrace, Henry."

"Why the terrace?" Entire body trembling, his hands slip on the wall as he can't find purchase, yet I'd venture to say he's a lot more awake now than when he walked in. Eyes alert, he manages to right himself but doesn't move from what I assume he thinks is a safe distance.

He more than likely thought I wouldn't shoot inside of a building filled with innocent people on every floor.

Thing is—I would, and I will. Everything comes down to precision and choosing the right spot.

Say, forcing my gun into his mouth will end him, but not go through to the next floor. Not with the concrete noise barrier. That alone will help slow if not stop the bullet.

I'm not going to, but I could.

I believe in gun safety and firing responsibly.

"Because I said so."

"De Leon, this is unnecessary. I'm not the enemy."

"I like your fear." Standing to my full height, I take the steps between us and bend my head a little so we're eye to eye. "You have two choices. Are you listening?" His shaky nod is a good enough answer. "Follow directions, or take a trip with me downtown. Your call."

And because I'm a saint, I give him some space to consider his options. Not that he's the brightest crayon in the box, because the moment he thinks there's room to escape, the asshole goes for the door and yanks it open, rushing toward the apartment to the right of his door.

He bangs on it.

Screams out the names of who I assume is the neighbor on vacation.

Leaning against the doorway, I bring the muzzle of my gun to my chin and rub it there. "You'd think being a criminal would make one more aware of their surroundings. Check the whereabouts of those who live next door."

"Did you kill them?"

"The couple that moved out, or your friend?" My smirk irks him, yet I don't make a single move to grab the cornered animal.

"Whatever I did can be fixed."

"Seems you've sobered up well, since we're making deals now."

"Please."

"No." One word. Two letters.

So simple, yet incites so much fear, and his need to escape overrides common sense. My position places me within seconds from the open hallway and when the idiot makes a desperate last-second sprint, I clock him.

A single punch, bare knuckles, and the fucker goes down. The loss of consciousness is immediate. His body stiffens and drops, skull bouncing hard off the ground. He also lands a bit awkwardly on his shoulder and arm, the latter appearing off.

"This could've been handled with dignity, asshole." Grabbing a foot in each hand, I drag him back inside and close the door, locking it before maneuvering his limp body up and over my shoulder.

The top units in this building have access to a private rooftop terrace they share, mainly used for sitting out in the evenings on the large, shared patio set. That, or taking care of plants inside of a small greenhouse that's sealed, cooled, and irrigated in a very specific way.

But more importantly, it's private. Every noise is blocked by the small bit of traffic down below and the occasional plane above as we aren't too far from the airport.

No one to hear me empty my clip in his head.

Chapter 10
IVAN

AN HOUR LATER the idiot rouses, groaning from his place on the floor a few feet from me. He's unaware, soaking wet from the hoses I pulled from his greenhouse after Israel confiscated every full-grown plant and the equipment.

The latter I'll toss somewhere or give it to a small farmer who's loyal to the family. This motherfucker purchased and used quality tools; it'd be a shame to waste them.

All in all, it wasn't much in the matter of bulk, but once ready for sale, the street value is easily twenty grand and I'll donate it to the cause. Because to remove a president in power, you need funds, weapons, and soldiers—in the end, this will be nothing more than a humble act of goodwill from a dead man.

"How much did I have to drink last night?" His cough is rough as if he'd smoked heavily for many years. There's also a small gash over his right eyebrow from where I struck him, and it's bled quite a bit. *Not enough, in my opinion*. "I've never felt this fucked up."

Rivulets of red mix with the low setting of the water hose, flooding the top a bit before sliding over the side of the building. To anyone that comes up and discovers his body between tomorrow and the next few days, it'll look like a robbery for his illegal farming. Just another drug deal gone wrong, and the case will receive little to no attention.

The difference is that Jaime will know. The message will be clear to him and his family.

I'm coming.

"A lot, from my understanding." At the sound of my voice, his head snaps in my direction, and his eyes widen in horror. "Morning, sunshine."

"What the…*shit*!" He made a move to scramble back, but the dislocated shoulder doesn't help his cause. The weight he put on it when trying to gain traction causes him to slip and fall forward, hitting his face on the cold concrete floor. "Fuck!"

"You might want to be careful. That looked like it hurt."

Henry doesn't answer me, too busy looking around and notices two things: his marijuana is gone, and so is his phone, which I now have in my pocket. In all this, he keeps flicking his gaze in my direction, trying to guess my next move while I sit comfortably in a folding metal chair beside a patio table.

There's no escape. No help.

Just an executioner and the convicted.

"Please don't."

"I suggest you start talking. My patience is thin at the moment." Reaching into my front pocket, I pull out a pack of cigarettes and light one up. I'm not one to smoke often, but the relaxing atmosphere seems to call for one. The idiot flinches at the sudden move but settles; Henry tries to stand once again, but I hold a hand up. "You can explain from your knees, and I'd be quick to drop to them. Either you cooperate and make this easier on yourself, or I begin to unload my magazine. Trust me, you'll drop immediately with a blown kneecap."

"Killing me is not the answer, De Leon."

"No. It's not." His rough exhale almost makes me chuckle, but I keep my expression neutral. Emotionless. "It's just the beginning." Holding the cig between my lips, I inhale deeply and hold it a few seconds before exhaling through my nose. I also hold up my gun and point at his horror-filled face, and at once, he gets into position. Watching me. Body is shaking. Maybe going into a little bit of shock. "Now, you know why I'm here?"

"Yes."

"Tell me. I want to hear you say it."

Tears pour from his eyes, bottom lip trembling. *Pathetic.* "I paid for an order with fake bills. Lied and stole from your family."

"And? What else?"

"That's all I did. Te lo juro." *I swear it. I swear it.*

Leaning forward in my seat, I glare at him. "We both know that's a fucking lie. Your friendship with the Uriels is enough proof of that."

"Ivan, please. It doesn't need to be like this?" Henry says, teeth chattering while his body tries to shy away from the cold puddle he's sitting in. A quick tsk from me stops him. "Can you turn the water off?"

"No." Another deep inhale; this time I stretch my neck from side to side before releasing perfect 'O' rings of smoke. "Pick it up. I want it over your head while we discuss a few things." Shaky hands reach over the nozzle not too far from him. "And turn the setting to full power."

"Okay."

"Point it at your face, right eyebrow to be exact." Doing as I ask;

Henry holds the sharp blast of water to his face and the gash I left earlier. A string of curses leaves his mouth, almost choking him as the water, tinged with red, rushes inside. There's coughing and sputtering as he tries to remove the jet, but I discipline him just as swiftly.

From my back pocket, I pull out the silencer attachment and shoot to his ear.

One shot, and it tears clean off. The torn cartilage now lies a few feet from him, and it's burned from the impact.

"Son of a bitch," he grits out, his hand loosening on the green hose to cup the injured area. Blood pours from the open wound at a rapid pace, and his hand becomes drenched—his arm and clothing bear the same fate. What was once a pale-yellow shirt is now red. Dark and bright. "How could you just shoot me? I'm cooperating."

"Pick it up and aim again, or you'll lose something more painful next time." One last puff, and I toss the remains at his head. The red ember bounces off his wet forehead and flops to the ground. "Remember, you hold the power here. How much you suffer is up to you."

"No more."

"Now."

"I'm begging you." Henry's face suddenly loses all color and then, like the pussy he is, the man bends over and empties his stomach. *Nasty.* Hacking and gagging, he unleashes hours' worth of drinking onto his front and below. "Please, no more."

"Pick. It. Up."

"Fuck," he screams out the second the sharp jet hits his cut and now the jagged cut where his ear once was. More water is poured, and the force of the stream opening the wound a little at a time while the floor is bathed in his life's essence, among other things. It's a foul smell. Henry looks pathetic. Nothing like the man who stole from my family conspired to help my enemy, and put my mermaid in danger. "Let's work something out."

The added pressure isn't helping the swelling either. The eye below the cut is half swollen shut.

My finger on the trigger twitches, and he flinches. "Like what?"

He licks his lips. Swallows hard. "I can pay—"

"First, what the fuck is your last name? I didn't care enough to memorize it." No sense in lying. That grates him, but he's smart enough to not react negatively. I'd kill him before finding out without giving a single fuck.

"Davila."

"Okay, *Henry Davila*." I smile and lower my Glock. "You have four minutes. This is your only chance to convince me that shooting you would be a mistake."

"I'll pay you double."

"Money isn't a problem for my family."

"You can have me work it off." Sweat trickles down his temple, mixing with the bit of blood there. "I'll tell you where they are."

"Now we're talking my language." Pressing the stopwatch setting on my smartwatch, I start running the time. "Convince me in the next three minutes, and we'll discuss other options."

"Okay."

"You can also lower the water. Take that as a gift for your cooperation."

"Thank you." Davila exhales roughly, dropping the hose. His shoulders hunch, and his hands clench and then open a few times. "They approached me with an offer to make a large amount of money while also allowing me to keep my counterfeit operations with police backing. I'd be essentially protected and rewarded, and all I had to do was hide Dalian here and do some small surveillance."

"Whose name are both apartments under?"

"This one is under my mother's." At my nod, he looks down as if he knows what he says next will piss me off. "Dalian's is under Amberlyn Ibarra."

That son of a bitch.

Every cell in my body vibrates in anger, yet I keep a tight rein on it. *Not yet.* "Who put it in her name? How did they get the information?"

Davila swallows, still not looking at me. "I did."

"Again, how?"

"A hacker I met online in a chat group. We exchanged goods."

"I see." Then I begin to pace. From one side to the other, while his bloodshot eyes follow. He jumps each time the hand holding the gun so much as twitches, but I ignore it for now. His audacity to involve others and obtain her information through a third party, one that could harm her as well, adds to my list of bodies.

"What can I do," he chokes out on my next pass, lips trembling. "Anything. Please, just ask."

For a second, I turn and give him my back. I'm a rational man, at times more than my brother, but right now the rage that consumes me is hard to fight back. So I breathe in deep and stare up at the night sky, taking in the many businesses on the street not far from us and those traveling through, a car here and there, but none the wiser to how close they are to a killer.

Life's funny that way.

As humans, we are complacent and unaware. Never truly seeing.

Instead, we ignore to protect our minds when that puts us in the most danger.

And then, occasionally, you run into an idiot like the one behind me.

He has the equivalent to the *I'm on vacation* syndrome. The it-will-never-happen-to-me mentality gets many in positions like this one: staring down the barrel of a gun and pleading to someone with no human compassion or morals not to hurt you.

"Anything?" I ask, looking over my shoulder at him. Completely filthy and pitiful.

"Yes."

"I want the name of everyone involved. I want addresses and details of each."

"Done."

“You have forty-eight hours, Davila. Get me this information and I’ll discuss relocating you out of Florida permanently.” Henry opens his mouth to respond, but I shake my head. “I’m not being understanding or have any desire to be. Don’t mistake this for what it’s not. Fail me, and I will not only find you but gut you and leave the body and entrails for all to see hanging off the Brickell Bridge. Understood?”

“Si.”

“Then clean this up. The clock is ticking.”

“Y-you’re leaving?”

Too much hope in his voice and I laugh, the sound sardonic. “I am, but I dare you to run and hide.”

Chapter 11

AMBERLYN

"MORNING, mi niña," Mom calls out the moment I step into the office early Tuesday morning. It's been two days since the wedding and since I last saw Ivan, and I'm worried. No text. No calls. Not so much as a late-night visit and it drills home the words I heard him say to Maribel.

Makes them real.

Not so much a mistake.

Not that he hasn't disappeared on me before, but there's a difference in knowing he's working and this time, having the fact he sees you as an obligation replay in your mind like an endless reel. It's why I took yesterday off; no matter how many times I went over what happened—heard—I'm left in a loop of confusion.

"Morning." It's a low grumble between sips of hot coffee, but she understands and then follows me toward the back where we keep a small lounge for those who work here. An employee is manning the front for now, and Mom wants to gossip. "I brought pastries and an omelet sandwich. Want half?"

"No, but I'll take a guava and cheese turnover." She makes a beeline for the coffee maker, her favorite mug in hand. "How was the wedding, by the way? Did you party that hard to call out yesterday?"

"Yes and no." Another sip from my latte, not looking at her yet. I'm keeping busy by grabbing a small platter and with the help of tongs, arranging the sweets for anyone working today to grab in between clients. Some days we are busy, and others it's a person here or there. "With all the last-minute wedding prep and helping Luna, I'm exhausted. Barely slept for a few days."

"Do you need an extra day? We're good if you do."

"Nah. Just need the caffeine to kick in…" unbagging my sandwich, I take a bite and chew, then swallow "…besides, I have two cases to catch up on. Court date is coming up, and I'd hate for them to skip. Both have a mom's signature on the debt."

"Gotcha." Mom studies me. I can feel the hard stare. The dissecting of my behavior. "Ask away, woman. What's got your curiosity?"

"You never answered my question, kid."

At that, I look over and raise a brow. "The inquisition hasn't begun yet. No clue what needs to be answered."

"Smartass." Grabbing a few pastries, napkins, and her coffee refill, Mom takes a seat at the small kitchenette set. Pats the seat beside her and waits for me to trudge along, and once I'm seated, she turns on the cheesy grin. *Yup. She wants to gossip.* "Okay, now tell me. How was the wedding…everything?"

"You were there, Mom," I chuckle before taking a second bite. When I don't say anything else, those eyes, so much like mine, narrow. Swallowing, I wipe my mouth with a napkin. "You're going to need to be more specific."

"Décor, food, and dances? Any surprises?"

"Same as the ceremony, catered from the restaurant and the couple's favorites, and they danced all night until leaving. Those two couldn't be pulled apart. So much so, the tossing of the bouquet happened right before she got in the car to leave for the honeymoon."

"Who caught it?"

"Is that important?"

"Yes."

She's an amazing woman, but nosy runs in all Latina mothers and it's best not to fight. The trick is always make them think they've won.

We were all standing in front of the house waiting for the newlyweds to drive off. Everyone there had a balloon in their hand with a wish for the couple, and as they descended, they were released one by one.

The idea had been mine. Something I saw in a wedding magazine and loved, and with how things are with me and Ivan—the lack of any commitment—I'd given Luna the suggestion. Something she loved and as they made their way through the group of family members and loved ones, she broke from the group and walked toward me and Nat.

Our balloon was a little different. The all-white plastic was hiding a naughty gift for the trip.

"I have a feeling this isn't meant for the public to see?" We shook our heads in unison, giggling a bit. "The extra streamers, glitter, and the three giant X's also give away that vibe."

"We thought so, too." Nat hands it to her, while Luna shakes her head. Even the man standing behind her snorts, the amusement and hunger for his woman clear to see. "More fun for us this way."

Luna shifts her gaze to me. "And you feel this way too?"

"Absolutely."

"I'm glad you do. Babe?" The bride holds a hand behind her, being blocked by her groom. There's a bit of rustling, whispered words from him that I can't hear, but beside me, Natasha groans.

"She wouldn't."

"Oh, cousin. I did." A few seconds later, I'm blushing and stunned into silence as I'm handed half of her bridal bouquet while Nat gets the other. Literally, she split it in half. No tossing, the woman just decided to hand it over to us. I'm going to kill her. "This is for my two favorite people—"

"What did you say?" Thiago growls, it's playful yet still full of jealousy. "Repeat that."

"Favorite after you, babe. Calm down."

And while they bicker a bit, Natasha taunting him with favoritism, my eyes search out his. Yet when I find him, I don't see the warmth in them from when we danced or the sweet smirk I'd been gifted after his mouth licked my release from them.

No. Nada once again.

Blank and uninterested and I shift away, smiling at some random person in the crowd. I'm sure I know her. Hell, I've been around for years, and yet, making out faces is past my abilities.

Instead, the flowers in my hands feel like thousands of pinpricks and I just keep repeating the words: trust me.

I'm brought back to the present by a throat clearing. "Well, kid. Who caught them?"

"No one caught them per se."

"Who?"

"Luna split it in half and gave the pieces to me and Nat."

"Oh, dear." That's it. That's all I get after answering, but the woman is smiling. Way too bright for this time of day. "That's one way to push her girls into finding someone to settle down with."

"And is that your way into peppering in that you want grandkids?"

Mom shrugs. "Maybe."

"Not happening for a long time, woman. I'd need a man first, and at the moment, I'm very much single." Those words feel wrong, yet the truth is the truth. The old saying *No puedes tapar el sol con un dedo* is appropriate. Covering the sun with one finger is impossible and burying your head in the sand makes it worse.

I was honest when I told him I can't keep doing this. Maybe we're just not meant to be, and I've been kidding myself for far too long.

"You need a man?"

"Yes. Unless you want me to adopt or go buy some—"

"Amberlyn!" Now she's red-faced, but there's sympathy behind that stare. Mom knows about me and Ivan, or better yet, I lied to her. Told her that *I* wanted to keep it a secret until taking over the business. That I wanted respect for my name and not fear because of who I dated. "Niña, behave. If your father—"

"What about her father?" Dad asks, walking into the room and straight for the baked goods. "Whose butt am I kicking?" At that, I burst out laughing and he looks over, giving me a wink. "What, kid? You know I could."

My father and mother couldn't be more different, yet they work. Where he's over six feet, Mom is barely five. While he's reddish hair and green eyes, my mom is dark hair and light brown eyes.

One is loud but believes in peace.

The other likes sports and enjoys a good fight. Kickboxing is his passion, as is being a bounty hunter.

She bails them, and he finds those who skip, while I'm certified to do both jobs.

"Last time, I gave you a black eye."

"I let you get that punch in." Coming over, he drops a kiss on my head and then pecks Mom's lips. So casual. They're in love, have always shown it and I look away, my eyes tearing up for a second. Blinking them back, I focus on my breaths but still catch the tail end of his response. "…your mother threatened to make me sleep on the couch if you so much as got a scratch in our last sparring match."

"Is that so?" My gaze shifts to hers, and I find understanding in them. There are also questions. A quick shake of the head and she nods, understanding that I don't want to talk about it. "That's mean, Mom. Poor Dad."

"Exactly, princess. Poor Dad."

"Oh, shut it, you two." Pushing back from her chair, she stands and walks over to the sink and rinses her mug. "I'm nothing if not sweet and gentile."

"Of course, love." Dad shakes his head at me and I bite my lip, fighting my amusement.

"I saw that, Joey."

"Yes, dear."

"Out, Joey."

"Yes, honey." With one last kiss on my head, Dad steals the other half of my sandwich and walks out, but not before calling out their plans. "Be ready for lunch by two."

Mom doesn't say anything for a few minutes; she's facing the wall while the water runs, and her fingers tap the countertop. But then she turns, and the sympathy is more than I can handle at the moment.

"I'm fine."

"Are you?" she counters, leaning back against the sink. "Is he?"

"To be honest…" I shrug "…no clue."

"What happened, kiddo?"

"Life. Reality." This is my cue to leave. Without understanding how we got here and what's true and not, I'm done speculating. What I need to do is talk to him. Confront this and let the chips fall where they may. Standing, I pick up my trash and then dump it before walking over to her. I kiss her cheek and meet her eyes; I'm not hiding. "But this mess is ours, and we will figure it out. We both need time, and I have clients to deal with. Just leave it alone for now. Si?"

Mom isn't convinced but smiles anyway. "Okay. I won't ask or interfere."

"Thank you."

"HEY, AMBERLYN." Anita, our front desk girl, taps on my door. "There's a woman out front who's asking to see you. Says it's urgent."

Looking up from my laptop, I scrunch my eyebrows. "One of my clients?"

"No. Never seen her before, but she looks...*twitchy*."

"Okay." Closing my computer, I sit back and crack my neck. It's been a long day so far with a few walk-ins and the two house calls I made, delivering court dates personally. Not something done by other companies, but at ours, we give people every opportunity to do the right thing. No excuse. We serve you a few days before and have you sign off a statement that says were made aware. "Offer her something to drink and send her in. Bring me a coffee, too, please."

"Right away." Anita pauses before slipping out. Hesitates.

"What's wrong?"

"It's not my place to—"

"You've worked here long enough to get a read on things. Speak your mind."

"Something's off about her, Amberlyn. I bet money on the fact she's under some influence—"

"Drugs?" I ask.

Anita nods, pursing her lips. "There are track marks and her eyes are bloodshot. Not the kind from crying, either. That, and her story makes no sense."

"How so?"

"Bar fight turned into arrest and the boyfriend is missing."

"Missing?"

"Yes."

"You pulled up the arrest records from last night?"

"Yes, ma'am. The name she's giving isn't in any Dade County facility."

"Send her in." Something's fishy, and I'm not in the mood for bullshit. "Pull whatever records you can on them both and bring them in with my coffee. Let's see what's this about."

Chapter 12

AMBERLYN

"THANK YOU FOR seeing me, Miss Ibarra," the woman says upon entering my office, taking a seat without me offering her one. She's pretty, about my age, but shifty—almost scratching her arms. There's also a lot of makeup on her face, her eyes are red, and the clothes she's wearing are better suited for a bar and not someone who's worried sick about a loved one.

She's a mess, yes, but not dirty after a quick perusal. Clothing isn't torn and her shoes are new; I'd say this is the first time she's worn them, too.

All in all, Anita is right; something's off.

"How can I help you…?" I trail off, needing her name.

"Sorry." A giggle and she holds out her left hand which I take, giving it a firm shake while checking out the ring. It's on the larger side and also obvious that she wanted me to look. Most people offer their right hands, rarely the left. "I'm Karen Lopez, but you can call me Ren—"

"I'll stick to Karen, thank you." There's a quick tightness around her mouth at that, but she quickly fixes her expression. "You wanted to speak with me?"

"Yes." Rubbing a hand down her arm, she tears up, and her bottom lip trembles as if on cue. In doing so, she failed to realize I noticed the needle marks on her arm, and they were fresh. "I can't find my fiancé."

"Okay." My cell phone beeps with an incoming text, but I ignore it. "Have you filed a report with the police?"

"They're the ones that took him from me!" Karen wails, covering her face with both hands while I reach into the right drawer of my desk and pull out a box of tissues, sliding it across my desk to her. Shoulders shaking and leg bouncing, she cries louder—nearly falling from the chair since she chose the one without armrests. "He's innocent!"

"Miss, there's not much I can do outside of posting bail," I say, keeping my voice gentle. Dealing with people under a lot of stress comes with the job, and while something is off, I'll give her the benefit of the doubt until proven wrong. "You do understand that, right?"

"But a friend of mine said you'd helped her." This is mumbled, yet I catch her peeking toward me.

"Please look at me."

"You got her a better lawyer and with your connections, the charges were dropped."

Connections? Lawyers? "Who is this friend you speak of?"

"Her boyfriend worked for the De Leon family." Not the name I need, but I'm understanding a little better. Either she wants special treatment or is trying to extort my company. Neither will end well for her if she doesn't tread lightly. "Last year he was picked up on carrying without a permit, a dumb charge, but she said you pulled some strings, and he was out before the following day."

"Name." The more she talks, the more I smell bullshit.

"I was asked not to say."

The last person I took care of was Ivan himself. He's who the MDP picked up, and before he was fully booked in, I had him out. It was a mistake by a rookie cop who didn't know the set of rules made specifically for the De Leon family.

There are certain concessions made for them. Miami doesn't want a bloodbath.

Moreover, it was his mother who called me in the middle of the night asking for help, not a girlfriend. I've accepted a lot over the years, but fidelity is the one thing I won't question.

Ivan knows where I stand.

What I'd never accept.

Dropping her hands into her lap, she wrings them together in a nervous action. More tears fall—faster—leaving behind black tracks of mascara in their wake. She's also a little more jittery. "Please. I don't know what else to do."

Coming around to Karen's side, I take the seat beside her, patting her back gently. "Please try and get a hold of yourself, Miss Lopez. There's not much I can do for you if I don't have the information necessary."

"Tissue, please."

"I've already laid the box out for you."

"Oh." That's it, but she does calm down. Creepily at once. "Didn't see them there."

"It's okay. I can see you're under a lot of stress."

"I am." She grabs a tissue from the box and dabs her eyes. Another to blow her nose. "They ruined our engagement celebration."

"Who did?" Trying not to cringe at the way she places the dirty tissues atop my desk. *Nasty.*

There's a knock at the door and Anita walks in with a manila folder, a bottle of water, and my coffee in a Styrofoam cup. "Here you go, miss." She places the water down first and smiles at Karen after she mutters a low *thank you.* "My pleasure. Please let me know if you need anything else." The rest is put beside my closed laptop before she walks out. Yet, before reaching the door, she tilts her head toward the folder, meeting my eyes.

Message understood.

A quick nod from me, and she exits. "Please continue, Karen. Who ruined your engagement?"

"I'm sorry, but can I have a coffee instead?"

"Sure."

Standing, I pause just outside my door and whistle. "I'm sorry, Anita. She'd like a coffee, please."

"Of course." Chiming comes from the front, and she rushes to greet whoever entered.

However, when I turn, I find a nervous woman. Pale. A little sweaty. Once again scratching her arm. "Are you okay?"

"Yeah." Clears her throat. "Why wouldn't I be?" *Because your fiancé is lost?*

"No reason." When I take a seat this time, it's back behind my desk. This is when I notice the papers peeking out from the folder, and the fact the coffee lid flap is open. The staff here knows I like the latter closed—keeps in the steam. *What the hell are you playing at?* "By the way, someone came in and Anita is helping them. It'll just be a few minutes for your coffee."

"Of course. No worries."

"So about your fiancé…"

"Oh, yes." Opening her water, she takes a deep enough pull to empty half the contents. "As I mentioned, we were out last night celebrating at a bar when we were attacked. We'd had a couple of drinks with some friends, nothing over the top…" she leans over as if sharing a secret, and I keep up the façade by grabbing a pen and opening the folder "…when some guy accused me of taking his keys. Mind you, I'd been sitting on Ramon's lap the entire time."

"Ramon is…"

"My fiancé."

"And his last name?"

"Isn't that in your paperwork already?" *Bingo. You looked.*

"That's not what I asked."

"Ramon Valle." Sulky, she sounds put off by my question.

"Where were you when this occurred?"

"I'm sorry, Miss Ibarra. I was told you were discreet and didn't ask for information, that this was an easy money exchange. Maybe I should've just called the officer that made the arrest." Karen begins to stand, and in an act of pure clumsiness, knocks over the water bottle. It soaks my paperwork and dribbles across and down onto my pants, but I remain calm. Too calm. "Oh shit! I'm—"

"Please sit down and collect yourself." Leaning over, I grab a few tissues and mop up the spill, then a couple more because it spread, before tossing all of it in the trash. A trash can that I hold up so she can also dump her used Kleenex.

"Thanks." Both are thrown in the bin, and I hold back the urge to Lysol the area. "Barging in and disrupting your day was never my plan. I'm just desperate to find him."

Taking a deep breath, I let it out slowly.

Also chuck the coffee in the bin, which makes her flinch.

There are two possible reasons why Karen made this visit, and I doubt it's pure love for Ramon Valle. Either she knows about my connections to the De Leons and wants to exploit that for gain I'm not aware of, or she wants to fuck mine or Ivan's family over.

The one common denominator in both is someone opened their mouth.

As a mistake? No clue.

As a favor to a worried friend? Maybe.

The problem will be in finding out the who, when, and why.

And I plan to do so.

"I know. I'm not upset, sweetie." Opening my laptop, I tap on the dictation app and give her a reassuring smile. "Now who is the officer you spoke of? I'll need his information to help you find Ramon and why he's not showing up in the system."

"Of course!" Karen quickly digs into her small purse, digging through before producing a small white card. This she lays on the desk and slides it across, careful to avoid the damp areas. "This is what he gave me. Asked me to call him if I had any questions."

Detective Jaime Uriel
Miami Police Department
Cell: 305-123-5847

"He was the arresting officer?"

"Yes."

"A detective?"

"Yes. That's him."

"I see."

"You think it's weird that an off-duty detective broke up a simple bar fight and then made the arrest."

"Yes and no. Being off duty doesn't mean they can't make an arrest or detain until another officer comes along. My problem is with him getting personal on this arrest. There's no large crime here, no reason for you to call him." While the dictation app continues to record what we're talking about, I pull Jaime Uriel's information through my phone. With a couple of clicks, his picture is on my screen. His bio is short, which doesn't give me much to go on.

I have his rank, years on the force, age, email, and phone number —different than the one on the card.

Next, I open the daily arrest report and check for any new inmates and scroll down the list. Anita already did this, but it never hurts to check twice, and still no Ramon Valle. Not in any of the jails.

"What county was this in again? Dade?"

"Yes."

"He's not reported to be in any of them."

"Christ, where can he be?" Tears form again, and they slide down her cheeks. "Please. I know you're busy and this isn't your usual case or work, but at the very least, can you call the detective? Maybe ask someone you know at any of the jails or precincts you might have a connection at?"

"Okay." At the very least, I will find out who opened their mouth.

Bails Bonds offices have to follow certain protocols and government regulations, and I can't have people sharing information—my business dealings—with anyone. Not even a family member. The wrong kind of attention could bring attention to my doors and worse, to the De Leons.

I'm not worried about myself, but him. Always him.

Karen exhales, her smile nearly ear to ear. "Really?"

"I'll see what I can find out for you, but I make no promises. Understood?" Opening the bottom drawer to my left, I pull out a basic NDA and pen, placing them in front of her. "Please read and sign. I'll need you to understand that anything shared through our interactions is to be kept private, and sharing business procedures outside of the parties involved will be cause for legal action on behalf of Mariposa Bail Bonds."

"No problem." Without reading a single line, she signs and stands. "I appreciate this. Anything you can do is appreciated, and money isn't an issue. My father will pay for it."

"I'll call you if I find anything. No guarantees."

"You'll find him. There's no doubt in my mind that you will."

ENTERING my home after a long day and endless phone calls—inquiries—I drop my shoes by the door and head straight for the kitchen. My footsteps are soft on the hardwood floors, yet inside the silence, it reminds me of a banging drum. This steady sound follows me. Torments.

It's easy inside the office to get lost within my work. To focus on helping someone, filing paperwork, and sometimes driving out to pick up a jumper.

Here, though, in my silence, it maddeningly comes rushing back.

My needs and desires. The lack of touch from the man I love.

His words and the limbo they've left me in while I haven't heard from Ivan in two days. Not a note, message, or smoke signal.

And this time, it stings worse than any other rejection.

"Maybe what he said to Maribel was the truth and once again, I fell for his act." In the kitchen, I open the freezer and pull out a bottle of vodka with a smile. Ice cold, it's just what I need and without hesitation, I remove the cap and take a sip straight from the bottle. There's not much left—at the most three double-shot drinks—and I take the bottle without a glass out onto the balcony.

The sun's slowly lowering as I sit on the lounge and take another small drink. From blue skies to darkness, it descends slowly while people begin to settle in for dinner.

Families talk. Couples share a kiss. Lovers curl around each other, offering pleasure while satisfying their hunger.

And here I am alone. Unsure of myself.

"He can't care for me and then turn around and hurt me this way." Something crinkles in my pants pocket as I shift and I slip a hand inside, pulling out a small white card. It's basic and like many I've seen in the past with the precinct information and officer's name.

"No reported incidents. Jaime Uriel is clean." Yet I'm unsettled. Something about Karen and the case—her fiancé who doesn't appear under anyone's detainment—worries me.

Those closest to me are not saints and have plenty of blood on their hands, but I'll be damned if anyone hurts them. Comes for *him*.

Because everything for me starts and ends with Ivan De Leon no matter how much I hate it at times.

The weakness. The pain. My never-ending cycle.

"He needs to know, though. What if something happens?" Grabbing my cell from beside the bottle, I press number one and wait. Five chimes and nothing. Straight to voicemail. Then I try a last time, but instead, my device goes off, and on the screen is a phone number I've only seen twice. I press the green button. "Hello."

"Miss Amberlyn Ibarra?" The man's voice is deep, a bit hoarse before they clear their throat. My skin prickles at the way he says my name, and I don't like it. Unpleasant. Ruins the slow buzz flowing through me while I also pick up the police radio in the background and the codes being shared. "May I speak to Amberlyn Ibarra."

"This is her, Detective."

"You've been expecting my call." Not a question. His tone is amused. "You can also call me Jaime. No need for formalities."

"I have a good memory, and your number crossed my desk today." *There's no reason for him to have my number or the informal interaction*. More cause for concern. "How can I help you?"

"Karen Lopez called me today and said you'd need my assistance. That something happened to her—"

"I'm not an investigator, Detective. We do bail bonds and bounty pick-ups when clients fail to show up. Nothing more." Either they're trying to catch me in some illegal activity or as an accessory. That, or they're after who I associate with. "This is something you or a superior should look into. Don't you agree?"

"My hands are tied, Amberlyn." Frustration is clear in his tone. I also don't feel comfortable with him using my first name. Doesn't feel right.

"How so?"

"Paperwork shows that I brought him in, when in fact, another officer did. I detained him, nothing more."

"Still doesn't explain why I'm being brought into this mess."

Screw it, I pick up the bottle and bring it to my lips. My sip is larger than the last. "Again, I'm not an investigator."

"No, but as a bounty hunter, you have certain legal pull and allowances. I need to clear my name, Miss Ibarra, and Karen needs her other half. Can you help us?"

"Where's the arresting—"

"He's missing, too."

Chapter 13
IVAN

"WHERE IS SHE?"

"At home, boss," Junior says, and a car door's alarm follows a few seconds after. He's stationed outside my mermaid's building and has been her tail now for a few days—since the morning after the wedding—and has my trust to protect her. Fail to do so, and he's aware of the consequences. Knows who will be pulling the trigger. "She seemed pensive on the drive home. Upset."

"That's later than usual." My watch reads a little before seven, and I frown. I've ignored her calls, stood outside her door at night, but haven't touched her since our dance. It's the only way to control my urges. This hunger that tears me apart, eats away at my flesh. Resolve. "Did something happen today at the office?"

"Yes."

"Speak." A knock on the open metal door announces their arrival, and Israel walks in with a reluctant Henry behind him. The latter has his bottom lip busted and his hands tied in front of him. He'd tried to run, as I expected, but the fear and stupidity led him to make a costly mistake.

He set fire to his *and* Dalian's apartment before running. Fucking idiot.

Especially when I had eyes on him at all times.

Cisco gave me the tip while his brother followed him to a pay-by-the-hour motel near Okeechobee known for catering to those needing a quick fuck. Most of the rooms are set up with garages that lead to a private entrance, and Israel had a key made for the one Henry rented not two hours later.

The female clerk was more than willing to make one after a hefty tip.

"A woman came in today and was there for a while. She's not a client, but Amberlyn saw her anyway."

"And?" I point at the empty chair, but when Henry hesitates, he's forced by a single shove down. "Hold that thought." Placing the phone down atop a folding table, I press the speakerphone key before narrowing my eyes at the bruised man avoiding my gaze. "Okay. Tell me."

"Boss, you were right."

Scratching my jaw, I stand and begin to pace the twenty-foot container. We're inside the port and near the back end of the lot where no one will bother us. Or stop me when I leave. "Go on."

"It was the same woman your lookouts saw with Dalian and Henry a few nights ago." Where he's at, the evening breeze off the coast sweeps and makes noise. "Anita gave me a copy of what she came for and the police info pulled. Her name is Karen Lopez, and she's looking for her wrongfully arrested fiancé. You can guess who the detaining officer was."

A low hum escapes. No originality. "Jaime Uriel."

"Yes, boss."

"Where's Dalian?"

"I believe he's the missing-in-detainment fiancé."

"Of course. Thank you, Junior." Pressing the end button, I tilt my head and watch as beads of sweat roll down Henry's pallid face. There are stitches on his face from our last encounter and the wound to his ear looks infected, yet he's alive. Should be thankful. "You made a bad decision, Henry Davila. Running from me was foolish and irresponsible."

He swallows hard but doesn't answer. Wrong move.

"Answer when spoken to," Israel spits out, placing the muzzle of his gun against Henry's temple, and pulling the trigger. It's empty, just a click, but my guest understands the rules. He also pisses himself. *Nasty.* "Next one won't be empty, Davila. Understood?"

"Yes."

"Good boy." I struck a nerve with that remark. His right hand clenches. "Something you want to say?"

"No."

"Then lose the pinched face and start talking." Israel hands me a folded metal chair and I take it, open it, and sit across from him. There's a plastic table between us. "I'm waiting."

"My stepsister is in love with Dalian. Karen can see no wrong in him." I'm surprised; this is something I didn't know. Can come in handy in the near future. "The Uriel brothers use her. I know they do, and I was dragged in as a favor to her. To win *his* favor."

"Dalian or Jaime?"

"Dalian, but I have my suspicions she's slept with both."

"And you?"

"Guilty." Henry snorts, the sound is a bit sarcastic. "Not that she'd care if I die. We're not close. She was brought up spoiled, self-centered, and never wanting a sibling. As you can see, we also don't share last names and in her eyes, that makes me beneath her."

"Then why get involved?"

"Because Karen met them through me. I'm responsible for our downfall."

"You're right about that. You decided to help them, to put Amberlyn Ibarra in danger, and then you ran from me. All that was on you." Israel pulls out a manila folder from inside his suit jacket and places it atop the table; I open it. My eyes skim through the papers and I find names, addresses, and bank accounts with an accumulated wealth of well over five million dollars. "Why, Henry? Explain to me how going against me and mine was a good idea?"

"Honest answer?"

I wave a hand for him to continue. "Please."

"Greed. The offer was too good to pass up, especially with the guarantees they presented."

"Nothing in life is ever a sure thing, Davila. Not a fucking thing. "The blood on his lip has crusted a bit, and I also notice he's swallowing hard, thirsty, and I look at my guard. "Get him some water."

"Of course, boss." Israel exits the container while I sit back. One of the papers has my attention and I read through it. This one has information on safe houses here and in Cuba, and the backup plan to grab her grandparents there. Not going to happen.

"Keep going." Tone terse, it comes out harsher than I intend and Henry flinches back. "Relax. Right now we're just going to talk."

"Okay." His hands try to stretch, but the tight rope prevents that. Reaching into my back pocket, I grab my matte-black balisong knife and with a quick flick of the wrist, tear through the bindings. At the movement, he jumps and falls back, slamming his head against the hard metal. "Fuck. That hurt."

"I'm sure it did. Now sit." Another twist of my hand and it closes; I place it to my right. Henry scrambles up, nearly tumbling again before managing to right himself. "There are two names on this list I do not know. Who are they?"

"Cuban military smuggled in to protect the brothers." Angry rope marks surround each wrist and he rubs them, occasionally stretching out a hand. "They're from an alliance exchange; they were trained in an eastern European country to specifically work as protection to the president. However, Jaime bragged they'd be coming here, instead. And they did, on the day of your brother's wedding."

They're desperate. Don't know how to control me. Which can be a dangerous thing. Nervous—afraid—people make mistakes. Some are more costly than others.

"Why that day?"

"Jaime claimed the De Leons would be preoccupied. That's what Dalian wanted to celebrate—to them, their time had come."

"Yet, I had eyes on you and him. Could've killed you both that night."

"They don't know how close you are."

And that's because I never gave him the chance to so much as send them a text. I gave him forty-eight hours, but my men were always near. In plain sight of him, and he saw them at every turn.

"Correction—how close *you're* about to get me." Sitting back, I cross my arms over my chest just as Israel walks in. He hands Henry the water, who takes it and then sips, before retaking his place a few steps from the nervous man. I smirk at that. "How much value do you put on your life, Davila?"

"Not much at the moment. I'm a dead man."

"That depends solely on you."

"I-I don't—"

"Help me, and you'll live to see another year. Maybe twenty."

His smile is wide, so much relief in his features. "Okay."

"Smart choice." Yet I'm not sure he's understanding how much another betrayal will cost him. Grabbing my knife, I open it and flick it at his shoulder, the black metal blade embedding three inches deep. His scream of pain reverberates, bounces off the metal walls, and helps to calm some of the ire boiling within me. He's not absolved of all his crimes, a payment is yet to be made. "Learn your place, and do it quickly, Davila. We are not friends, partners, or associates. Fuck me over again, and I will deliver on my promise to hang your corpse over the Brickell Bridge. Go near Amberlyn or anyone I love, and I will chop off your dick and watch you slowly asphyxiate as you fight to breathe through the intrusion. Mind your choices, and know that I am always watching."

"Understood," he whimpers, holding his arm while not touching the blade.

"I'm glad we could come to an agreement." Turning my gaze to Israel, I give him a quick nod and he grabs Henry's arm, hauling the weak man up. My knife is still buried in his flesh and will stay that way until later tonight. For now, though, we'll take a ride. "Take him out to our boarding dock. I'll meet you there shortly."

A nod and they walk out.

I'm left alone with my thoughts. With the need to check up on her, and before realizing it, my cell phone is in my grip. Yet it vibrates before I can call, and it's Junior's name on the screen.

"Is she okay?"

"Yes, boss. Miss Ibarra hasn't left the building, but there's a problem."

"What?"

"An unmarked white SUV has been making the rounds in the area. I've seen it twice on her street, and the others watching the surrounding blocks have as well. They're looking for something." *Or taking note of any protection in the area.* "Do you want me to approach?"

"No, and keep out of sight. Let them think she's alone for now."

"And if they come near—"

"Put a bullet between their eyes and leave them to bleed out on the sidewalk as a warning. She's untouchable."

"Done."

"Is there anything else?"

"Thiago called and said he needs to talk to you."

"I'll get a hold of him now; thank you. Call me if anything

changes." Hanging up, I pull up the camera to her bedroom on the app and find her asleep. No toys. No light sheen of sweat on her skin. *My sirenita.*

Knowing she heard the blasphemous words I'd said to Mirabel, that she was hurt by them, guts me, but knowing she more than likely believes them right now is a bitter pill to swallow.

But that's my penance. Her doubt. Anger.

But the one thing I can't allow to happen is for someone she loves to be hurt.

For the woman I love to ever be in danger or mourn her family.

I'd die for Amberlyn and those she holds dear.

They are mine to protect, too.

"I'll be back to you soon, my love."

Chapter 14
AMBERLYN

"THANK YOU FOR meeting me on such short notice, Miss Ibarra." Detective Uriel stands from his seat, holding a hand out toward me as I make my way to the table he's occupying the following afternoon. I take it, and a shiver runs through me. It's small and unpleasant and I pull it back just as quick, which he catches, face tightening a bit around the eyes, yet his smile remains in place. "Would you like anything to drink? I'm heading to the—"

"Here you go, Amberlyn." Lily places my café con leche down along with a large slice of red velvet cake before heading back to the counter. They know me here. It's a small bakery in a strip mall near the office that I frequent when needing a pick-me-up. They make the best sweets, and today is one of those days where indulging is how I'll get by.

I'm frustrated and miss him.

His smile. His touch. The way only he can make me come, and the tension left in his absence continues to grow.

I haven't touched myself either while thoughts of the last time we were together keep me awake. No toys or replicas of his cock. No release for this tension. And it's not just the sex; I need our connection. This all-consuming nirvana that his mere presence gives me. It's raw and sweet and us. *But was it ever real? Or was it all an act?*

"Amberlyn?"

The way he says my name snaps me out of my thoughts and I refocus, giving him a professional smile. "It's already taken care of." Taking my seat, I pick up the oversized white mug and take a few small sips since it's still very hot. "Now, what did you want to show me?"

"Does this mean you'll be taking the case?"

"I'm here, Detective."

"I need a yes or no answer, Miss Ibarra."

"This is me giving you the chance to explain yourself and gain my interest," I say instead while sitting back in my seat. For the first few seconds, there's quiet. He's studying me, and I flick my gaze around the semi-empty establishment before meeting his stare head-on. Detective Jaime Uriel is tall, and I'll admit many would consider him to be handsome with his tan skin, chocolate-colored eyes, and sharp jaw currently sporting a five o'clock shadow. Yet, he does nothing for me. Not so much as a twinge. *Will I ever be attracted to anyone but Ivan? Can I move on?* "That's the most you'll get from me at the moment."

"Noted." Tone terse. A hint of annoyance.

"Or we can end this here. This isn't my headache."

"Why are you being difficult?" he hisses, hands tightening into fists. There's also the restless leg, that moves him and rocks our table a bit.

Something about his presence isn't right. I'm a believer in following my instinct—heavily in tune with that tiny voice inside blaring out in warning, and I place my cell phone face-up on my lap. My father and mother are at the office today and will get here quickly if something were to go wrong. That, and I'm carrying my weapon in plain sight for him to see.

I caught him looking at my cross-body shoulder holster and the loaded SIG inside.

I'm not afraid to shoot. Have a damn good aim, too.

"What you decide to share is up to you, Detective. However—lie, and you'll make an enemy out of me." Again, the skin around his dark eyes becomes tight and this time, there's an added tick to his jaw. "Are we clear on this?"

"Are you threatening an officer of the law? Do you understand the implications—"

"I don't make a habit of saying things I don't mean."

A grin stretches across his lips at my response and his body relaxes, amusement coloring his features. "You're a spitfire, aren't you?"

In return, I level him with an impassive stare. "If I am or not, I don't see how that pertains to what I've been cited here for. Am I wrong?"

"You are correct." Bending to the right, he lifts a work bag and undoes the zipper before pulling out two yellow folders and placing them atop the table. No names on them, but one of the papers sticking out does have the city embossment in the corner. "We're here for business, and I apologize if I—"

"You're fine. I've had a few rough days, and I'm not at my peachiest."

"Are you okay?" While his tone is sincere, I'm still not sold on him. The man's job as a detective is to investigate, not pawn off work on a bail bond office and their bounty hunters. Bullshit seeps from every pore of this meeting, but I'll see it through. If he's a threat, I'll find out and deal with it myself if it comes to that. "Anything I can help you with?"

"No, but can you explain the need for my services?"

"Of course." Detective Uriel opens the first folder and shows me the picture of another police officer. Below his name is a handwritten note with the word *rookie.* The guy is of Latino descent and from the picture, he has a slim build with a recognizable tattoo of praying hands on his left forearm. His bio is short, having been officially on the force for a few months, and works in the Hialeah precinct. "This folder is on the rookie and the other is on the man I detained."

"Tell me what happened." I'm skimming down the few notes, nothing large. He's dependable, a likable guy by his peers. No wife. No kids. "I'll need full details, please."

"I was just having a couple of beers with a few friends, watching a Marlins game, when the fight broke out. It wasn't near me; I was on the opposite side but jumped in to help when it got too rowdy for the employees to contain."

"And you noticed this from across the establishment?" Opening the second folder, I skim down the perp's details. Young, male, and again of Hispanic heritage. Not much on him either, not even a speeding ticket. "Who was involved in the altercation?"

"After separating the two men with the help of my friends, I asked the owners what the issue was and if they wanted the police called."

"And they said yes." My gaze lifts to meet his. Uriel nods.

"They said yes."

"Hmmm."

"Good or bad?"

"More like I'll need a minute. Are you still going to get a drink?" Nothing to do with the conversation, but I need a moment to text Anita the names. There's a discrepancy between what the fiancée gave us and these reports. Same name, two different spellings. "I'm going to read through what you have here before asking more questions."

"Sure. I can go for a coffee." For a second, his eyes narrow but then relax. "Anything you recommend eating?"

"Sweet or savory?"

"A little hint of both." I don't miss the way he licks his bottom lip.

"Try the medianoche sandwich. It's legit the best I've ever had."

"I'll do that." He raps his fist on the table once and stands, pushing his chair back. "Be right back."

"Take your time."

Detective Uriel gives me another studying look before turning and walking toward the front. We're a bit out of sight of the counter and my back is turned to him, so I easily send off a quick text to Anita. Some things don't make sense; their insistence on my working with them is only a small red flag.

Angling my cell, I take three pictures of each document while pretending to read. Her reply is just as quick, her worry clear.

> Got it and already jumping into research. Do you need an out? ~Anita

Fingers tapping a quick ***not yet*** on the screen, I hit enter and place the device down before picking up the document with the perpetrator's name and info. As my eyes scroll across pictures from that night, I notice something interesting.

Uriel is smiling. As is the man being arrested.

In fact, they look more as if posing for a picture than someone documenting the altercation that led to this man's detainment. There's also the question of who took this photograph, and why was it included in this file?

Usually, you get a booking mugshot and detailed report. That's it.

"So what do you think? Can you help us?" Uriel says from behind me, close enough that I feel his hip graze my arm. That extra contact wasn't necessary, and he knows it, but I don't call him out on it. Not after he sits down. Nor when he takes a bite from the sandwich I suggested.

Instead, I smile, and it isn't a professional one. Whatever they want, I'm in and have all the time in the world to play.

I'm a woman scorned, vengeful, and who needs an escape from her problems.

"I can and will."

Grabbing a napkin, he swallows and wipes the corner of his lips. "Thank you."

"Don't thank me yet..." Uriel's head tilts a bit to the side, his mouth opening to say something I assume to be positive, but I shake my head "...you will, though. I'll find them both for you."

"Both?"

"The officer and perp are equally important, and both have stories to tell. Don't you think?"

"What if he's in on it?"

"Then all the more reason to find the guilty, and I won't rest until I do."

"Good." His tone of voice doesn't agree, though. There's a hint of something I can't quite put my finger on, but it raises goose bumps on my arms. "But I'm going to need a final favor if you will."

"Favor?" That word leaves a bitter taste in my mouth. Because the last time a man asked me for a *favor*, it hurt me and people I've come to care about like family.

What Ivan asked of me was a test—used my emotions against me.

I should have never agreed back then to pretend to help Thiago deceive Luna into thinking he cheated, even if it came from a place of love and worry for her safety. I'd rather know the truth than being fed bullshit, and I regret my stupidity over the need to please the youngest De Leon.

"It's nothing serious. All I ask is for complete discretion, please."

"Discretion?" My café con leche has gone cold, but I take a few deep sips anyway. "Explain."

"Amberlyn, if I get caught sharing private information..." he trails off, and I understand the implications. Yes, he can lose his job, but I bet a month's salary that he could give two fucks about that. This is larger than he's letting on; I'm more intrigued by his reasoning for targeting me.

Is my family being investigated and this is how they get inside?

Am I a key to information on the De Leon dealings?

What are you looking for, Detective?

"And that worries you?"

"Yes."

"Then so be it. I'll be prudent."

Chapter 15
IVAN

SHE CAN'T SEE me, but I'm watching from across the street through the windows. They're sitting toward the back and beside a tintless glass. It's a little away from the main door, but in his idiocy, Jaime didn't pay much mind to the public view.

The again, why would he when his uncle sent two trusted hitmen to guard his prodigies?

This is where it becomes a simple lesson: comfort makes you cocky. Sloppy.

Or he's tempting me. Trying to draw me out.

The problem with that is—I know how to play this game.

"Where's the other singao that arrived with you?" The muzzle of my gun digs in deeper into the back of his neck, and his knees scrape against the dirty asphalt when he shifts away. He was easy enough to find, but what he has in size and skill, he lacks in common sense.

This isn't Cuba or whatever country trained him.

This isn't a simulator or controlled assignment.

My eyes and ears reach far deeper than this country or the island. One email sharing the photo, and plenty came forward with information. Seems they've been enjoying their time here, entertaining whores and gambling, the latter of which comes from casino footage of three establishments within city limits.

"Yo, no hablo ingles."

"Yes. You do." Junior, who's here just to remove the body before going back to his bodyguard duty, hits play on a small recorder from the bar they visited a few nights back. They were all there. Each of these assholes had a role to play, and the owners were more than willing to hand over the footage and erase the rest from their server for a small donation.

That video corroborates the audio Cisco and his brother provided.

"I wouldn't mind living here one bit," one man says while another chuckles in the background. You can hear music playing and the occasional cheer from those watching a game on a giant screen above the bar. "Acere, the pussy here alone would be worth the relocation."

"Amen." You can hear the clinking of bottles and what sounds like snorting after. "My brother, I never want to go back."

"Don't let my uncle hear you say that. He'd take offense." A feminine voice mingles with theirs for a minute or two, asking if they need another round, which is declined by Jaime.

"Coño, the ass on that one."

"Stay loyal to me, Pirro, and I'll make sure you have her and any other woman you want. Anywhere. Anytime."

"For her, I'd be loyal."

"And you, Silvio?"

"Keep me in la Yuma and I'll pledge my life to you."

"Now the question is…which one are you? Pirro or Silvio?" The man doesn't answer, and I'll wait a few more minutes. I'm too busy watching as Jaime walks away and my brilliant girl takes pictures of the folder in front of her and then sends off texts.

Whatever he's selling, Sirenita isn't buying.

Makes my chest puff out with pride; I know what she's capable of. How strong she is.

The entire time, Jaime doesn't look our way. Doesn't acknowledge the added security that he assumes watches his back and takes care of any issue that arises. *Dumb motherfucker.*

"Step forward." The moment I say this, the other person in attendance does as I ask, coming to a stop a few steps to my left. He's beside Junior and I look over, finding his focus on the ground. "Look at him, Henry. Meet his eyes."

The unnamed guard tries to stand, his fists clenched tight, but one strike to the back of his head ends that. He slumps, not unconscious but enough to know his place down on his knees. This soldier is a pet of the Rodriguez administration, and I'll teach him as such.

"Sir?" Henry asks, so unsure of himself.

"Name and rank."

"Don't you fucking dare, you piece of mierda."

"I thought you didn't speak the native language of this country." Not a question, but a sarcastic remark. The man is angry—nearly shaking—and my grin broadens. "What happened, asshole? Afraid?"

"Of you, hijo de puta? Never."

"You should be." One bullet with a silencer, right on the shoulder bone, and he cries out. Yet I'm quicker and stuff the end of the tie around his neck deep in his mouth, causing the jackass to choke. Gagging, he coughs around the material while I pat his cheek. "Breathe through your nose." Turning my attention to Davila, I urge him closer with a nod. "Do you know him?"

"Personally? No."

"In what capacity, then?"

"He's Pirro Cruz. One of the two men who came from Cuba under strict orders from the president to protect and help his nephews. He's the younger of the two and seems to get along the most with Jaime."

"Military or mercenary?"

"Both, and they speak fluent English. It's mandatory for anyone who works for Rodriguez."

"Thank you."

Pirro spits out the necktie then, dribble falling from the corner of his mouth. "You're a traitor to your people. You'll pay for this."

"He'll receive penance when I allow it. Not a second sooner."

"Boss, they're shaking hands," Junior says, and I look toward Amberlyn only to find her nodding at something Uriel is saying. The exchange is quick and when Jaime extends a hand, she takes it, but not before saying something that causes his grin to drop.

Sirenita, what are you getting yourself into? You're making it harder to keep you safe.

"Take his body and burn it. I want nothing, not even his teeth left behind."

"Yes, sir."

"Fuck you! You can't—"

My release is quick, and two shots to the back of the head end his time on earth. His body falls forward, blood splattering across the pavement and my shirt, but I only focus on the beautiful woman drinking coffee not far from me.

So beautiful. So mine.

I'm almost home, baby. Just a little more time.

My conversation with Thiago moved my trip up a bit and with a minor detour. My brother received an invitation to meet with President Rodriguez, and I've accepted.

"He's angry, brother. Very careless after finding his general's mangled body." Thiago's amusement comes through the secured line a few days ago. He's outside and the wind is a bit heavy, but being

they're so close to the water it's normal. His private estate isn't far from the family compound near the Mariel port. "You did quite a number on him."

I snort at that. "Nothing they wouldn't do to one of our own if given the chance."

"Agreed."

"What's going on?" Taking out a cigarette, I light up and take a drag. "Why are you calling me instead of enjoying your honeymoon? By the way, when's your flight out to Tahiti?"

"A presidential invite arrived today via Amberlyn's family, and in two days." There's a pause, and I know what he's going to say. "I can post—"

"No." Grip tightening, I hear the plastic in my hand protest, nearly cracking. "Who delivered, and to what home?"

"Her grandfather arrived at the compound, and the maid called me, Ivan. The old man had a busted lip and black eye." My brother exhales roughly. Even from miles away, his anger is palpable and mirrors my own. "Rodriguez wants to meet. Says we have a week to show our faces before he forces our hand."

"I'll be there when the time is right."

"You've always had my back. Let me—"

"Alone, Thiago. He's mine to deal with."

"I know."

I'll also be arriving with gifts.

The heads of his nephews, to start.

Fingering the beads at my wrist, I play with the latch and extend the solid steel wire within, thrumming it once. I've been saving this for someone special, and the who has been revealed.

And when Amberlyn stands from her seat, I step back into the shadows. When she exits after taking the folder with her, ignoring the tightness on Jaime's face, I watch her every step until she's inside her car and the taillights disappear around the corner.

Then from the dark alley, I meet his eyes from the inside the window.

The asshole waves at my silhouette, and I do the same. He's confusing me with his now-dead guard, and I smirk, still toying with the steel wire for another second before snapping it into place within the bracelet.

"Your hours are numbered, Uriel. Tick-Tock."

Jaime walks out the door and I turn, stepping inside an unlocked door a few feet away from me. It belongs to a laundry shop owned by a family acquaintance who's been nice enough to let me borrow the back room as storage from time to time. She's also old and crotchety, but Mom likes her, so I hold nothing but respect for the woman.

"Grab a clean shirt from my office before you leave, kid. I'll burn this one."

"Thanks." Pulling my soiled one off, I hand it over while taking a small, wet hand towel she's offering. Both items will be burned once done, but not before being soaked in commercial-quality bleach. "This one got a little messy."

"You, or the dead man I saw your guy dragging away?" Raised bushy brows assess me, lips pursing. "The deceased didn't look local, either."

"You're too perceptive for someone nearing eighty, Dora."

"No. I've just been around long enough to pick up on certain things." Turning, she walks over to a large metal drum that's rusty and has a caution sticker on the wall behind it. We're now inside the back room I use, away from customers, and with a filtration system that keeps the harsh odors away from those roaming the front. "You okay?"

"I will be." It's the truth. No use in lying.

"Good." Dumping my shirt in, she opens her palm for the towel, but I toss it in for her. I also open the lever that controls the bleaching agent, its strong odor infiltrating my senses at once. "God, that stinks. I'm getting too old for this."

"Blasphemy."

"Shut it and call your mother. She knows you're here."

At that, I raise a brow while closing the spigot. “How so?”

“Easy. I called her.” She shrugs.

“Snitching isn’t attractive, old woman.”

“Neither is coming here without my favorite cookies.” That pointed look is harmless to me. Her huff of annoyance tells me she knows it, too. Thiago, on the other hand, has fallen for it. “That’s a horrible thing to do.”

“You’ll have three dozen first thing in the morning and dinner catered all week.”

“Much better.” Slowly, Dora walks over and taps my cheek with her small hand. Her expression is knowing. “Never make that mistake again, De Leon. I’m old and small, but mess with my sweets —our arrangement—and I’ll complain to the woman you fear the most.”

“And who’s that?”

“Amberlyn Ibarra.”

Chapter 16
AMBERLYN

FIVE AND A HALF YEARS AGO…

I'M FLOATING, water lapping at my bikini-covered breasts while the sun warms my cheeks. The shore isn't far from where I am, and yet, I hear the group laughing—the loud music playing—as if I were sitting among them.

Instead, though, I'm in my own world.

Thinking. Daydreaming. Eyes closed while tipping my head back; I pretend I'm somewhere else.

Living in Miami is fun, and exciting at times, but to me, it's still not home. I miss Tampa, my family, and my friends there. I miss being accepted and not looked at like a favor they're doing. Like someone who tags along without being truly invited.

Not all do. Just a small few, but they matter more than most.

No one is outright rude, but you get that feeling. A look—a fake smile. If only they paid attention to where my eyes always wander. Who my smiles are really for.

Not that I don't understand; after two years, I'm still an outsider to them. Or maybe I try too hard.

Luna is as possessive as Thiago.

Natasha is protective of her family.

The rest follow the leaders.

While Ivan continues to ignore my crush. Yet his secret smiles when no one is looking give me hope. That maybe he sees me too.

"What're doing, Mermaid?" His voice comes from behind me, close enough that I feel his warmth on the back of my neck, and at once, goose bumps rise on my skin. Shivers rush through me. "Why are you out here by yourself?"

"Because I enjoy my solitude."

"I don't like it."

"But I do."

"What if I forbid it?"

That makes me turn, meeting his warm, soft eyes. Like he understands more than I want him to. "Why does it matter?"

"It does."

"That's not—"

"Come with me," he interrupts, hand raising to push a few wet strands of hair back and off my neck. Those fingers linger there and then trace from my neck to jaw before cupping my face. "You shouldn't be out here."

"Why don't you stay with me instead?" It's hard, but I fight the urge to nuzzle my face into his palm. "Maybe take a swim further out?"

"Swim?"

"Yes."

"Okay." His thumb traces over my cheeks before dropping and Ivan moves back, running a rough hand down his face. "Just promise me you'll stay close." I nod, but his eyes narrow. "Use your words, Mermaid."

"Why do you call me Mermaid?" I answer instead.

"Does it matter?" While the response could be taken as rude, his expression is playful, his grin delicious. "Would it make you happy to know?"

"It would." More than he could ever know. Since we met, that's been his name for me, much to the annoyance of almost every girl in our school. Rarely does he use my first name. It's always *Mermaid this* or *Sirenita that*, and in Spanish, it sounds sinful coming from him.

This crush controls me. Ivan De Leon is my weakness.

"Miss Ibarra, I call you Sirenita because you remind me of a movie my little cousin used to watch on repeat." Once again, he steps closer. Our skin touches this time, and his hands grip my waist —fingers flexing against the mostly bare skin there. "It was about a pretty girl who loves the water and who has bright red hair and expressive eyes looking for acceptance. Always curious. Always sweet." Ivan lowers his face toward mine and inhales deep, this low, rumbling sound building in his chest. *What would it feel like to kiss his lips? For him to make that sound against my skin?* "I also call you Mermaid because when I look at you, I'm reminded of my favorite things. Is that enough of an explanation?"

"Yes." It's nearly a whimper, and his smirk deepens.

"Will you swim with me now?"

"Okay."

"Good girl." Heat sweeps across my cheeks and I turn my head away, hoping he doesn't catch my blush. Those words cause an ache in me, a need I try to control, but the pebbling of my nipples and clenching of my thighs are unstoppable; thank God he doesn't call me out on it. There's no doubt he noticed both. "Don't look away, Amberlyn."

And I return my gaze. As if I have any control over my actions.

I also swallow hard because the slight darkening of his eyes unnerves me.

"You ready?" Tone breathy. A slight whimper.

Ivan doesn't answer me. Instead, he turns and without a word walks us deeper into the warm waters. Moreover, I follow without hesitation. Let him lead me until my feet no longer touch the ocean floor and I lean over, hands gripping his shoulders to keep myself afloat.

We stay like that.

No swimming. No movement other than the gentle sway of waves.

Ivan and I watch the horizon while ignoring the world around us. In the distance, someone calls his name, yet he continues to look ahead with an arm low on my back.

Peace surrounds us. This quiet is comforting.

I never want this moment to end.

But then he clears his throat. "Sirenita, we need to talk."

"About?" Low. A little meek.

"A favor."

"A favor?"

"Yes." Regret flashes across his expression, but it's soon replaced by the smile that causes butterflies to take flight in my stomach. By a soft touch to my back, fingertips dancing up and down my spine while his mouth lowers to hover over mine. His exhale is my inhale. His scent infiltrates my senses and had I not been leaning on him, I'd have found myself submerged. "I need you to do something for me."

"Anything."

"Pretend to mess around with Thiago."

PRESENT...

I AWAKE WITH A GASP, my heart pounding while sweat beads across my forehead. My mouth is dry and my muscles are tight, thighs clenching, and the wetness there is unmistakable. As is my shame.

I'm needy and tired. Wanting and angry.

Yet my mind gives me no reprieve as the day our relationship crossed over the line from mild flirtation to indecent touches replays in my dreams like a punishing reel. Over and over while my body remembers that I haven't felt his touch in days.

No relief. No soothing words telling me it'll be okay.

Sitting up, I flick my eyes to the bedside alarm and groan when it reads a little over two in the morning. "Freaking detective and his stupid *I need a favor* crap."

Why did he have to use that precise word during our meeting three days ago? One I loathe, and yet, it was the beginning of *us*...

My affair with Ivan De Leon.

It reminds me of something I'm not proud of yet can't deny; he is my weakness. My ever-present inability to deny Ivan anything hasn't changed since then, and a part of me knows he'd do the same for me.

My battle: common sense argues with my heart.

His words to Maribel don't match the actions of the man I tried to reject before his brother's wedding. How he touched me—made me come for him with a desperation that rivaled the first time, and even now, I remember how easily I gave in.

Then. Now. Yet my clit throbs just the same. I feel the way my wetness soaks my underwear.

"When will he stop tormenting me?" I ask the silence of the room, but the reply is another memory. "This limbo is driving me insane."

Images flash behind my eyes. Our story. Him.

We were walking on the shore later that night and stop at one of the empty bodyguard towers, climbing up the steps to be away from public view. Giddy would be the only way to describe me, so freaking happy as he squeezes my hand and turn us so we're facing the night's sky.

"You're so beautiful, Sirenita. A perfect doll," Ivan croons, his voice low, yet the deep velvet tones slide across my flesh like a sinful sweep. At once, goose bumps rise on my skin, and my nipples pebble beneath the thin material of my bikini top. I shiver. Can't stop it. "You cold?"

"Little bit." A lie. Yet Ivan doesn't call me out on it. Instead, he moves so he's behind me with an arm wrapped around my midsection.

That's the first time I feel him.

All of him.

"Better?"

"Yes." This time it leaves me on a low whimper, and he chuckles, the low rumble causing his chest to rub against my bare skin. I'm in tune with his every minute shift. The rough exhale against the back of my neck a few seconds before he nuzzles me—leaves open mouthed kisses that make my knees weak.

Not that he lets me fall—I'm pulled tighter against his muscles while the hardness digging into my back throbs. Flexes in time with my pulsing clit.

"You feel so good, bebe. Always knew you would." Voice gravelly, he brings two fingers to my lips before dipping them inside, just the tip against my tongue, before drawing them down my neck and chest. Lower, and Ivan caresses my skin—circling my belly button and the piercing there. He's toying with me. Causing me to squeeze my thighs together, and right when a moan slips from my lips, those same two fingers dip beneath the waistband of my—

"Fuck me." My hand moves without prompting, reaching inside my bedside drawer for one of the toys I keep there. Fingers skimming, I feel the texture of one I know too well. The silicone girth and veins make me suck in a deep breath; my mouth waters and chest expands, yet it feels as though I can't get any air in.

I remember him.

The day he gave this to me.

How he used it to fill my pussy while buried deep inside my ass.

"No. No." A chant. A demand I force myself to follow and remove my hand, ignoring the need clawing at my flesh, tearing me apart. Instead, I reach a little deeper and grab my thrusting vibrator. It's not the real thing, nowhere close to Ivan's perfection, but it'll have to do.

With the click of a button, it buzzes in my hand, vibrating on a low setting. *More. Need more.*

It feels so good when I run it across my naked chest, nipples throbbing to the point my eyes roll back, and I bite down on my bottom lip. A hard shiver runs through me, and I'm wetter—hips lifting a bit and I lie down, situating myself so my back is slightly up.

My knees spread wide after I kick off my sheets so they pool at my feet.

My walls tighten and then release, anticipating the orgasm I desperately need. And when the tip of the toy touches just above my clit, I moan as warmth spreads through me. It's a gentle sweep, yet in my head, it's his lips that kiss me there.

His tongue dragging across my swollen bundle of nerves and tortures me with hard strokes. The vibrations pick up, a pulsing rhythm that makes me cry out when I circle my entrance. From hole to clit, I spread my juices as I remember just how he touched me that day.

Ivan wasn't tentative or slow, and petting me wasn't enough. No.

He slowly lowered to his knees as his hands pushed down the unbuttoned cutoffs I'd put on after exiting the water. They didn't make it past my knees before his warm breath was teasing my flesh. I never got to fill my lungs with air before his tongue dipped over my clit and then my folds, those same strong hands yanking me against his mouth while the waves crashed behind me.

We were in our own little world and the darkness covered anyone from seeing how I was his at that moment.

"Fuck, bebe. So fucking sweet." That groan reverberated through me, vibrating against where I was most sensitive, and my body rewarded him with a rush of wetness. And the moment it coated his senses, I'm raised off the floor by two hands on my hips that forced me to ride his tongue.

"Oh, God," I moan as the silicone enters me, bottoming out while the air suction attaches to my throbbing clit. That's as far as I get while the air in my lungs gets trapped. In my mind it's his fingers inside me, two thick and unrelenting fingers thrusting, while his lips suck and nip at me. Sweat mists over my shaking form, a few drops rolling down my flesh and I arch, body strung tight.

I'm so close. It hurts.

But then I hear him as if he were here. Right next to me, that gravelly tone borders on a growl that's his tell before he fills me with his release.

"Come for me, bebe."

"Papi." It's a scream, my entire frame wrought tight a second before pleasure consumes me, and I let it. The torturous wave slams into me, and I don't know what's real or fake or even if this is all a dream, but it doesn't matter either way.

Not when a second later I let the vibrator fall and I'm languid. So spent I don't turn the toy off and simply kick it toward the end of the bed where it will eventually die off.

All I can do is melt into my mattress and close my eyes.

Yet the last thing I hear before succumbing brings a smile to my face.

"I'll be home soon."

Chapter 17
IVAN

ROPES OF COME coat my hand and stomach, the proof of my inability to stop thinking of a woman I love more than rationality dictates. Maybe it's a sickness. An obsession.

I could give less than a fuck either way.

And the evidence of that is how I continue to stroke my cock as her breathing evens. How I wring out another spurt of my release while she sighs in contentment, body stretched out in her bed. Those sheets smell of her—a sweetness I crave more than anything in this world.

Again, my fist tightens and my eyes close. Another bead drops. It rolls down my fingers as I stroke up and then over then sensitive head when I hear her murmur *Ivan* in her sleep.

A shuddering breath escapes my lungs and my cock jerks, the near painful throb coming from the dissatisfaction of not being there. With her. Keeping my little mermaid cuddled close and warm.

"I'll be home soon." Gazing at her once again, I touch the keypad of my laptop and turn off the mic. She's mirrored on a large screen inside the penthouse suite of a hotel room in Atlanta after my short flight here, having connected the device to the TV from a remote private server.

The accommodations are large, ostentatious for the few short hours I'll be here, and not too far from the strip club where my enemy snorts his way through endless amounts of cocaine.

My job here is simple: grab and escort back home.

Nothing else. No more than a couple hours of sleep, yet the moment I open my camera inside her room—watching on the screen as she pleasures herself—that resolve always hanging by a thin thread whenever she's concerned snaps.

It's why I couldn't resist and let her hear me.

I needed to be the reason she came.

Yet my sirenita *destroyed* me. Hearing her say *papi* in that whiny tone, one that drives me crazy right before reaching her peak, is my kryptonite.

"Always mine." A ringtone blaring pulls my attention from the TV and I look over, finding Israel's phone number on the screen. He's stationed outside the club, monitoring who enters and who leaves. With my clean hand, I press the green button while ignoring a text from my father, then hit the speaker option. "Talk to me."

"He's here and not alone. There's a brunette with him and a man, one I've never seen before."

"Silvio?"

"No. This one is American and older."

"Okay." Grabbing the still-wet towel from my earlier shower, I wipe my hand and stomach before standing from the bed. I'll need a quick rinse before heading out, but for now, I wrap the bedsheet around my waist. I've made a mess, but it's her fault and I look over to where her figure still sleeps peacefully on the monitor. I can't help but bite back a chuckle when I find her hugging my pillow. She sleeps on the right, while I've always taken the left side of the bed. "Dalian doesn't leave. If he tries, shoot him. Blow out both kneecaps if you must, but don't kill him. He owes me a conversation."

"Consider it done."

"I'll see you in a few." Before I drop the phone, I read Dad's message.

How was the flight? ~Viejo

Parents never stop worrying. Yet before I get the chance to respond, there's another text.

Answer me, so I can calm your mother. If not, she'll be calling in sixty seconds. ~Viejo

I bark out a laugh, shaking my head. She would, too.

Good, and I'll be driving back once I pick up. See you around two. ~Ivan

At once, three dots appear.

At the docs or warehouse by 49th? ~Viejo

Neither. We're taking a trip to the swamp. ~Ivan

THE PARKING LOT IS FULL, and the music can be heard from where I'm parked a few hours later. I'm next to a party bus; the lights inside are on, but the driver is long gone. He drove my prey here, and did a little coke, too.

Yet a few bills were enough to send him on his way. Alive.

"In and out. Keep it clean." I'm an asshole, but killing innocent people isn't how I get off.

"Yes, sir." Israel steps outside the all-white SUV with black tints and the two others traveling with us follow. They check their weapons and move to the back and wait for me.

It's late at night.

Those on our side of the world sleep, yet a few lurk.

Work. Party. Or fuck.

Dalian's mistake was doing all three without fear of being found. Every move he and his family took against mine wasn't well thought out. A trap with too many exit points, especially after the unhidden fiasco they created to reel in Amberlyn.

Bringing in the female as bait to gain Mermaid's trust, as though she—I—wouldn't see through it, almost makes me laugh. Almost, had it not pulled me away from my girl and forced decisions that keep us apart for now.

Pulling out my phone, I open the camera again. I just need to see if she's still sound asleep.

The sight that greets me tugs at my lips and my heart, and the owned fucker thumps harshly inside my chest. There she is, warm and sweet and waiting for me. Now she's snuggled up in a soft blanket that usually stays at the foot of the bed. It's big enough for her and in a dark purple tone she loves.

Closing my eyes for a second, I breathe in deep and then out, craning my head from side to side. All noises in the back minimize. They feel like a low thrum, yet I can pinpoint the direction of each: the guards at the back of my vehicle talking lowly, the two men laughing at something while walking past us, and then my breathing.

It's harsh, but not from nerves. No.

Rage flows through my veins and burns me from the inside. My hands clench, the phone in my hand making a low cracking noise, and I look down. The plastic groans again, and I drop it beside me on the seat.

I want my pound of flesh.

For her. For us.

The darkness in my soul, the baser instincts, demand blood. Retribution.

A sigh comes from my phone and I gaze down, seeing the microphone turned on. She can hear me, and I, her. Amberlyn turns then, just a slight shift, and gives another content sound. It's low, almost indiscernible, but to me, it's as if she's moaning beside my ear.

Beneath me. Sweaty and so fucking wet.

"Papi."

"Fuck, Mermaid." My voice carries and she stirs, almost wakes up, but then settles. Nestling deeper into the soft blanket, she grips my empty pillow beside her, and I turn the camera off. If I watch for even another minute, I'd head back.

I would murder every person inside that strip club just so I could end it all sooner.

Instead, I place the device inside my pocket and exit the vehicle. Those with me straighten and remain silent, eyes on the establishment while I tuck my gun in the waistband of my dress pants. They have their instructions and quickly fall into step behind me, Israel to my right.

The closer we get to the entrance, the music becomes louder, and a blaring guitar riff shakes the glass on the large doors. There's a bouncer there, and understanding dawns on his face when Israel hands him an envelope.

No questions. No pause.

We walk straight through and bypass the hostess waiting to walk us to a table. Or sell services.

VIP, dances, or an extra, if I go by the look sent my way.

Not interested.

The establishment is large with a few stages, but the main one is surrounded by men and three women. They're watching the show, some cupping themselves while throwing a few dollars on the stage, yet my eyes aren't on the two dancers kissing for the crowd.

It doesn't take long at all to find Dalian and company. I make my way over, ignoring everyone but them.

"What the fuck are you looking at?" a female's voice hisses and when I find their location, the one with Dalian isn't Karen. Yet she's hissing as if she's the wife, her twang unmistakable Miami, and more so when she adds a *fucking pata sucia* at the end. That's a 305 insult all day. While many outside the city culture won't understand, you're calling her dirty. One of those nasty women that will take off their shoes in a club or street and strut/dance without care where people have tossed garbage, drinks, and who knows what else.

For the women in Miami, that's a large insult. Cleanliness is drilled into your head since childhood and if you're willing to do that, how low will you go?

I find it hilarious.

Especially the lost expression on the waitress's face. "I'm sorry. What did you say? I don't—"

Before the brunette can answer, I slide into their booth while the others take a small table a few steps away. "Ignore her. They don't go out much."

"Oh. We get people like that in here occasionally." The blonde's smile widens, arching her back a bit after getting a good look at my face. "Is there anything I can do for you, handsome?"

"No. I'm here to pick them up."

"Limo driver?" She giggles, and the sound grates on my nerves—it's too nasally—but I keep my smile polite.

"Party bus." Dalian and the female shift uncomfortably to my left, while the other man remains quiet. "I'm parked outside."

"Those are fun. You got a business card on—"

"Excuse me, miss." A man taps her shoulder, and she looks over. "I'm here with a city employees retirement party, table of fifteen, and we need some service. We've been sitting for twenty minutes now, and no one has come by. Can you help me find our server or the manager?"

Talk about divine interruption.

He turns and glances at the table, looking apologetic. “Sorry for the interruption.”

“No worries.” I wave them off. “Go ahead, miss. We’re fine.”

“Are you sure?”

“I am.” The two turn and leave while my guards stand. My eyes shift to Dalian first, and then the others. “Get up.”

“Who the fuck are you?” The one I don’t know sneers before raising a beer bottle to his lips, emptying what’s left, and then burps. Disgusting. “You got balls, kid. But I’m not the one you should be fucking with.”

That makes me laugh. Loud. “Know your place, *old man.* This isn’t your problem, but I can make it so.”

“Who the fuck—”

“Ivan De Leon.”

Recognition dawns on his face; I notice the subtle shake of his hand still holding the bottle. “I thought you said he was in Miami. That they didn’t know about our arrangement.”

“Interesting.”

“I want no issues, De Leon.”

“Name.”

“Kyle Montgomery.”

Arms dealer, but his business is mainly with the US military. I’ve never met the man but know plenty, and it makes sense in a way. While I deal more with the narcotics department—you can call it perico, yayo, or simply cocaine—it’s the same thing, but Thiago’s brought black-market weapons into our arsenal. Untraceable and handmade, the pieces coming out of the Philippines are shipped to us using the scraps from the family yard in Hialeah and are better than anything you can find in the country. We provide the metal, but the supplier is a true artist and can recreate anything the large companies produce for a fraction of the cost.

Montgomery knows this. Has wanted to buy from us, but Thiago dealt with and denied him.

That’s the only reason I’ve never seen his face before today: I trust my brother and his judgment in the matter while I've been watching our deliveries through our ports.

"You have some explaining to do, Montgomery."

"I meant no harm."

"Yes, you did." Sliding out, I stand and fix the watch on my wrist. "Let's go. We have a lot to discuss."

"Me too?" the woman asks.

"All of you." Dalian's been quiet, too quiet, and I find him looking toward the emergency exit. So does one of my soldiers, and I give him a nod. Within seconds, the muzzle of a gun is at the back of the bastard's neck and his two companions pale and nearly yell out. "Draw attention to yourself, and I'll kill you here. Don't tempt fate."

"You can't touch me, Ivan. My uncle—"

"Made a grave mistake in trusting an irresponsible cunt like you." Before the last word slips past my lips, there's a loud commotion near the main stage, howling, and Dalian is struck at the base of his skull. At once he slumps forward, his face meeting the tabletop and his empty glass cracks at the impact.

Blood begins to pool, and the woman whimpers.

Montgomery is grabbed from behind while Israel handles Dalian.

"Miss, I suggest you don't make this hard on yourself and follow me outside. I'm not going to hurt you."

"I'm just an escort. He paid me to spend the weekend with him through an agency," the brunette pleads, tears brimming in her over-made dark eyes.

"And as long as that's true, then you have nothing to worry about."

Chapter 18
IVAN

"YOUR NAME, please."

The woman sitting across from me on a picnic table is shaking, tears running down her face. Those ten pounds of makeup have begun to melt and the mascara tracks make her look like shit, so I hold out a napkin and bottle of water. She doesn't grab them right away; it's smart to be wary, but I don't hurt women.

Never have and never will.

In our family, if a woman is to be dealt with, my mother or another trusted female does. That's always been the rule, but this time I take the lead while my parents arrive. They've caught a bit of traffic.

We're away from the other two: a still knocked-out Dalian, and Montgomery, who's tried to buy his way out of this mess.

Placing the items atop the table, I push them forward. Now she grabs them. "Thank you."

"No worries." I give her a few minutes to right herself. Standing from the table, I walk over to Kyle and remove his blindfold. I'm not worried she'll try to run, not in the Everglades. We've brought her deep enough that one freaked-out wrong turn will land you face to face with a gator, or worse, a constrictor. Both will kill her. Both these dominating species have overtaken the wetlands and grow to be huge and aggressive. "Kyle, I'm going to ask that you please stop talking. When I'm ready to deal with you or hear out your plans to make amends, I'll let you know."

"Ivan, please. Let's—" My knuckles meet the bridge of his nose while the second punch lands on his mouth, busting his lip.

"Not another word. Understood?" He nods. "Good." When I turn back around, she's standing but her eyes are not on us. Rather, she's looking at a decent-sized banded water snake slithering toward a wet area not far from her. "It's harmless and nonpoisonous."

"Snake."

"Sit down. It's only passing through." When she doesn't, I pick up the animal gently and walk over to a bush farthest from her. There, I release it and return to take my seat at the table. "Now can you sit?" She does. Still terrified. "Your name?"

"Cindy."

"All right, Cindy, let's make this quick." At her quick indrawn breath, I hold both hands up while maintaining some distance. She's on the opposite side of the table and to the left, and I'm more than okay with that. "I'm not going to hurt you, but there are questions I need answered."

"Then I can go?"

"Yes."

"Okay." She adjusts the suit jacket Israel gave her, closing it tighter around her front. The water and napkin are in front of her, unused. "Ask me anything."

"How do you know Dalian Uriel?"

Her brows furrow and her fists close, yet I notice her hands shaking. "Who's that?"

"That would be the unconscious man on the grass."

"Pero like, that's not the name he gave me or the agency. His I.D. reads Wilmer Santos." *Bingo*. Only the natives use "pero like" instead of "but like" on everything. Just like *irregardless* and *supposably*. The lingo in South Florida is different, and most outside of the locals don't know these idiosyncrasies. Are the words said and spelled incorrectly? Yes, but we understand, and that's all that matters.

"Where do you work? And is Cindy your real name?"

"Craving Sugar, and yes."

"And your last name?"

"It's Johnson."

"Cindy Johnson from Craving Sugar?"

"Yes, sir." Grabbing the bottle of water, she twists the top and pours a little onto her fingers, then dabs her eyes while looking away. All that does is further smear her makeup, but she carries on like nothing and I don't say anything either. The silence stretches for a few minutes before she releases a sigh and meets my eyes again. "At first, it was a sugar baby/sugar daddy dating website, but recently, they've expanded into escort services for those needing an event or weekend companion. Those short-term contracts make me the most money, and that's how I ended up here."

My fingers thrum on the wooden tabletop. "Is the company based in Miami?"

"Yes, but they take clients nationwide. I work in the Atlanta area. Born and raised there."

"And you reside?"

"There as well." *Liar.*

While I've heard of the website, her story is too convenient. I also haven't forgotten how she insulted the waitress at the strip club, once again using terminology only Miami girls say. However, I don't call her out on this. Instead, I'll let the brunette walk and hang herself later.

"You're free to go. Thank you for your assistance." Standing, I point at one of the men who's standing guard over Dalian. He jogs over at once. "Get her on a plane back to Atlanta. First-class, and make sure she's compensated well for her trouble."

"What's going to happen to them?" Cindy moves toward me, calmer now. "Is this about a girl named Amberlyn?"

My head snaps in her direction, eyes narrowed. "How do you know that name?"

Cindy points a shaky finger at Uriel. "He spoke about her shortly after picking me up. Wanted me to wear a red wig, but I denied his request. And then—"

"Then what?" I snap and she jumps, yet a hand on my arm makes me pause.

"Let me talk to her, mi niño. I got it," Mom says from beside me. "You handle those two, while we go get a coffee and something to eat."

I nod, gritting my teeth. "Take one of my men with you."

"Miguel will go with us. He's in the car waiting."

"Okay." Without taking my eyes off the woman, I bend down and kiss my mother's temple. "She doesn't leave until I'm satisfied with what she knows. I don't trust her."

"Of course, son." Mom pretends to clean something from my collar, her lips barely moving. "You know I'm protective of our girls."

"Thank you." Rising to my full height, I give her and Cindy my back while Israel ushers them to the awaiting vehicle. Dad hasn't said a word all this time, but I catch his eye and he gives me a nod. We wait in silence for a good fifteen minutes while my guard comes back, knowing the women are gone and won't hear any of this.

The area we are in is mostly closed off to the public and leads to larger bodies of water where you're more likely to find dangerous animals. Not that the entire park doesn't have wildlife everywhere, but the deeper you go off trails and into the marsh, the terrain changes and so do the encounters.

No barriers separate you.

No illusion of safety.

"Wake him up." My father does the honors, landing a solid kick to his face with his favorite pair of church shoes, breaking the idiot's nose. For an old man who uses a cane, he's still strong and his violent tendencies are slightly below his son's. Not far, though.

"Motherfucker," Dalian groans from the floor, twisting on the ground while blood drips from his nose. A hand comes up to cup his face but then halts midway. His eyes open, the fact he's on a patch of dry grass and not in a comfortable bed inside of an Atlanta hotel hitting him. As is the harsh sunburn growing across his face and neck, then lower to his bare chest.

I can see the recognition on his face, the slight shake of his frame.

"Get up." At my voice, his face pinches tighter. There's fear in his expression, but more pronounced is the anger. "Now."

"Fuck you, cabron." That earns him a foot to the neck, pinning him down and cutting off some of his airflow. Dalian sputters and tries to push it away, but my father doesn't budge. "Get off!"

"No, hijo de puta," Dad sneers before adding a little more pressure. It's entertaining to see him this pissed. It's been a while. Orlando De Leon is strong, loving, and above all else, protective of his family. The only reason he's relaxed a bit is because of my mother. She wants to relax and enjoy what's left of their lives, and he lives to not disappoint her. "Fucking scum. I should chop your head off and ship it to your uncle."

"They'll be reunited soon enough."

Dad's gaze snaps to mine, and his lips curl into a grin. "I trust you have a plan?"

"Was there ever any doubt?"

"You've always been the more creative one of the two. Your brother's more—"

"Straightforward in his approach." I match his smile, and the men here chuckle. "We each have our strengths, Viejo."

"You are my kids, after all." Cocky bastard puffs out his chest a bit. "I expect no less."

"Funny." Shifting my gaze to Israel, I wave him toward Dalian. "Stand him up. We need to have a little chat."

A whimper comes from just a few feet to the left of Israel, drawing my attention. "Is there a problem, Montgomery?"

"Please let me go."

"Why should I?" While my attention is on the arms dealer, my men stand an unsteady Dalian up, but not before Orlando elbows him in the gut twice. The Cuban president's nephew coughs and groans, then sputters out a pained *fucking shit* before my father steps back. "This is your chance to save yourself."

"I meant no disrespect, De Leon. That's something I need you to understand, please."

"Go on." Pulling my shirt over my head, I toss it to a soldier near me. Next, I remove my gold watch, two rings, and then stretch my arms out. The ink on my skin glistens under the hot sun, the story on my body an homage to who and where I come from.

The island. Our culture.

Yet the scripture on my neck comes from an old poem my mother loves written by a famous Cuban author. It speaks of the land, the treasures unseen by the eyes of most, but for those that know of its beauty strive to hold close.

Montgomery swallows hard, the blood on his face mixed with sweat and he licks it off his lip. "They approached me with an offer too interesting not to entertain."

"Isn't that always the story." Stretching, I extend both hands back and feel a pop at each shoulder. Feels good. "Get to the point."

"I was told your family had been overthrown…" He trails off when my eyes narrow on him. I take a step forward and he flinches back, falling to his ass from his knees. "I'm just telling you what they said."

"They who?" The bracelet I've kept on shines in the sunlight, the black azabache beads at the end near the clasp drawing his attention. These stones are used heavily in Spanish countries to ward off the evil eye. Babies especially wear them after birth, and Thiago gave me this special one as a joke since I'm the baby of the family. *Asshole.* Yet it does come with a special extra that I've saved for this piece-of-shit family. "Give me a name."

"Jaime Uriel."

At that, I snort and meet Dalian's eyes. "You're nothing more than a puppet they use."

"Fuck you, De Leon."

"No, thank you."

"You won't kill me. Motherfuckers like you don't have the…*Christ*," Dalian cries out at the end, bending at the waist after my father stabs him once in his stomach. One. That's all it took for a few tears to fall.

"Pathetic." Turning back to Kyle, I wave him on. "Finish the story. Jaime called you, I assume?"

"Yes," he whispers.

"Louder. So everyone can hear you."

"Yes, he called with President Rodriguez on the line listening in."

"The fuck did you say?" Dalian's face pinches tight from his position, but he still hasn't straightened up. "That can't be true. My brother wouldn't lie to me."

Dad meets my eyes briefly, his knuckles white as he grips the teak cane tighter.

"I'm not lying. I have a recording of the conversation in my office back in D.C." Little Uriel's face becomes red, angry, but when the muzzle of a gun is placed at the back of his neck, he's smart enough to keep those lips shut and lower himself to his knees. Montgomery, on the other hand looks troubled. Very much so. "I never questioned the call or how they got my phone number—things in this business move fast—but Jaime did ask me to be discreet. To not tell anyone about the call, not even his brother, as he supposedly knew and wasn't interested in the details."

"And why do you think that is, Dalian? Are you discardable?" No answer from the man. "Continue, Kyle. Tell me everything discussed."

"Of course." Again, he licks his blood-stained lips. "Jaime assured me there had been a takeover of the De Leon operations and that you and Thiago stepped down. That the business had been sold for a reasonable sum to him after a bit of forcible persuasion, but you'd be staying on as intermediaries between them and the suppliers for the time being. From my understanding, your family agreed to keep a member safe and that your next shipment, which includes Mac-10s and other military-grade weapons, will be here next week and would be mine. I already have a client waiting for these."

"That's a lie! You're in a bidding war with a South American country; I promised you the rights to it if you doubled your original offer."

"What else?" I ask, not giving much thought to Dalian's outburst.

"I'd be given first right's refusal to all shipments following this first purchase."

"Hmmm." Walking over to Dalian, I crouch down and meet his bloodshot eyes. "Wonder why they made you their bait? What made them betray you?"

"They wouldn't."

"Are you sure about that?" He's right, but I'm not going to tell him that. Betrayal stings on his face, this pain-filled look that comes from family cutting deep, but I do keep my smirk. "Sounds to me as though you've been set up."

"Lies. All lies."

"Are they, though? Is Cindy as easy to manipulate?"

"They'd never." Yet at the mention of her name, he twitches. "She's loyal."

Exactly. She's dirty, and I'd bet my left nut that's not her real name.

Chapter 19
IVAN

"YOU'RE DUMBER THAN you look, Dalian." Eyes narrowing, he tries to rebut, but I grip his chin tight. The force grinds his teeth and hollows his cheek, while I hold a hand toward my father. "Knife, please, and text Miguel."

"Here you go, son."

"Thank you." I grip the blood-stained gold handle, weighing and testing my hold. "You'll get this back in a minute."

"Kill me, and you'll never find out our plans for your bitch." It's muffled by my grip, but I understand Dalian clearly and refocus on him.

"Keep talking."

"You can't protect her from us, Ivan. We know her schedule." Spit dribbled out the side of his mouth, and I smear it against the opposite cheek in mocking. "When she wakes up. When she eats. Every fucking thing Amberlyn Ibarra does in her day-to-day."

"So you say, but I also know those you hold dear."

"They'd never betray me." His defiance is almost admirable. "I trust my family."

"Okay."

"Okay?" he asks, confused by my lack of taking his bait. I've played this game too many times to fall for his bullshit.

"If you trust or don't, it makes no difference to me."

"Let me walk, and I'll give you the chance to save her." A different tactic. *Next, he'll beg like the bitch he is.*

"No." With my unoccupied hand, I flick open the blade Dad passed over and dig the tip into his cheek, carving out a T, then an I, and finally, an O. The letters once put together, say *tio*, the Spanish word for uncle, and if his body is ever found, or just the cheek area, they'll look toward his family. And while President Rodriguez is the catalyst, those letters stand for Thiago, Ivan, and Orlando: the three male De Leons he tried to fuck over.

"We already have a grip on her," he hisses through clenching teeth, trying to shift away, but my hold doesn't allow that. Blood drops seep from the wounds and onto my fingers. They're not deep enough to have an open flow, but *drip, drip, drip* they do. Nevertheless, I pat them to make sure they sting a little more before releasing his chin. "One call from me or my brother, and she'll be taken and shipped to another country. She'll be used as a pet. Used like a—"

"Isn't that the job of Karen Lopez? Stepsister of Henry Davila?" At my response, anger flashed through his eyes, nostrils flaring. "From my understanding, she's looking for her fiancé at the moment. Crying and begging for help, while you rent a hole to fuck."

"You won't get a word out of her. She's conditioned to be loyal."

"I'm not the one you should worry about when it comes to her or

Cindy, Dalian." My smile grows and I bite my bottom lip, sending the asshole a wink. "The De Leon women are ruthless when betrayed."

"Amberlyn isn't claimed." That idiocy isn't worthy of a response and I tilt my head to the side, casually standing from my position and walking to his back. There, I watch him squirm like the rodent he is. Dalian goes from cocky to scared. Human nature never fails to bring in the fight-or-flight impulse at the right time, and I watch as his eyes bounce from man to man, landing on a crying, sniveling Montgomery.

The man is now praying, the front of his pants soiled, and the stench of piss hits just as a warm breeze sweeps through us. *Why do they always pee?*

Bending at the waist, I lower my head just enough to place my mouth beside his right ear. "Just so you know, it was easy to find you and the woman you paid to suck your dick. The tip given to me paid its dividend."

"How did you find us?"

"Ahhh. There you go." With two fingers, I undo the latch on the wrapped-twice-around-my-wrist bracelet and it falls open, exposing a long, flexible wire hidden within. It's sharp and thin, just long enough to reach around a person's neck from side to side, and after gripping each end, I pull it tight against Dalian's neck. "Finally, an intelligent question."

"Stop!" His reaction is automatic as my knee digs into his back and I begin to saw from side to side. The flesh gives under the stress, cutting a straight line across his skin with ease and then deeper through the first layer. "You can't. No mas!" Both hands try to grip the wire, but all that does is cut his fingertips. The slickness of each doesn't help him find purchase, and I watch from above as his face becomes redder and redder, reaching an almost purple tint quickly.

A chuckle escapes me, my grip tightening. "Knew you'd be begging soon enough."

"What do you want, Ivan?" It comes out in between coughing—choking—but I don't ease off. "Ask, and it's yours."

"To know everything. Talk, and we'll come to an agreement at the end."

"You pissed off Tio Rodriguez and he asked us to remove the threat to his regime." A little deeper and a tiny bit of blood squirts from the wound, his coughing causing more of his life's essence to flow. Dalian tries to bring a hand up to the area again but a quick tsk from me and it falls back to his thighs. "H-he wants you and Thiago dead."

"Keep talking."

"We agreed, with one condition." His chest shudders, and I ease the pressure.

"Go on."

"Jaime wants your operations, and I, Amberlyn."

"Why?" When he's not quick to respond, I begin the side-to-side motion again, ripping through a little more flesh. "Last chance."

"Did you know I met her at a city function a few years back?" No. I didn't, but don't say this. Instead, I raise a brow as a silent request to move on with his story. Dalian exhales roughly, reality finally sinking in to that thick head. "It was a charity fundraiser hosted by the police department and my brother dragged me along. He wanted me to meet someone. Turns out that those someones were the owners of Mariposa Bail Bonds and their daughter, who's set to take over in a few years.

"Why did he want you to meet?"

"Because he knew her family is close to yours, and Jaime has always wanted to own Miami. In his eyes, they were an in. She could lead me to your family, or at the very least, introduce us."

"But that didn't work out, did it." Not a question.

Yet before he can answer, there's a rustling near the trees where I released the small snake earlier, and our heads turn in that direction. Nothing moves for a beat and it's silent, too quiet before a head slithers out.

It's large and so is the attached body, larger than any snake I've seen in the past. However, with all the invasive species that call these lands home, I'm not surprised that at some point we'd end up here.

Years ago, during one of the worst hurricanes the state has seen, there was total destruction in the city of Homestead. In 1992, Andrew, a category 5 storm, tore through South Florida leaving behind a loss of power, structures, fatalities, and lastly, the escape of many exotic animals that made their way to the swamps they now call home.

The breeding facility that bred pythons and other countless snakes created a problem.

One that now has made the need for a snake hunting season a reality in these parts.

Yet, this isn't what I thought it to be at first glance. No.

More than likely from another problem we have in this state, a lesson human beings haven't learned. We're not meant to own exotic animals such as these. They are easy to handle when small, but a specimen this large…at the very least fifteen feet in length, will kill you easily.

A green anaconda stares at us but makes no further move. It's coiled now and still, tongue flicking out to catch us in the air just outside the tree line. Everyone stills while watching the animal.

"Go on, Dalian. Tell me why it didn't work out with Amberlyn?"

"We need to go. That snake—"

"Is not the biggest threat here. Finish."

The animal shifts its head, and the pathetic cunt whimpers, "I'll help you stop him."

"I'm not hiring, but you have ten seconds to start, or I'll feed you to it myself." Still too afraid to talk, I force the metal to dig through a little more; the flesh now truly bleeds. The wound isn't enough to kill, but he's sitting on that razor's edge where another thin cut will bleed him out. "I can make this easy on you, or drag it out to the point you'll claw at your flesh and tear it apart just to end it. Tell me, Dalian. Now."

"She wouldn't even dance with me." He's choking, breathing labored as panic sets in.

"Is that all?" My men take a few steps back as the large animal slithers closer but not enough to strike. This is a waiting game.

"Please." Wheezing. Hands scraping at the ground, trying to find purchase and move back, but fail. "No mas. Por favor."

"All she did was turn down a dance? That made her your target?"

"She couldn't muster more than a hello, while I couldn't pull my eyes away."

"People always want what they can't have. It's a sin."

"We need…" he coughs and blood splutters, falling to the ground by his knees "…please. It will kill. I don't want to die."

"But you will, knowing Amberlyn Ibarra is mine. That you were never enough." Dropping the end of the wire from one hand, I pull it hard with the other and Dalian falls forward. His body is spasming, his breathing labored while I move out of the way, but not before leaving him with a final thought. "Henry Davila was your downfall. You told him where you'd be, and he told me after your last phone call."

Then, as I back away, another predator makes its way slowly into the small clearing. The gator is clearly more than eight feet, reminding you of a prehistoric beast. His hiss is clear, a warning to those in his domain and the snake takes notice, raising its head. How they interact reminds me of Georgie and Kline in the lake behind my parents' home; one testing the other.

For a few minutes, neither moves.

Both sizing the other up, but to my surprise, it's the snake that backs off. And while it coils into itself by the trees it emerged from, the gator moves toward Dalian at a speed I'm impressed by.

His head looks our way, another warning to back off his meal and we do.

One foot at a time, until the animal feels comfortable and clamps his jaws on the barely-alive scum. Teeth digging in, it overpowers the man in one death roll, breaking bones and tearing flesh while the younger Uriel gives one final scream.

You see the moment his body stops—eyes vacant—and that's when I turn to leave.

If it eats him or not, I don't care.

If Dalian is dragged into the marsh and torn apart by the various animals there, so be it.

I call this divine fate.

Meeting Israel's eyes, I nod toward a passed-out Montgomery. *No wonder his crying stopped.* "Get him up and in the car. We'll be heading out soon."

"Yes, sir." Israel rounds up the others and while they carry Kyle away, I look at my father.

"Will you be okay while I'm gone?"

"We'll be fine." Dad's pensive for a moment. I can see he has questions.

"Go ahead and ask." Leisurely, we walk back toward the tourist trails and parking area. "What's on your mind?"

"Are you sure this is how you want to handle the situation with Amberlyn?"

"Do I want to be away from her? No. No, I don't."

"But—"

"But I'm doing the best I can to make sure that woman never knows fear or the pain of losing someone she cares about. Staying away *is* how I prove my love. The only thing I'm guilty of is being selfish in my belief that she'll be there when I come back."

He nods, rubbing his chin. "Will you be back after D.C.?" I shake my head. "Then where are you going?"

"I'm going to personally deliver some bad news to President Rodriguez."

"Do you need me with you?"

"No, old man." I bump his shoulder with mine. "This is something I have to do on my own."

"You're carrying too much weight on those shoulders, kid. What happened five years ago was not your fault."

"We all have different points of view, and mine sees a picture that others don't."

"And the truth is, you're being stubborn. Let it go, and live."

"I am living." *I'm building our future.*

Chapter 20
IVAN

I'M SITTING INSIDE Amberlyn's living room later that evening, watching as the sun begins to set while flicking my eyes to the front door every few minutes. The silence inside her home is comforting and brings forth a sense of peace I've been missing and couldn't help but return to.

Being here was never in my plans. Not until I could offer her what she deserves.

And maybe my father's right and I'm carrying five years' worth of recrimination, but failing my family isn't something I can get past.

Did I save my father's life? Yes, but at the same time, I made a costly mistake that led to Thiago's arrest.

Stepping outside the Versailles Restaurant in Coral Gables after a last-minute fishing trip, I was full and tired. My job today was simple: guard the two old men talking shop and about my brother's ascension to head of the family. This man is a client, someone who buys large quantities of perico for private consumption while entertaining in the Bahamas.

Cocaine is his drug of choice, and we have the best quality. With imports from Colombia and the UK, the De Leons have managed to overthrow all other vendors while evading local police and DEA.

"So you'll have my order in two weeks?" We're at the client's trunk now, my eyes surveying the parking lot. "I know it's last minute, but there's a private swingers meetup I'm hosting and—"

"Done deal. You'll get it two days before." Dad extends a hand while with the other, he accepts a briefcase the older gentleman pulls from the inside.

The black case has a number lock, and I raise a brow. "I'll need the code to verify."

"Of course." He pulls out his phone and shows me the screen. 0916

Once the last digit is turned and set, the latch disengages, and I open the top. There's an envelope inside and after a rough count, I know the agreed fifty-percent deposit is there, if not a little more.

He'll get his briefcase back with the merchandise.

After my nod, Dad gives him a final handshake and steps back, a clear signal that we are done here. No further words are exchanged and the client leaves, getting inside his BMW while we turn and I press the fob to unlock our doors.

We each make it to our door; my father's hand is on the handle when the first shot rings out in the parking lot. Immediately, I move to his side and drop us to the ground, my body covering his.

The second round hits close, too close, and I pull my Glock from the back waistband of my jeans and fire in the shooter's direction. "Did the first one hit you?" I ask, keeping my voice low.

"No. At least, I don't feel anything."

That's not reassuring, but I focus on keeping him alive. Adrenaline courses through me. My hand wants to shake, but it's not fear. Not for myself, at least. Mom's face comes to mind, and I take a second to breathe in deep through my nose, then exhale.

I can't allow anything to happen to us. Mom won't mourn us.

Neither will Amberlyn.

She's been on my mind more and more as of late. I've always noticed how beautiful she is, how sweet, but have kept my distance. Haven't allowed more than innocent flirting while everyone is oblivious to my attraction.

Focus, asshole. Kill the asshole.

Lifting my head, I scan the area the first two shots came from and make out a pair of dark glasses, a mistake from the shooter as they reflect the moonlight, glinting as a target. I don't hesitate, moving a little to the side so I can get better aim.

We exchange fire at the same time.

His next fire zips right by my ear, while I empty my entire clip into the motherfucker. There's a specific sound that bullets make when hitting flesh, this low, almost thud before his body hits the ground. However, as he does, one more round dislodges and my father screams from beneath me.

Panic sets in and I drop my gun, not giving a fuck about anything but making sure he's okay.

"My leg, Ivan. Hijo de puta got my leg."

It was my bullet—my panic and forgetting to call for cleanup—that eats at me. That body with my bullet holes was dumped in Thiago's home and pinned on him because I forgot a simple rule.

He lost five years because of something drilled into our heads since we were old enough to hold a weapon.

An oversight like that is unacceptable.

Killing those threatening my woman and family is how I repay my sins.

The sun sets lower in the sky, filling the night with various shades of orange and pink with touches of purple mixing in. It grows darker by the minute, and I look over at the clock on the wall, noticing it's just after eight and she should be walking through the door at any moment. Later than usual, but the calendar on her fridge says there were errands to run.

My sirenita had mundane things to do and the fact makes me smile. It's what I want for her.

That the most she worries about is buying groceries, picking up meds from the pharmacy, and sometimes getting tires rotated on her car.

The latter is something I've taken care of for her in the past and failed to do so this time. It bothers me a bit, but I ignore it in lieu of the bigger picture: my sirenita is safe.

She's independent. So beautiful and strong.

I need her more than she needs me. A thought that's steeped in truth, and I can't deny a small part of me hates it. Abhor that her world continues without me, while mine revolves around hers.

I don't doubt her love for me, but my obsession—this need mauling at my chest—overshadows anything Amberlyn feels for me. It's what brought me here instead of stopping at my parents' home to handle the Cindy—or whatever the fuck her name is—situation. Why I barely showered in my penthouse overlooking the South Beach waters and didn't hesitate to unlock her door and sit in this oversized chair while waiting for Amberlyn to return.

That is what this kind of love does to a man. I can't stay away, no matter what vows I make for myself.

I'm crazy and irrational. Near desperate to feel her again, but won't.

Not until I can come back and place a diamond on her finger. Because I will. I'll lay the corpses of our enemies at her dainty feet before sliding my ring where it belongs.

For eternity. *Till death never do us part.*

Keys jiggle in the door and the knob turns then, her small fingers pushing it open while my heart picks up its beat. She doesn't see me; there's a couple of bags in her hands, nothing heavy, but when I stand, her eyes dart my way.

My mermaid screams, yet I'm proud of the way she quickly grabs her gun and aims at my chest while dropping what looks to be paper goods. "Don't make another move."

"It's me, bebe. Just me." At the sound of my voice, her shoulders drop, and the gun ends up pointing at the ground. Her chest, though, is rising and falling fast. Her lips part, words sitting on the tip of her tongue, but my sweet girl has gone mute. "Are you okay? Do you need to sit?"

I take two steps when the hand not holding the gun darts up. "Stop right there."

"Babe, you need to sit. I'll bring everything to the kitchen."

"Don't. Move."

"Okay." I'll give her a minute or two, but that's my limit. "Do you need some water?"

"Ivan?"

"Yes."

"Please grab my bags outside the door. I'm going to need a minute."

It's her professional tone, the one she uses while making phone calls or talking with clients. I don't call her out on it. Instead, I give Amberlyn a small smile and do what she needs me to. "Of course."

"Thanks." Without another word, she turns and heads toward her bedroom, closing the door once inside.

"That went well." Walking to her door, I grab the bags outside and head for her kitchen, depositing them on the counter. Then I go back for what she dropped and begin to put everything away.

One thing I learned soon after we began to date; my girl is organized.

Like the kind you see on social media with special containers for their eggs and orange juice. She rotates her stock, everything needs to be front-faced, and the newest in the back. It's a quirk I find adorable, and also know better than to mess with.

So I do as she does and make sure it's to her standards, with the shopping bags put away to recycle later.

My eyes shift to the clock and realize that thirty minutes have passed and she still hasn't come out yet. I worry. I also didn't miss the fact she took her gun with her. Not that I'm worried she'll harm herself—Amberlyn will shoot me, not herself—yet I can't help but want to check on her.

"Order dinner first." Pulling my cell out, I open my texts and send one to Junior downstairs.

> Pick up two pizzas from the place three blocks down. Tell them it's for De Leon and they know what we'll want. Get dinner for yourself, too. ~Ivan

His response is immediate. Not even thirty seconds later.

> On my way. Thank you, Boss. ~Junior

> Please leave it outside the door and knock once. I'll message you again before leaving. ~Ivan

Tossing my cell atop the counter, I make my way to her room. It isn't locked when I test the handle, turning it easily in my hand before I push it, and poke my head inside. She's nowhere to be found. The bed's empty, *but* then I hear it…

Water.

Her shower is on, and my naked and wet sirenita is inside.

I don't think twice about removing my clothes or making my way over. I'm hard and need to feel her against me.

Steam billows when I open the wooden door, yet it's the sight of her lithe form through the glass door that I focus on. The sight consumes yet lifts every single weight I carry while filling me with a different kind of demand.

That I take.

Own. Love. Cherish.

"Fuck, bebe." It leaves me on a pained groan and her head snaps in my direction, those piercing eyes meeting my own. There are so many emotions in them: anger and love being the dominating ones.

Those I can handle. Understand them.

But the tinge of disappointment that lingers behind the others is almost too much.

"Are you going to come in, or just watch?" The sassiness in her tone helps to ease this ache in my chest and I smirk, knowing my grin is one of the things she likes.

Amberlyn has always loved making me smile or laugh. Claims my eyes crinkle at the corners and it makes me adorkable. Her word, not mine.

Crossing to her shower, I open the glass divider and step inside, welcoming the hot water on my tired frame. It's been days since I've gotten a good night's sleep. It's been days of nonstop hunting and removing threats while finding every hiding hole and blocking them from our enemies.

I have one more Cuban sicario to find, but my gut tells me he's no threat.

Jaime Uriel will die by my hands.

I'm going to hand over the women to Luna, Amberlyn, and my mother.

All before decapitating the snake that President Placido Rodriguez is.

And all that while helping a country rediscover its footing and monetary position in the world.

"You look exhausted, Ivan." Her voice is low, almost tired, but I detect no anger. No resentment. "What's going on?"

"A lot." Reaching around her, I turn the water a little hotter and turn us, her back to my front. She fits perfectly there. Those sinuous curves mold against me and each shiver, every indrawn breath moves through me. *She's my heaven.* "Things I never want you to see."

"I'm not as delicate as you think I am."

"I know." Doesn't make things any better for me. If anything, I worry more. "But I've always wanted a different world for you."

"What about what I want?" While she keeps a calming tone, I can feel her strength. That fire draws me in, forcing my will to become one with hers. And while I'm a dominant man and I'll admit I'm hard to deal with at times, this woman owns me.

Turning her in my arms, I wrap both arms around her back and pull her in, chest to abdomen. Heads tipped toward each other. "What do you want, Sirenita? What do you dream about?"

"A life with you."

Four simple words. So honest. Pure.

Yet, they destroy me where I stand, and I can't stop myself from taking that sweet berry mouth in a passionate kiss. Our lips crash, and I'm reborn while branding her taste into my DNA.

Her tongue sweeps across my bottom lip and I shiver, yet my hold never wavers. If anything, it tightens while moving from her lower back to supple hips. They fit perfectly in my hand, so sexy—

The rain shower feature turns on and I pause, smiling down at her. "Did you switch it mid-kiss?"

"Guilty."

"Bad Mermaid," I growl against her lips, not upset in the least. This is something I've enjoyed about us—the ease and comfort to switch from playful to ravenous to nearly demonic with yearning. "Am I not enough to hold your attention? To blind you with need?"

"Ivan, you've always been my everything."

"Motherfuck, bebe." That's all I can say. No words would ever suffice, and I show her instead. Bending my knees, I drag my hands to her thighs and lift her and then tap the skin there. Amberlyn understands and wraps her legs around my waist while her back meets the still-cool-to-touch tile away from the still-running showerhead.

Her tan skin looks beautiful against the white. More so, when she arches, offering me her chest while gyrating in search of my dick. "I need you just as bad. Why can't you understand that?"

Dropping my forehead to hers, I try to remember all the reasons why we should wait. How I don't want to add another reason for her to hate me, but then Amberlyn sneaks a hand between our bodies and grips me, fist tight.

One stroke, and I growl. This animalistic sound builds in my chest, shakes every muscle in my body, and I pin her hips with mine, forcing her fingers to cease moving. She's trapped, yet I don't know if that's worse.

A sinful groan slips from her swollen lips. She's rubbing against her hand and my cock, searching for a release that belongs to me. "This is right. See that."

"Of that, there's never been a doubt, Mermaid."

"Then why stop." She's soft skin and warm eyes, so eager for me to impale her—wring an orgasm from her tight body.

"Because tomorrow I'm leaving again."

While her fingers flex around my girth, she cups my face with her other hand. "Will you be safe?"

"Yes." I throb against her palm, balls drawing tight. There's nothing I want more than to be buried deep inside her warm cunt.

"Will you come back?"

"Always."

"Then fuck me, papi. We'll figure out the rest later."

I don't respond. Can't. Not without blurting out four little words, and she deserves the world, not to be told in the heat of the moment and later abandoned.

The day I tell her is near. So close.

And while my lips mouth the words against the skin of her throat, loving the sweet flesh there with nips, I pray she sees my sacrifice. How much I adore her.

As if she understands, Amberlyn grips the hair at the back of my head and holds me tighter to her. "Ivan, I—"

"No words, mami. Just feel me." Lower, and my teeth drag

against the top of her breast before attaching myself to a pretty pink tip. Her nipples throb against my tongue, swelling a bit, and I bite down hard enough to draw a short cry from her. "That's it. Let me take care of you."

Pulling her in deeper, I tease the sensitive tip with my tongue and then rake my teeth over it before applying the same attention to the neglected tit. Goose bumps rise on her skin. Her eyes become hooded. *Motherfucking perfection.*

My hands wander across her skin from ass to thigh and then back up before resuming the same path. My mouth leaves open-mouthed kisses across her breasts and then I suck hard, bruising the skin right above each nipple so she remembers me every time she looks in the mirror.

I do the same to the area between them and then back up to her neck where I bite down hard enough to break the skin a little. She screams, loosening her grip on me, and I position my cock between slick lips.

Hot. Wet. Heat.

She's velvety against me, feels so good, and I slide through her labia again, and again, her clit throbbing against my head on each pass.

Amberlyn is wet, and I'm drenched in her—us—the bead of pre-come and her juices mixing as I pull a deep moan from her. The sound so fucking decadent, I pause with the tip at her opening and breathe in deep.

Ambrosia, her name is Amberlyn.

"Need you inside me, papi. I'm so wet for you." Between the heat of the shower, her flushed skin, and those dirty words…

I slam in deep and hold still, knees nearly buckling when her walls stroke me. They pulse and pull me in deeper, her sharp cry and the way her hands grip my arms—nails digging into the skin—

"Motherfuck, beautiful." I'm breathing hard, trying to regain control, but I'm lost in the feel of her. She's slick, so fucking tight, and I take hold of her right hip with one hand while the other grabs her neck, fingers flexing as she swallows hard.

Those sinful eyes darken and her tongue sweeps across her bottom lip. Tempting. Pushing.

I pull out a few inches and stab in again, just short strokes and her eyes roll back, the walls of her sex tensing. They clamp around me, try to pull me in deeper, but I don't stop.

"More." Desperation sweeps across her features, thighs shaking while she tries and fails to gyrate in my hold. Instead, I press her harder against the wall, loving the small whine she emits. "Please, Ivan."

"Say you're mine. Only mine."

"There will never be anyone but you." No hesitation. Just her love open for me to see—feel.

Looking away is an impossibility and so is getting air into my lungs; I'm drowning in the open emotions clear on her face, and it's a heady yet humbling combination. Yet I never pause; I'll show her with my actions just how much she means to me.

And even as my chest burns, I thrust in deeper while grinding against her clit, forcing deep moans from the back of her throat. Those sweet orbs never move from mine but watch me as I take in how she falls apart a stroke at a time until I'm left with a quivering mess.

"Good girl." Another tight flex of her walls and I give her what she needs, stroking in deep this time while shifting my gaze between us. I'm watching her juices coat my cock, her upper thighs, while I stretch her in the most beautifully obscene way. It looks nearly painful, but when our stares connect again, the look of rapture on her gorgeous face tells a different story.

This is us without restraints, and I give in to my baser instincts; I fuck my mermaid brutally without reprieve. I don't stop or breathe; all I can focus on is the way she grips me and the slick juices that bathe my cock in claiming.

Because for as much as I own her, I'm hers.

We don't look away from each other, lips hovering as we inhale the other's exhale. I can almost taste her unique sweetness in the air around us while pistoning in and out of her pussy. A pussy that's squeezing just a little tighter.

"I'm close, Ivan."

"I know," I hiss through clenched teeth while she clamps down again. A small wave of pleasure crests over her—it's almost too tight to move—but I buck my hips hard enough to move her up the wall before sliding down hard on my cock. "Come for me, Mermaid. Let go."

"Oh, God!"

"That's it. *Fuck*, bebe." The moment I ease my hold on her hips, she bucks against me, matching my every move. She's wild and lost in her pleasure, taking from me what she needs. "Give me what's mine."

My name falls from her mouth like a prayer while her muscles seize momentarily, her walls making it difficult to move while her orgasm takes her under. I give her a few seconds, ten at the most.

"Papi!" she screams, clinging to me as I pump in time with each pulse of her walls, chasing my own release. It's there, hovering close, and when the next rush of wetness almost forces my dick out of her, I lose control.

I'm almost feral, lip curling back as I force her to ride me, back sliding against the wall as I fill her with my come. Rope after rope, mixing with her own until the combined mess slides down my shaft and skims my balls.

And still, I ride her a little more until she's slumped against me, and this time, when my knees shake, I lower us to the shower floor. I let her curl up in my lap while I kiss her temple, my hands stroking her back and arms while the water soothes our muscles.

There's still so much to say, to talk about, but for now, I just want to stay like this and close my eyes.

Because when I open them again, it's time to tell her the truth.

Chapter 21

AMBERLYN

WE'RE SITTING ON the living room floor with our food spread out on the coffee table while I contemplate if eating a fourth slice of my favorite pizza is smart. It's sausage, pepperoni, black olives, and lastly…*pineapple*. Some might call it weird, but it's my thing and this man knows my weaknesses.

He's clever, I'll give him that.

Favorite food and cold beer? Check.

Warm guava cake and a slice of molten lava to split? Check.

Organized pantry? Double-check with a chef's kiss attached.

No shame in the fact I double-checked the moment we got dressed and he grabbed our food from a quiet Junior. At the time, I needed something—a few extra seconds to center me after the intimacy inside the shower.

Because even though he tries to hide it, Ivan let his guard down, and it was his openness that crumbled my walls. I couldn't deny the pull when he's being open and sweet—his actions showing me what he hasn't said with words.

"You know you want another slice. Go for it, Mermaid." He's smiling and more relaxed than the man I found sitting in my dark living room. Sure, sex is a great de-stressor, but it's more than that. I just wish I knew what the more was.

"Shut it."

"Make me."

"You more than anyone know I can hold my own." My quip elicits a foreign response, not the playful banter I expected. What I got was a man who put his sandwich down and grabbed me, placing me astride his lap as if I were a doll he can manipulate to his liking.

And as much as it's unwanted at the moment, my reaction makes me blush.

His strength—the way he can hold and bend me—has always been a turn-on.

"Behave, Sirenita."

"I've always been a saint, papi. The devil in this relationship is you." He tenses at the word *relationship* but before I can seize the opportunity and call him out, Ivan places a finger over my lips.

"Eat. We'll talk after."

"Promise?"

"Yes."

"Okay." Grabbing another piece, I bring the cheesy, salty goodness to my lips and take a big bite. Ivan, on the other hand, resumes eating his cold-cut sub while giving me indulgent looks here and there. Almost as if he enjoys spoiling me, but there's still something off.

Not negative, more like a secret I'm yet to be made aware of.

Once I'm down to the crust, I toss it on my plate and pat my stomach. "No mas."

"Overate?"

"Thanks to you!" With mock indignation, I slap his chest. "Go for it, Mermaid."

"Your imitation of me is ridiculous at best." His chest rumbles with a laugh while the fingers of his right hand skim up my bare thigh. There's also the flex of his cock beneath me, pushing against my bottom. One, twice...three times, and I can't help but blush. "Is that how I sound to you?"

The question is simple enough, yet I'm squirming. *He's doing this on purpose.* "No."

"This I got to hear."

"Not really." I try to move from his lap, but Ivan holds me in place while thrusting up. "I'm just going to put the leftovers away. Give me two minutes."

"I'll let you get up if you answer me."

Bastard. "To me, it's sexy," I say, voice low while trying to avoid his eyes, but the man is having none of it and with the tip of two fingers under my chin, he forces our stares to connect.

"Don't be embarrassed. To me, you're my kryptonite."

Why is this man so confusing? Why can't he just be straight-forward?

I can't judge him based on actions when one minute he's ignoring me, and the next, worshipping me. When he caters to my pleasure and then lets small truths slip out that knock the proverbial floor from under me.

Buck up and ask him. It's the only way.

"Ivan, I—"

"I can't stay away from you, sweetheart," he says, tone gravelly.

Just like when he's about to come, holding me a little tighter while breathing out a low *fuck* against my ear. "I'm tired and ready for more than what we've been these last few years."

"Why do I feel like there's a 'but' coming?"

"But there's something I need to take care of first."

"Does this have to do with where you're going after you leave me?" Ivan nods in response. "Does this have to do with the family? With all those trips to Cuba?"

"It does."

"Hmmm." For a few beats, we stay in silence, neither saying what we want. He's holding back, while my mind is running a thousand miles a minute. Yet, I can't help but come back to one thought. *She's nothing more than an obligation.*

She's nothing more than an obligation.

An obligation.

"Ask me."

His warm voice pulls me back to the present. "I'm sorry."

"I said, ask me. Anything, Sirenita...I promise to answer as much as I can."

"Why?" That's the only thing that comes out. A lump forms in my throat right after, those same emotions I've been pushing back—burying deep in the darkest recesses of my soul—slamming into me with the power of a wrecking ball. For a second, I'm back in that moment and listening to the man I love more than my own life talk about me as if I'm a nuisance. A pesky bug he tolerates. "How could you say that about me? Us?"

"Because I knew you were listening." It's his truth; I can respect that, but it stings worse knowing he said it to hurt me. I try to stand, though my legs are shaky. Once again, I'm kept in place by his arm around my midsection. "I'm an asshole, bebe. I know that and I accept all the fault here..." Ivan's warm breath is on my neck a second before he leaves a kiss over the bite mark from earlier "...but I need you to believe me when I tell you it's a lie. That all I was trying to do is push you away while I settled a few things."

"Settled things?" While I'm not okay with this, the hurt has lessened. It's becoming anger, a little resentment, but then it dies when I truly take in his expression.

Because I see him. Always have.

Ivan De Leon is loyal and protective, especially over those he loves. I've seen it firsthand, have been there when those walls came down and his family was threatened. His father. His mother. But it all came to a head when Thiago went to jail and at the age of twenty-one, he was stepping into the role of boss and righting wrongs that he was never at fault for to begin with.

I was there then. And damn everyone to hell, I'll be here now no matter the outcome.

Because that's what you do when in love. We give and give and give without asking for anything in return.

"Who's in danger, Ivan? Is there anything I can do to help?"

Lip curling up at the corner, he taps my nose. "I appreciate the offer, but we both know I'd never allow you to put yourself in danger. Least of all for me."

"You're worth it to me."

"I'm going to come back for you, but I have sins to atone for first."

Those words throw me back; I've heard them before.

"Ivan?" I'm shocked to find him outside the bail bonds office, leaning against my car after work. There's no one else in the parking lot; my parents left an hour ago while I finished filing some reports. "Is everything okay?"

"No." He exhales roughly, the billowing smoke from his cigarette swirling around him. He taps the end, breaking the ashes, and watches as they meet the ground before scattering in the wind. "The verdict came in today."

"I heard." And I did. It was all my parents could talk about. They were trying to see if bail could be posted while the lawyers appealed the decision.

Because of his family ties, no one was surprised, but Thiago has no prior conviction, or charges, and that goes in his favor. That, and the evidence presented was trash and anyone with two working neurons can see it. Then, there's the sentencing, which has been pushed back to a few weeks from now as they decide his fate.

Because of that, they can plea for a release while the appeal is presented.

No one thinks it'll work, but there's nothing to lose for trying.

"Had I not been stupid enough to leave evidence at the scene, none of this would be happening."

Leaning against my car beside him, I lean my head on his arm. "You mean the corpse of the man who tried to kill you and Orlando? You did the right thing and saved your lives, Ivan."

"It's not that simple."

"The blame is on the hitmen and whoever hired him. That's who should be paying."

Ivan's hazel eyes meet mine while a cruel smirk grazes his lips. "They will, Sirenita. Their lives will atone for my sins."

Suddenly, fingers snap in front of my face, and I find Ivan giving me a quizzical brow. "Lost you there. Are you okay?"

"Why are you punishing yourself for something that happened over five years ago?" I say instead as things click into place. The extra hours at work, the constant travel—his constant jumping in to take care of everything and everyone over the last few years, but it's worse since Thiago got out of prison. "You're still paying for something you're not responsible for, papi."

"I'm not—"

"You are." Shifting, I turn and straddle him before cupping his face. Immediately, he nuzzles my palm and I melt. That single action takes away any question or doubt; he does care. Yet, there's a piece of the puzzle I'm missing an answer for: me. "You did it when they locked up Thiago and you're doing it now. Stop hurting yourself."

"Bebe, I promise I'm okay. There's never a need for you to worry about me." There's a stubborn set to his jaw that I'm all too familiar with; he's shutting the conversation down. "Everything will be over soon, and I'll be back to fix this."

"Fix what?"

"Can you wait for me?" My nod in agreement isn't because I'm afraid to make him angry, but because I'm picking my battles instead. My love for him won't allow me to do anything but be what he needs, and I'll push, but not right now. "Thank you."

"I've always been your friend first, Ivan. That's not going to change."

"You're too good for someone—" He's cut off by the ringing of his phone on the countertop, and by the dark look that crosses his face, he's not happy. Ivan taps my thigh and I get up, walking toward the device, and pick it up. The screen reads *Israel* and I toss it over before picking up our mess. "What did you find?"

I try not to listen and give him space, but in between cursing and now pacing, there are a few things that stick out. This is also when he finishes getting dressed, and I miss seeing his tattoos immediately.

Hacker.

Leave tonight.

No D.C. and change of plans.

Dead.

And when he turns around to face me, I know this is where we part. Not as heavy as last time, and I'm somewhat at peace for the first time since my best friend's wedding.

"Promise me you'll call, Ivan. That's non-negotiable."

"Will it help you if I do?"

"Yes."

"Then you have my word." Ivan walks toward me with purpose and without another word, steals the air from my lungs with his kiss. It feels different from all the others before; I taste his passion, but behind it, there's something deeper. An emotion he's kept hidden but is now giving me a tease of.

His tongue runs across my bottom lip before biting down on the abused flesh. He nibbles, drawing a moan from me, and then steps back.

Ivan appraises me from head to toe, his want palpable, before turning for the door. Hand on the handle, he pauses. “You never answered my question, Mermaid.”

“About?”

“My voice.” The mirth in his voice tugs at my lips. “Tell me.”

“Like sex and chocolate.”

I hear his amused chuckle as he walks out, but what’s important is his *wait for me, love* before the door closes.

FOR THE LAST forty-eight hours I’ve been on autopilot, reliving moments from his visit while going through the motions for those around me. I’ve also been going through my contacts in four precincts and haven’t found a single hair of Karen Lopez’s fiancé.

No one knows who her fiancé is.

There are no records of Ramon Valle being detained, much less arrested.

Not even a friend or family member on the news demanding answers, which leads me to believe I was right all along. This case is full of blaring warning signals and lies.

As if on cue, my office line rings. I look over, and it’s Detective Uriel, and it’s also not the first time he’s tried to get a hold of me over the last few days. His last voicemail came hours after Ivan left my home, and his speech was a little slurred.

“You have to help me, Amberlyn. It’s your duty and my—”

The recording stopped there, but the short message left me unsettled. More than when we met face to face; Uriel came off as scared.

“Are you going to pick that up, or do I forward your line to the front?” Mom asks, taking a seat across from me. Her eyes are on the paperwork I’m going through. “You’ve been off for days, kiddo. Talk to me.”

"I don't know why I'm wasting my time with this case." A frustrated huff leaves me, and I crane my neck from side to side, the crick there growing more pronounced as of late. I'm beat. "If I could find this man, I'd feel better. Know that there's no danger—"

"Did you tell Ivan about this?"

"No."

"Why?" Mom gives me a pointed look. "You know he wouldn't hesitate to help you."

"We're on break." It's a weak excuse and total bull crap, and by the look she gives me, Mom knows this too. "Or maybe I just didn't get the chance. There was so much going on when I last saw him and I. . .*what*?"

"Like the hickey on your neck that you're failing to cover up with that scarf?"

"Mom!"

"What? You think I'm blind, or stupid?"

"It's not that." The phone rings again, but this time it's Karen's number and I hold a finger up. "Mariposa Bail Bonds. This is Amberlyn speaking."

"Can I please speak with Amberlyn? It's an emergency."

"Karen, it's me."

"I know." Voice low. So meek. I can also make out a male speaking nearby and the slamming of something, and my brows furrow. I also decided then to attend the call through the speaker option. "Is there any way we can meet today? Do you..." her breath hitches, the sound a little scared "...can we meet today?

My eyes meet Mom's, and she's shaking her head at me.

"My schedule is full today, but I am working on your case." Mom leaves for a second but comes rushing back with Dad on her heels. His mouth opens to ask what's going on, but his wife's hand slapped over his mouth prevents that. "I'm actually waiting on a phone call from a private investigator who's been helping me as a favor."

All lies, but she doesn't know that.

"Oh. Okay." Still off, she sounds nothing like the woman who came here begging for help. "Do you have any new information? Has anyone contacted you? His family?" A choking sound comes from the background at the word *family*, but it's covered by a sudden sob. "Karen, what's going on? Are you okay?"

"Yes." Sniffle. "It's just all so hard. I miss him."

"Understandable and expected, but please know I'm doing the best I can to help."

"Thank you." She mutters something that sounds like *no one can save us,* which my parents also pick up on. Dad grabs a notepad from my desk and writes something down while Mom grabs her cell and begins to record the conversation. "What you're doing means so much to me. No one else has given me any answers or even looked into this mess. I just want my love to come home."

"Let me call the investigator and see if anything has come up. If so, can you meet—"

"Please. I'll meet with you anywhere and anytime."

"Okay, Karen. I'll call you if I hear anything."

"Thank you, Amberlyn. For everything."

The call disconnects and our expressions mirror each other: worry.

"Something else is going on here, kid. Her reaction and wording make me think she's being forced into whatever this is." Dad scratches his jaw and turns the notepad around to me. "Call him."

"You think it's necessary?"

"If you don't, I will."

"Okay." At this point, I agree. Luna's uncle would be the best person to call. "Do we alert the De Leons, too?"

"Get ahold of Ivan or his parents. They need to know just in case."

"In case of what?" I ask. For the first time since meeting Karen and the detective, I feel a frisson of fear. "What do you suspect?"

Mom places a hand on Dad's arm while giving me a small smile.

"Because I'd bet money this is an attempt by the feds to gain information or—"

"Or what, Mom?"

"Or an enemy trying to get close, mi niña. They might feel as though you are their in."

Chapter 22
AMBERLYN

"GOOD TO SEE you, Edgar," I say, bending at the waist to kiss Luna's uncle on the cheek. We're inside a restaurant owned by the De Leon boys, where the staff here knows me and a waitress is quick to place a Materva soda in front of me before giving Edgar his coffee. "Have you had lunch yet?"

He chuckles. "Already ahead of you. They're cooking my vaca frita as we speak."

"Damn, that sounds good." Neither of us has a menu.

"You thinking of ordering one?"

"No. I don't need to put in an order." There's only one thing

I eat each time I'm here, and that's not changing today. "The imperial rice is all I ever get, and I'm not about to break tradition."

"Sounds good." Edgar smiles at a waitress while waving her over. She's not more than halfway to us when he points at me. "I'll take the vaca frita to go but blame this one for tempting with the arroz imperial. All. On. Her."

"Men." Jenny laughs. The older woman has been around for years. Before I met the family. "Always blaming women, when they're the ones with constant cravings. Right, mi niña?"

"Amen." I hold a hand up and she high-fives it, giving Edgar a huff. All in good fun, but the man pouts until she smiles and then leaves to put in the added order.

"So."

"So," we say in unison, which I snort at. "This isn't a social call, and you know it. Might as well get to the point and enjoy our meal after? Sound good?"

"Go for it, kid. What do you need help with?" Edgar has been with the Miami Dade Police Department for years; he's respected and has the kind of in I need to get information on Detective Uriel. "By the way, is Ivan aware of this meeting? You know I'm loyal to the family."

"No. And I'm also not sure if what I'm going to tell you is cause for worry or not."

"Do you plan on telling the De Leons either way?"

"Yes. I haven't heard back from Ivan, but my next stop is Maritza or Orlando, depending on what you have to say."

"What's going on?" he asks, leaning forward in his seat while every few minutes sliding his gaze to the entrance. Edgar is in uniform, not sure if on duty or just got off, but the cop in him is ever vigilant. "Are you in trouble?"

"That's what I don't know." Opening my oversized purse, I pull out an envelope and hand it over. "The man in this file is missing, and his fiancée came asking for help. She believes that through my connection, I can find the detained prisoner that no one has ever heard about. Detective Uriel—"

"Has that asshole contacted you?"

"Yes. Multiple times over the same missing person." Tilting my head toward the file, I purse my lips. "The report and info are inside, all given to me by him and the fiancée, but something is off."

"You're not a private investigator."

"My thoughts exactly."

"I know him, and he's rotten. Jaime and his family hate the De Leons." *Fuck.* My gut instincts were right, and they're trying to use me against them. And right before I convey that, Edgar laughs at something, and I am lost. "Those motherfucking snakes."

"Excuse me?"

"Amberlyn, the person you've been looking for doesn't exist." That sinking feeling I had earlier returns, my eyes studying the grainy picture of the man he's pointing at. Then, he turns the page and pulls out one given to me by Karen of herself with whom she claims is Ramon, hugging her. "The person in this picture is Dalian Uriel, sweetheart."

"What the hell? Uriel?"

"Detective Jaime Uriel's younger brother." Edgar pulls out his phone and sends off a short text. Within seconds, there's a reply and he meets my eyes again. "I'm having someone pull records. Shouldn't take long. We'll go from there."

"We will?"

"You're not alone. Ivan would kill me—Luna's uncle or not—if anything happened to you." Then he gets an amused look. "Not to mention my niece. Luna can be intense."

Ignoring the mention of the younger De Leon, I raise a brow. "Does she know you're scared of her?"

"Her and Natasha." His bark of laughter catches a few eyes, but people look away just as quickly. "My daughter is trouble, too."

"I'll make sure to let them know."

"Good. Maybe they'll take it easy on an old man." Bullshit, but I won't tell him anything. I know that once he retires from the police department, he'll be working with the family full time. To what extent, I don't know, but he won't be a cleaner or work on the docks. "But back to your predicament." All traces of humor are gone as the phone vibrates in his hand.

Edgar goes through the information first, skimming it before handing the device over.

And right there on the screen is a picture of the siblings, maybe a few years back, at an event.

All of it comes back.

Why didn't I recognize him sooner? "Shit."

"What?" Jenny places our plates down, but I've lost my appetite. I feel stupid. How could I miss something so important? "Sweetheart, you've gone pale. You need me to call Ivan?"

"No." Grabbing my soda, I take a sip and hope the caffeine helps give me a boost. My hands are shaking. "Just remembered something."

"About the information I gave you?"

I nod. "I've met them before. Spoke to the younger one, in fact."

"Where?"

Noticing our untouched food, Jenny brings over some to-go boxes. "In case you need to leave."

"Thanks." Taking the offered container, I quickly shove my food inside before pulling out my credit card. "Just charge everything here. We need to go."

"Family doesn't pay."

"I'm not—"

"Just following orders, sweetie." Jenny doesn't stick around, and I'm left with Edgar, who looks at me strangely. As if he sees something I don't.

"Where did you meet him, Amberlyn?"

"You don't think that was a coincidence, do you?"

"Maybe. Maybe not, but either way, it's suspicious."

Taking in a deep breath, I let it out slowly. "It was at a city function my parents attended a few years ago. I was dragged along under the pretense of meeting officials and high-ranking officers whom I'd be doing business with. You know how it is. Everything is money and rubbing elbows and pretending to like each other for personal benefit."

"I do understand that."

"Well, as the future owner of Mariposa Bail Bonds, I needed to play the part. Get to know who my allies were."

"And?"

"And they were there. Both walked up to my parents and introduced themselves as detectives, claiming to be appreciative of a fugitive we found by mistake." I shake my head and take another sip of soda. "Dad picked up the wrong guy, but the man we turned in was also running from a double homicide charge. Our guy looked like him, down to the same bald head, but his criminal charges were all theft related."

"Did you socialize with them at all? Something other than being polite?"

"Edgar, I couldn't even muster more than a hello. Especially with the younger brother. He seemed too eager."

"Hmmm." Luna's uncle goes quiet for a minute, pensive, before standing and offering me his hand. He grabs our food bags and then walks me out, all the while his eyes keep shifting around. For a second, he pauses right beside my car with his eyes toward a section of vehicles farther down. Whatever he finds isn't a threat, but he nods at something or someone before looking at me again. "You were right to come to one of us, Amberlyn. Whatever those two want, it has to do with you and the De Leons, and I won't let you be in danger. It's time to speak with the family."

"CALL HER. Let's gauge her reaction," Maritza says from her seat behind a large desk. We're inside her office in the De Leon home while her husband left to grab his wife a drink from the kitchen. They've been calm while we explained, understanding of my concern, but I don't miss the sympathetic looks she gives me here and there.

There has been no yelling or shouting orders.

No angry man with tattoos coming inside to grab and hide me away.

Where are you, Ivan? I need you.

It's been days and once again, no communication. His promise was nothing more than words spoken to the wind and disappearing just the same. And even when I called him before we arrived, my attempt was shut down after the third ring.

Disappointment sinks into me, but I shake it off. "She seemed nervous last time we spoke. Almost fearful."

"They must've known Dalian was missing then."

"That idiot has been dead nearly a week, and they're panicking." Not a hypothesis. That was a statement from Orlando as he walks back into the room, and it's clear they know more about the brothers than I ever did. "When was the body recovered, Edgar?"

"About three hours ago." Luna's uncle takes a bottle of water from Ivan's father and passes it to me before grabbing another for himself. My stomach is in knots, though. I'm nervous. "I haven't been able to get ahold of my source inside. Right now, the media's reporting and the headline ties Jaime to Dalian, and they're asking the public if anyone knows how he was mauled by a gator."

"Where was the body found?" I ask.

"Deep in the Everglades by a now-traumatized park employee."

"I can imagine." Every person in this room has seen things they'd rather forget, but were unavoidable. Turning my attention back to Maritza, I give her Karen's number and wait as she punches the numbers in. No one talks as it rings, the speaker loud, and after the fourth ring, there's an audible click.

"Hello? Who's this?"

"It's me. Amberlyn."

"Hey. How's it going." No reaction. Very calm.

"Have you seen the news today?" I ask, hedging.

"No." Small laugh. "I'm just waking up. Felt very sick all night, think it's something I ate."

"Karen, they found the body of your fiancé at—" The phone sounds like it dropped, and I can hear the word *fuck* being repeated, but no crying. No, this is panic. Pure fear in the one word. "Karen? Miss Lopez, are you listening to me?"

"I'm dead," I hear her say this clearly and so do the others in the room, but before I can ask another question, I'm met with a disconnected call. Immediately, I try to call again but it goes straight to voicemail.

I try one more time and get the same.

"We need to find her."

"We do. Something tells me she's the key to understanding this mess," I agree with Edgar. "The sooner we take her into custody, the fewer chances of someone else nabbing her."

Standing from my seat, I pull out my phone and head toward the door. "Dad can help. He'll start mobilizing our resources to see where she could be hiding."

"I'll contact Ivan," a voice says, and my head snaps toward the female so fast my neck cracks. "He should be made aware of what's going on."

"Who the fuck are you?" The brunette is pretty and curvy, but the gleam in her eyes as they stare into mine hold malice.

"I'm a guest of the younger De Leon brother."

"Are you, now?" No one denies it, and I feel sick. "Since when?"

"A few days now." She's wearing a man's shirt but as my eyes water, I can't tell whose. Both Maritza's sons leave clothes here for emergencies. In fact, they have stashes everywhere, even in my home. "He saved me from Dalian." Her smile is wistful, as if remembering something that causes her heart to flutter, while mine feels as though it dropped to my feet. "I knew he would. Ivan promised to come back."

My heart clenches and the air escapes my lungs, yet I remain standing.

This betrayal stings, feels as though I'm being stabbed all over, and the look on Maritza's when I gaze back at her says it all. "Explain."

"Don't speak to my mother-in-law like that. Who the—" Before I can comprehend my actions, I have my hand around her throat and she's on the ground. I'm straddling her, my grip choking while she tried desperately to claw at my arms.

"Who is she?" The question is open to whoever wants to answer, but no one does. What I do feel is someone pulling me off, dragging me away and to the opposite side of the room. "Who is she?"

"Mi niña, you need to calm down. There's an explanation—"

I hold a hand up, and Orlando quiets. "I'm going to ask three questions, and I expect the truth."

"Of course," Ivan's mother agrees. Yet I also notice that she's now standing in the middle between me and the other woman. Edgar is helping the brunette up while Orlando is using his phone to message someone. "But we need to keep our hands to ourselves. Understood?"

Strike one. They are protecting her.

"Did Ivan bring her here?"

"Technically, yes. But it's not what you think."

"Why?"

Maritza's eyes plead with me to understand. To back down. "That's something we can't discuss with you. Just know that she's innocent and was under the Uriel brothers' thumbs."

"Are they involved?"

"That's something only my son can answer."

Strike two. His mother knows and doesn't care that I'm being torn apart where I stand.

"Why are you even discussing anything with her? Is she someone important to Ivancito?" the brunette cries, clutching at Edgar's sleeve while she put on quite the show. Had I been a spectator, I'd be laughing at how ridiculous she looks and the clear marks I left on her neck.

I wait and no one responds, which says everything. I'm no one to him.

I'm an obligation. Moreover, who knows what else he's done behind my back while everyone smiles to my face.

"Enough." The older De Leon cuts in, his eyes narrowed. Not at anyone in particular, but more at the situation. His hand holding the cell phone is clenching, knuckles white. "My son has been made aware of the issue and will call you. Please remember your role in this family, Miss Ibarra."

"You want me to leave?" Voice low. They've cut me deep with this.

"At the moment, yes. I'm sorry, mi niña."

"Not sorrier than I am. Never come near me again." With that, I turn and leave the room, ignoring the raised voices and what they're saying. Someone tries to follow me. They call my name, but I run out of the house as if the hounds of hell are on my heels.

I'm done.

She can have him.

They can all go fuck themselves.

I need to leave Miami. I can't be here.

Chapter 23
IVAN

I'M STANDING ON a veranda overlooking the city of Havana a few hours before my meeting with President Rodriguez. The sun is high and the palm trees sway while the people below continue with their day-to-day activities as if there isn't a palpable change in the air. With the way they carry themselves, you'd never know that the standard government trucks parked outside are mine and what they're delivering to the bodega on the first floor of my building is much-needed food and medical supplies.

It's been a routine here for the last few years while we use the ports. The agreement was simple, but then Placido Rodriguez became greedy. Ambitious. Had he left well enough alone and let us give back in the memory of my grandparents, he'd be a powerful and obscenely rich man.

But human nature is one of envy and morbid hunger for what belongs to another, not once bothering to see that what you have is enough. Wanting more isn't the problem. It's all about how you go about achieving those goals.

The ten commandments are simple, and while I'm the poster child for most of those sins, I do understand that there's a place for everyone. That some basic needs should never be trampled on to become successful.

You don't starve your people.

You don't take away their safety.

And while I agree that ruling with an iron fist is necessary to stay in power, you also create bonds and loyalties to stay on top. Take care of yours, and they have your back. They'd take a bullet for the hand that feeds versus the one who abuses.

Taking in a deep drag of my cigarette, I watch another large, high-mobility truck drive down the street and turn out of sight. The two men inside the cabin are natives and dressed the part of military while delivering my weapons to a separate location. One where a select few have access.

Every political branch, including the army, is infiltrated by people in the De Leon pocket and they all have a role to play—to execute—for the country's takeover to work. Because the current administration's hold is on a timer, and the countdown is near done.

But not yet.

First, I have other things to address.

"Henry, come here." The man stands from his place inside. He'd been sitting on the couch for two hours now without moving much. There's been a twitch here and there, sweating, but for the most part, he's the perfect companion on this trip.

Silent. Dutiful. Nervous.

Moreover, he has every right to be.

"Yes, Mr. De Leon?" he asks, coming to stand beside me. I'm on the fourth floor of my building on a popular road that leads to a few touristy restaurants that serve food catered to their taste buds. It's old architecture and indoor water features inside of open courtyards where the waitstaff is taught to serve and entice while offering a milder taste of our cuisine.

"Dalian is dead." I've kept that tidbit to myself just to watch his reaction now, and he doesn't disappoint. There's a quick, indrawn breath and gripping on the metal railing in front of me. I also don't miss the abject look of horror that mars his features, but it's to be expected. They were close friends, the best of, and something as little as lying to me won't change that. "It was quite the spectacle."

"Oh."

"Is that all you have to say? Oh?" Turning so my back faces the veranda, I motion for Israel to collect my laptop. See, while this asshole was busy lying and feeding me bullshit, I began to look past what's in front of me.

There's always another picture. Another version of the same story.

Karen Lopez isn't his sister.

She isn't willingly sleeping with the Uriel brothers.

Yet Cindy Johnson, also known as Jasmin Davila, who's at my parents' home under surveillance with a long enough rope to hang herself, is related to the idiot. Actual sibling. The dots connected themselves. I just needed to look a little further into the theatrical performance they set up.

If anything, how quickly he was willing to sell his own best friend out to save his skin is testament to Henry Davila's lack of morals. His believing me to be stupid enough to fall for and not capitalize on his incompetence is his penance, not mine.

MacBook in hand, I unlock the screen and pull up a small feed—security camera from another business that shares parking lot space with the bar. Same bar where Cisco and his brother reported from, while these men partied. This is the beginning of their ends. Pressing play, I let him watch as the other Cuban sicario brought to protect them is attacked from behind by a now-dead Pirro while the woman, Karen, cries and thrashes.

She's calling out to the unconscious man. Begging them to stop, but no one listens, and all the while Dalian and Jaime laugh. The younger of the two Uriel boys has an arm around her waist while palming her tit with the other.

No regard for her distress. No shame in touching a woman who's clearly disgusted by you.

I have no respect for a man who abuses women, and Dalian deserved worse than what I gave him.

"I-Ivan, I—"

"Finish watching." I press another button and enlarge the angle. "Describe what I'm seeing."

"I'm sorry."

"You will be." A sardonic laugh escapes me. "Now, tell me what happened here."

"I'd gone by then."

"Go on. Amuse me with this story."

His eyes shift toward the exit. I see the intent to move away from me, but one blow to his leg from my boot sends him to the floor. "Not in the mood to talk now? All right." I snap my fingers at one of the guards, a man from the Cuban capital, and he forces Henry to his bruised knees. "I'll fill in the blanks for you."

"I'll tell you everything."

"You're disposable, Davila. A puppet." Placing the laptop on the ground, I pace the small space. All the while, his eyes are on me. Waiting for the strike. "I had men on you that night and they did as I asked—more than, but once I pulled them away, this happened. Not their fault, but mine, and I see that. Had I paid better attention, I would've noticed how Karen slightly cringed while on Dalian's lap. How when she came to see my mermaid with fresh heroin tracks on her arms, she was fidgety. Twitching and crawling in her skin while the woman has no prior record of drug usage. If anything, she's intelligent and resourceful—was only looking for a way to bring her husband here after his service. That's where your friends came into the picture…isn't it?"

"Yes."

"Who approached her?" I ask, even though I'm sure the answer is him. Because that's who this man is; a glorified gopher and nothing more. "Who made the offer to help her?"

"I did."

"And what did you offer? What was her role in this mess?"

"To act as Dalian's distraught fiancée while Jaime moved in on Amberlyn." Henry swallows hard, tears falling from his eyes. "If she gave them this, they'd bring her husband to Miami and let them leave together with money and a secured home in Cape Coral."

"You used her."

"Yes."

"Sexually?"

Davila looks down, his fear palpable. "We forced her to get high and took turns."

Closing my eyes for a second, I exhale roughly. I have a mother, cousins, and a soon-to-be wife.

Had someone done something similar to those I love, I'd want them chopped up a piece at a time and fed as chum to the animals roaming in open water.

"What else do I need to know? Is there a hidden skill you've kept from me?"

"You know."

"I do." Birds fly over us before landing in the adjacent buildings. That's the old-world charm of this city; the structures are old and reminiscent of an era where this country was a tourist destination that rivaled the world's most exotic destinations and casinos. We're called the Pearl of the Antilles for a reason, and it's more than the long-standing Tropicana club. On this block, though, I own five buildings and they are occupied by those who work for me to distribute food and necessities from the capital to smaller cities and out to the more remote farmlands. "But I'd like to hear you admit it."

"I'm the hacker who stole Amberlyn's identity."

"Good boy." Reaching a hand toward him, Henry flinches but I simply pat his head. "Now pray."

"Let me work it off," he pleads instead. Wasting his breath. "I'm good at what I do and can be useful."

"I've told you before. Our organization isn't recruiting." Shifting a glance at the watch on my wrist, I give a short whistle and Israel comes forward with my gun. "Two minutes. Do we have word from Junior?"

"Yes. Karen is in his care."

"Good." After taking the Glock, I reach into my right back pocket and pull out a silencer attachment and affix it to the muzzle. "And Silvio Lopez? Have we found him?"

"Word is he's here on the island and held in a private high-security jail."

Henry clears his throat. "My uncle runs the president's personal prison here. I can get you in if—"

"Would you get my men inside and out safely?" I raise an amused brow. "Out of the goodness of your heart?"

"If it kept me alive? Yes." Low. Meek. Nothing at all like the man who lied to me and terrorized an innocent woman for personal greed. Where's that cocky son of a bitch now? "Just ask, and it's yours."

"Open your mouth." Expressions—from fear to almost relief—cross his features in rapid succession at the command. Yet he does it. He kneels on the cold ground while the sun beats down on the city, lips parted and eyes closed. The latter of which I didn't ask him to do. "Loyalty, Henry, is all that matters to the De Leons. What we pride ourselves on, from the lowest soldier to the head of the family. If we can't trust you, you are of no use and will be dealt with."

"I'll take my punishment." Opens his mouth further. *What the hell does he think I'm going to do?* Yet he's making this game of bull's-eye too easy.

Three steps separate us and I take two, stopping just shy of touching a wet puddle on the floor. *I hate when they pee themselves.* My aim is good, maybe even better than Thiago's. "You seem to be confused. Open your eyes." Muddy brown ones meet mine and widen. He tries to snap his mouth shut, but before he does, I've already fired, and the bullet breaks his teeth and tongue and exits out the back of his skull before he's successful.

The muted sound is barely discernible in the busy afternoon bustle where many pass the building below on their way to and from my store, and after he slumps forward, I turn and head straight for the door.

Those here fall into step behind me while dragging Henry's body. There's a cheap casket down in the bodega for him that I'll be taking with me to the meeting with Placido Rodriguez.

I couldn't bring Dalian back with me, but his best friend should suffice. I'll even give them enough time to bury the asshole before decapitating the president. Because that's the only way to get rid of a snake. A body is useless without the head, and his administration will crumble.

Chapter 24
IVAN

WE MAKE IT to the Placido de la Revolucion a little after four in the afternoon and are met with a new general and his body of force on the steps. They're standing guard, weapons drawn while I walk past them but make clear eye contact.

His facial expression doesn't change, but there's a subtle tilt to his head no one else catches. Or maybe they do, and those here are mostly my men.

Either way, I make my way inside the grand door and into a large open room where those dressed in military honors line the room. They don't move. Don't blink.

It's quite impressive to witness.

The place is opulent yet a bit sterile, gleaming from corner to corner with history and the money hidden from its citizens. To think those in here feast while the nation starves.

And sure, things are a bit different with the youth finding ways to survive and grow—becoming entrepreneurs while pulling their families out of the molds they'd been forced into—but the country needs more.

As people, Cubans are resilient and proud.

Fighters, and as I stand inside this room, my chest swells with emotions I didn't expect.

I've always been proud of where we are from, but this moment is one I wish I could've shared with the generations that were lucky enough to see this. The future.

Patria y Vida.

"Mr. De Leon, President Rodriguez is waiting," a woman says, pulling my attention away from the flag slightly swaying ahead of me. "If you'll please follow me."

"Of course." Israel isn't with me; he's coming from another entry point with my gift in a special box. A demurely dressed woman in her thirties turns and I follow, walking past those in ceremonial uniforms while they stare straight ahead. She takes me and the four men with me toward the end of a long hall where a set of double doors awaits me. They're wide open and with the man of the hour sitting at the head of a long conference table.

President Placido Rodriguez is a greying, pompous motherfucker with a slight beer belly to finish his look. He stands when he sees me, fixing the cuff links at his wrists before holding a hand out in a very diplomatic fashion. He's smiling, as if he knows something I don't, while giving the escort a nod.

The door closes and so do the pretenses, my grip tighter than his. "I'd say it's a pleasure, but we both know that's a lie."

"Likewise, but I will insist we take a seat and talk like men." Placido eyes my men, more specifically their faces, and his grin morphs into a smirk. "Did your parents let you off the leash to play with the big boys? How generous of them."

"No more than your wife leaves you unsupervised so she can bend over for the gardener." My expression is neutral, unmoved by his earlier shot. "But her private extracurricular activities are none of my business. Heck, you might enjoy being a cuckold."

"You're skating on thin ice, kid. I could kill you, and no one would lift a finger against me." His old hand clenched. "This isn't Miami."

"I'm well aware of where I am, yet you're the one who seems to be confused." Opening my suit jacket, I pull out an envelope and place it atop the dark wood tabletop. "You're surrounded by your enemies, Rodriguez. People who are waiting for the word—a reason to snap and slit your throat."

"And you're man enough to do so?" To his right is an ashtray and cigar inside the marked holder. The end is already cut, the sharp tool right beside it, and the president lights up. A few deep pulls and the end glows amber before it's overshadowed by his exhaled smoke. "We both know how this will end, Ivan. It's only a matter of time before Jaime and Dalian—"

"I didn't know the dead could walk, much less cause harm."

"What did you say?" The cockiness is gone and his voice shakes. Something the president tries to hide behind a cough, but it's too late. "Where's my nephew?"

"Morgue. In a gator's stomach." My shrug is nonchalant. "Both are true."

"You're lying."

"Are you willing to place a bet on that?"

"Hijo de—"

"Careful, old man. You're surrounded by your enemies; one wrong move and I will give the command." He's nervous. Sweating a bit. "Now, would you like the proof or are you willing to take my word for it?"

"Proof." Gritted teeth. The cigar is now back in the ashtray and wasting away. "How do I know it's not a lie?"

"Here." One of the men with me has my iPad, and it only takes a few clicks to open the browser and search. At once, headlines with links attached appear and I hand over the device. I don't care if he breaks it in a moment of rage. I'll buy another one. "Read one or several, but it won't change the outcome."

Rodriguez's face changes from pallid to nearly purple as the reality of what happened to his nephew sinks in. I'll do the same to Jaime and then him. He knows this. Yet he slams the tablet on the table so hard the screen cracks and shatters at the corner, but the image from the report on a local Miami station, a Spanish one at that, remains.

Dalian Uriel is dead.

Mauled. Unrecognizable.

"You will pay for this, cabron. From your mother to the puta you fuck, I will kill them all."

"Is this the route you want to go with me?" Standing from my seat, I tap the wood twice and the man to my left walks to a secret door no one but those at the highest level of intelligence know about. It's an exit made for the first family and the leeches who kiss their asses to escape through in case of a coup or assassination attempt.

Israel is on the other side of that door and the wooden box, half the size of a normal casket, is wheeled inside. It's plain white and has a few holes dotted in red where blood has begun to seep through.

"What's the meaning of this? How did you—"

"You have seventy-two hours to step down or bend the knee for the De Leon family, Mr. President. Seventy-two, and not a minute more." The lid is removed and inside, you can tell there's a male body about the age of Dalian. "And this is my gift to you. Henry Davila was Dalian's close friend and the snitch that told me where to find him when I pointed a gun at his head. You can burn him or pretend it's Dalian while having a fake service to mourn another life lost because of your idiocy and greed. Whatever you decide is on you, Placido, but remember one thing: I'm everywhere. I see everything."

"I won't let this go." Voice hoarse, he stands and leans over the table with both fists holding his weight. "What you've done—"

"Your call, and I could give a single fuck either way. Bend or die, it's up to you." Going around to his side, I place a hand on his arm and squeeze. "My deepest condolences. It didn't have to be this way, but the clock is ticking nonetheless. Make the right decision, Rodriguez. Don't be the reason your entire family dies at my hand. Take this as advice; I'm not the bad guy here."

I leave him to think and consider his options, then walk out of the room and the building without anyone asking questions or attempting to stop us. To be honest, everything was too smooth and when I get back to my chauffeur on the island, a sinking feeling hit.

He's worried. Wringing his hands together, but before I can ask, he tosses the cell phone I'd left inside the car at me. "Your father called me after you didn't respond. Says it's urgent and has to do with Miss Amberlyn Ibarra."

"WHAT DO YOU MEAN, you let her walk out the house?"

"Son, it's my fault. This is on me," Dad says, rubbing a hand down his face the same way I do when frustrated. "We thought she knew. That you told her, and she was just playing along to help Davila's sister hang herself. Even after she left, at first we thought it was her playing a part, until your mother called and found herself blocked."

"But Amberlyn doesn't know. I told you she isn't to be touched by my—"

"Papito, I'm sorry. I didn't mean to hurt her." The FaceTime call freezes momentarily, and Mom's blotchy face makes the situation worse. My ire cannot be contained; I'm shaking and what's worse, Amberlyn won't respond to any of my texts. I've been trying to get ahold of her since the plane took off, begging for her to reach out, but nada. *Is this what she feels when I've ignored her in the past?*

I'm an asshole for it. Deserve to feel the worry clawing at my skin because there are still risks I can't control.

A car accident.

Wrong place and time incident.

Fuck, even lighting strikes in Miami aren't that uncommon.

"This is beyond fucked up." Exhaling roughly, I type out another message to her and then one to Junior, the latter of which responding right away.

I have Karen and should be in Cuba by tonight. Am I heading to Havana or the compound? ~Junior.

Neither. Stay in Miami. I'm on my way back. ~Ivan

Three dots appear on the screen. Then the phone pings.

Is everything okay? What do you need me to do, boss? ~Junior

Try to find Amberlyn. No one knows where she is. ~ Ivan

His reply comes in just as fast.

I'll start searching now. Karen will be kept at my apartment; she won't run. ~Junior

Thank you. I'll call when I land. ~Ivan

The screen of my laptop unscrambles and my parents are there, still wearing upset expressions.

"My sirenita thinks I'm sleeping with and keeping a woman at your home? Do you realize how bad that makes me look?"

"I've never seen her so upset, Ivan. But again, we thought she was just playing along. We would've never let her go intentionally thinking that."

"Mom, to be honest…I don't know what to say right now. All I know is I need to find her."

"We fucked up, kid," Mom says and sniffs; she's been crying. Her face is blotchy while Dad looks miserable. "It all happened so fast, and I went along thinking nothing of it. I really thought she knew, yet her expression before running out is something I can't get out of my head. Baby, it's like she expected this and at the same time accepted it."

"Where was Miguel? Why didn't Edgar react?"

"Miguel was preparing for Cindy's transfer, and Edgar grabbed the bitch while your father sent that message to you. We were hoping you'd get in contact with Amberlyn to discuss what she came for, but instead, everything blew up in our faces." Dad passes Mom a Kleenex, yet she bats his hand away. She looks so sad. "I'm sorry, papito."

"Not your fault." Knocking back a drink, I pour another few fingers' worth of whiskey. "I'm the idiot that's let this go on long enough. She believes it because I've let her down."

"You'll find her. She has to listen." Dad tries to lighten the mood, to give hope, but the reality is much too somber.

Yet I refuse to lose her.

I can't and won't live without my girl. That gorgeous woman with the reddish-black hair and tattoos—with a sense of humor that rivals mine. She's sarcastic and beautiful and likes to read, but is ready for a night on the town just as fast. Amberlyn is the other half of my soul, taken from my rib as my perfect counterpart, and I will make things right between us again.

I love her. Simply and honest.

"I'm not letting her go either way."

OWN

"BEBE, PLEASE ANSWER. LET ME EXPLAIN." This is the third burner phone I've bought since landing. It's been twenty-four hours, and no one has seen her. Her parents don't know where she is, but know I'm involved and demand I make it right.

Not a promise hard to keep, but it'd be easier if the stubborn woman would just pick up the phone. Every time I call, she avoids or sends me to voicemail, and if I make her angry enough, I'm blocked.

Silly girl has no idea I'll burn through a million of these if it gets her to give in, even if it's just to curse me out. I'll take that any day over the silence. The cold shoulder.

I try again and get the same response.

Two rings and to a voicemail that's full at the moment. I'm more than positive ninety percent of those messages are mine.

The separation—this wall between us—is not something I can deal with. It's brewing, eating at me, and a part of me worries about the explosion that will follow our reunion.

Worry and anger mix while my love for her nearly suffocates me.

She'll be lucky if I let her out of my sight again.

Even my parents have noticed the change. I've always been possessive of her, needed her attention, but this surpasses anything I've experienced before. If what Mermaid wanted was to be claimed before, now she'll be handcuffed to me at all times. If what she needed was validation, now she'll bear my last name as proof of who owns her.

"Sir, I got Natasha on the phone." Junior rushes into my home office, phone extended toward me.

"Thank you." Sitting back in my chair, I place my legs up and cross the ankles atop the desk. The door closes and I breathe in deep before letting it out slowly, trying to calm myself so I don't snap at my sister-in-law's cousin. Nat is also my friend. Like a sister to Amberlyn. "Where is she?"

"Ivan, I think she just needs a couple days to cool off. Back off for a bit."

"Where. Is. She."

"I can't betray her trust. All you need to know is she's safe—"

"There's a plot to kidnap and sexually exploit her, Nat, by the nephew of Cuba's president. The man is a Miami detective, you know Uriel and should also be aware he's been missing since Dalian's body was found," I manage to grit out without completely losing it on her. This is my fault, not hers, but right now she's keeping me from what's mine. "Please, Natasha. Where is my mermaid?"

"Dominican Republic." Her voice is low, but I hear it clearly. As if she shouted the answer. "Amberlyn checked into an all-inclusive resort in Punta Cana."

"Thank you."

"Will she be safe?"

"She's mine, and I'd die for her."

Chapter 25

AMBERLYN

TWO DAYS BEFORE…

MY PHONE RINGS again, the thirtieth time and counting, but I hit ignore and pick up my drink.

I'm stewing in my anger. Drowning in a heady concoction of regret and hurt that makes it nearly impossible to breathe, but I do. One inhale at a time while one of my best friends sits across from me at an airport bar inside of Miami International.

My flight leaves in three hours, but I've avoided being found thus far and I'm praying they heed my request to stay away. I don't want to see anything of them. Ever again.

A sardonic laugh slips from me, and I down what's left of my second sex on the beach. "Maybe that's what I need."

"What do you need?" Nat asks, picking at her order of chips and salsa. The girl is obsessed with them and never fails to order some whenever they're on the menu. "You've been muttering a lot, and I have no clue if I missed something."

"A good hard fuck with a stranger on the beach."

"Okay," she says, dragging the words out. "Not at all what I expected you to say."

"Couldn't hurt to give it a try now." I shrug, but even that is listless. It's as if all the air inside my words has been sucked out and I've been left to gape and choke until it's my time to die. "Casual sex could be beneficial."

All this time, for years, I trusted him. Blindly. Like a puppet.

Not once have I looked at another man, and not for lack of attention. Men have always flirted—threw out a cheesy line or two—but I never entertained the idea of being with anyone but Ivan.

How can I when he's been scaring away anyone who tries to get close since high school.

But there have been plenty of women who've tried and failed to date him. At least, I thought so until the chick inside the De Leons' home. His parents didn't rebuke her or try to defend me; I was the outcast.

Always have been. Always will be to them.

She's nothing but an obligation.

Well, screw them.

They can figure out the dead body's meaning, and the threat I want no part of. As of today, right this second, I don't care.

For years, I've silently fought my doubts over my importance in his life. My place.

I'll never be that ignorant girl again Can't afford to be.

"No mas. This is it for me."

"No more what, chica? Be more specific."

I haven't seen or heard from Ivan since he left my place. Since I once again proved my weakness and let him take me in the shower. *I begged for his touch. I instigated everything.* Moreover, for years I've accepted the scraps of attention without shame—to just feel him next to me was enough—and all of that is my fault.

How can a man take you seriously like that?

No reproach. No demands for an explanation.

Instead, I've always been there with my legs spread. Literally.

"I'm an idiot, Nat. A total fucking pendeja for continuing to put myself in this position." A flight announcement comes through the speakers, but it's not mine and I wave my now-empty glass at a waiter. The bar and grill we're inside of isn't far from my terminal, yet it seems empty suddenly, and I scan the surrounding areas just in case. *Nothing. He's not here.* And I let out a huge sigh of relief at that. Now more than ever I need to get away from my responsibility. From life. *Him.* "Why can't I just send him to hell and be done with everything? He doesn't deserve me."

The truth tastes bitter on my tongue because the pedestal I've always put Ivan on has crumbled and the rubble lies at my proverbial feet. It's left me shaking. Unable to breathe without feeling his absence.

"Maybe there's a good explanation?" By Nat's expression, even she doesn't believe it. Her response irks me, but before I can respond, my cell phone rings again.

At this point, I'm ready to break the device.

But it's not a De Leon this time. No. It's Jaime Uriel, and in the mental state I'm in, I have no patience for the man. It's why I answer while baring my teeth, welcoming the anger I hold for all males at the moment.

"What?"

"Amberlyn?"

"Again, Detective. What?" Our waiter places my drink down, and I take another healthy sip.

"Where are you?" His tone is aggravated, demanding, and today is not the day to test my inner gangster.

"How is that any of your business, Detective?" I demand, yet don't give him the chance to answer. I could care less about his reasons. "What I do or don't isn't any of your business, and since what *was* our agreement is now null after the man's death, I suggest you lose my number. Don't call me again."

"Where. Are. You?"

"On vacation…so fuck off." With that, I hang up and turn the damn thing off. My parents and Nat are the only ones who know I'll be out of town for two weeks and heading to the Dominican Republic. They're aware I'll be staying at an all-inclusive resort, but not which one. "That guy just rubs me wrong."

"He's pushy," she notes.

"Very much so, but he shouldn't be calling again." That call's put me out, and I push the drink aside before standing. Our bill isn't large, less than sixty, and I leave a hundred-dollar bill on the table before coming to Nat's side and pulling her up and into a hug. "I'm going to go sit at the gate. Love you, babes."

She squeezes me just as hard, rocking us a little from side to side. "You sure you don't want me to tag along? I've got some vacation time saved up and—"

"I need some time on my own."

"Fine." Pulling back just enough to see my face, she pouts. "Go be all alone and mopey while I dodge that man of yours."

"He's not mine."

"He is, Lynnie. And I have no doubt he'll be coming for you."

Tears build, but I won't let them fall and blink rapidly. "For the first time, I don't want him to come. A person can't live like this…I can't live like this, mami. I want more than empty words and false promises; Ivan will never be what I need him to be."

"Are you sure that's what you want?"

"Yes."

"Then I'll hold him off your trail as long as I can. Go find yourself."

PRESENT...

A WARM BREEZE sweeps over me while I nurse a shot of Mama Juana out on the water. I'm in a hammock watching the trees sway and birds fly overhead while silence surrounds me. It's both depressing and therapeutic, yet exactly what I need at the moment.

There's no escaping reality when the noises cease and you can hear yourself think.

And for forty-eight hours, that's what I've done on this private slice of paradise that I've paid a fortune for. I'm but steps from the warm Caribbean waters at all times and far enough away from noisy tourists and the horny men offering me a private tour of the island.

Guest and staff alike.

Since landing, I've been hit on and asked to become someone's Mrs. several times.

"Yet the one I want doesn't see me." I won't deny it's a blow to my self-esteem. That I wasn't enough to fall in love with, but that's life and if this place has taught me anything within my solitude, it's that there's a reason for everything.

Accepting reality hurts—that he's not the man I thought he was—and causes my chest to feel as though it's caving in, but there's a lesson in that, too. I'll survive. I'll be stronger one day soon.

So I close my eyes while enjoying the last sip of my spiced rum and repeat my mantra:

I am enough.

In the distance, a merengue song starts playing, and it's from a live band. It's soothing and lulls me; I'm safe enough here to let my guard down, and I do, sinking slowly into a nice, relaxing nap. It's easy to forget the world and those around me while the sun filters through the thin shade, warming my skin. While the water below laps at the shore.

This is what I needed.

Here, I find peace.

THE ATMOSPHERE IS OFF TODAY. I don't feel as alone with my solitude, and while swimming not far from the shore, there are eyes on me. The sensation is unmistakable, and goose bumps rise on my skin.

Hairs at the back of my neck stand up, too.

My first instinct is to think Ivan had something to do with this, but that notion is squashed just as fast. He won't come for me. I'm nothing to him.

Yet I can't shake the feeling while eating lunch out on my private deck or while sunbathing near a group of women near the resort's main activity area. It's also why I find myself heading toward the concierge service desk to ask them to search the surrounding areas around my villa.

"How can I help you today, Miss Ibarra?" the woman behind the desk asks, her smile so infectious and bright. But that's everyone in the Dominican Republic you meet; they're happy and full of so much life—a positive attitude. "Are you finally ready to book a tour out to—"

"No, but I do need help with something."

"Of course. What can we do to make your stay more enjoyable?"

"I feel like I'm being watched." The smile falls from her face at that, but there's also a bout of nervousness that makes no sense. "Could you please have someone check the surrounding areas of my villa? Just as a precaution?"

"Of course, ma'am. I'll send security out there now, and again later tonight."

"Thank you. I really appreciate it."

"It's our pleasure. We want you to feel safe and happy during your stay with us." She taps a few keys on her computer, filling something out before giving me another warm smile. "I've just sent an alert to the head of security for us. He should be answering soon and will take care of it."

"Perfect."

"Are you heading back to your accommodations, or joining us for dinner this evening?"

"To be honest, I was thinking of going back."

"I insist that you don't, miss. Not until we get the all-clear from security."

"Okay." My stomach rumbles then and I laugh; since arriving here, this one isn't forced. "Which restaurant do you recommend? And I want authentic. Not something touristy."

"Lolo's is out on the pier and above the water. They serve the real deal, home cooking that our country is known for. Trust me, it's delicious."

"Sold. Do I need a reservation?"

"No. I'll take care of it." Glancing at my clothes, I grimace a bit. I'm in a simple tie-dye dress in different shades of yellow. "Will this be okay, or do I need to change? I didn't plan on going anywhere tonight."

"It's a casual setting. You'll have no problem with it." The woman grabs a walkie-talkie and sends out a quick call for a golf cart transport. Their response is quick, and the young man assures her it'll be less than five minutes before he arrives. "You're all set. I put the table under your last name, and the hostess knows to expect you shortly. Is there anything else I can help you with?"

"Not that I can think of."

"Great." Another mega-watt smile. "I'm glad I could be of assistance. If you need anything else, please don't hesitate to ask."

"Thank you."

"It's my pleasure."

"Wow," is all I can say, dropping my fork down after the final bite of the cinco leches dessert that's knocked me on my proverbial butt. It's sweet and a bit creamy with just the right amount of cake. "I'm in love with this."

But then again, everything about this place is amazing. Designed to make you feel as though you're out on the water, the entire restaurant is an open concept with nature providing the biggest draw. We're on the water with the late evening sky surrounding us while you can hear the water splashing against the pillars holding the place above the warm waters below.

From the waitstaff to the food, it's been an experience.

"We're glad you enjoyed the food, miss."

"Delicioso. Everything was amazing," I tell the waitress after she delivers my coffee and takes away my now-empty plate. "I'll have another of that to go or I'll be thinking about it all night."

She throws her head back and laughs. "You're not the first to request it. I'll get right on that…they'll be something extra too. You have to try the coconut dessert."

"Thank you."

"My pleasure." Once she leaves, I begin adding a little sugar to my coffee and begin observing the others dining tonight. There are a few older couples, but the majority I've run into are all adults. People are laughing and drinking and for a second, I'm a little jealous.

Always alone.

"Evening, Amberlyn," a male voice says from my right, and I'm startled, but more so because it's familiar. And when I flick my gaze in his direction, I understand why.

What the fuck? "Detective Uriel, what—"

"Jaime, sweetheart. Say my name."

"Again, Detective," I say, adding emphasis on his title, "what are you doing here?"

"I'm here to pick up my girl." That calms me for all of two seconds, when he's grabbing my arm on the next. His grip is tight as he tries to pull me up, causing the couple a table over to look our way. "Did you miss me, bebe?"

Coming from him, that word is all wrong. Disgust me and I shiver, something he mistakes for pleasure.

"Let go, Uriel. I'm not finding this funny."

"Neither was the death of my brother, but your cunt of a fuck buddy made sure I felt that blow." He bends down so his mouth is next to my ear, his hot breath causing my stomach to revolt. "And you will pay for his sins, amor. I'll take your pussy as deposit and your asshole as liquidation of said charges. Over and over again, Miss Ibarra, and you have the De Leons to thank for the cruel future you've been sacrificed to."

Yet a few seconds after the last word leaves his lips, there's an audible click of a gun, and men surround the table. It all happens so fast. One second Jaime has a grip on my arm, and the next he's on the ground a few feet from me with a vicious predator straddling his body and landing blow after blow to a now-unconscious man.

Those inside the restaurant look on in fear, while the staff seems unperturbed.

"What the fuck?" It leaves me and as if on cue, those eyes that haunt me turn and our stares connect. His hands are a bloody mess, while there are specks of red across his cheeks. His lips are curled up into an angry snarl, and yet he's never been more beautiful to me.

I sway in my seat and he's off Uriel's body in an instant, sauntering toward me. His gait is powerful, too much, and in my panic, I rise from my seat. "Stay back."

"Mermaid, I need you to calm down." Ivan grabs an untouched glass of water and napkin from a nearby table, making quick work of wiping his hands. The ease in which he does so show his comfort and quit wit, ridding himself of Uriel's blood quickly. Not completely, but enough you can't tell without inspecting carefully. "You know I'd never hurt you."

"Liar."

"Bebe, please. Let's cool off and talk. There's—"

For some reason, my world breaks at that moment and fight-or-flight takes over. There's one of his men to my right with a gun at his side, tucked into the waistband of a pair of dress pants, and I grab it before anyone can react. It also goes off just as quick, adrenaline making it difficult past the lies and betrayal—my need to hurt Ivan is larger than my body can contain.

"No one touches her," he barks out, the sound a little pained. "Step down."

"No, De Leon. You step back." My feet are trying to reach the exit, one step at a time. "No mas. We're done."

"The fuck we are," he roars, his harsh—angry—tone causing me to almost drop the weapon. "There will never be an end to us, Sirenita. I'll kill the devil himself to keep you."

Chapter 26
IVAN

I DON'T THINK twice, tossing her over my shoulder in three strides while ignoring the punches landing on my back. My mermaid is livid, and I love it. Prefer this to ignorance.

That cold shoulder shit taught me a valuable lesson; she can be cruel.

"Put me down, De Leon. I'm not going anywhere with you!"

"Out," I hiss from between clenching teeth while her body squirms over the shoulder she lightly grazed with a bullet. It's not a huge wound, just stings, and I'll take care of it—and her for it—later. No matter what, we don't shoot at each other. I'll admit my girl has good aim and had she been calm, there's no doubt I'd be removing a shell and not planning the ways to fuck her into submission.

One by one, everyone inside the restaurant vacates without hesitating. The moment the last person leaves, I give Israel a nod and he picks up the unconscious waste of sperm from the floor, nearly dislocating his shoulder with the way he jams it into the table's edge. "I want him in the plane's cargo area within twenty. Make sure he's treated like royalty while you wait for us."

My sirenita huffs, but the hard punch to my side will leave a bruise. *Brat.*

She'll pay for that later.

On her knees or back. Maybe on all fours with her pretty holes on display.

I'm not picky at the moment. Not after living with the fear of not knowing where she's been for a few days.

"Yes, boss." With that, he exits, meeting Junior at the door and they make quick work of getting the detective out of the restaurant and then off the pier.

Now, it's just the two of us:

Alone. Angry. Hurt.

Her skin is soft against my fingertips as I slowly drag the pads of each up and down the back of her leg, pushing the back of her dress higher with each pass. I also don't miss the low sigh she emits after each caress.

"Are you ready to talk?"

"Yes." Low. Meek. It's completely false. Yet I don't hesitate and lower her to the ground, making sure to ease her slowly, rubbing my hard cock across her clothed front.

Christ, the sight that greets me once she's standing is delicious, and I step back. "Hola, bebe."

Hard nipples. Goose bumps. Parted lips.

"You asshole!" Amberlyn's hand connects with my cheek, and the sting feels like a jolt of electricity in my veins. Thrumming and heated. It's harsh and fast, leaving behind this all-consuming yearning for her touch. *I'll never be without her again.* "This isn't a date. He followed me here, like you, apparently."

"I've missed you, too."

"What part of *leave me alone,* don't you understand? Leave."

"No." I take a step closer while she moves back, trying to evade me, but I'm done. She wanted me, she has me. We're not leaving this island until she understands how devoted I am.

"Are you insane? That's an MDP detective you picked up. If they pin this on you, it'll bring heat the family doesn't need. What were you thinking?" She could care less about Uriel; this is just another weak attempt to create conflict, so I don't touch her.

"That you being in danger is not something I'll ever tolerate."

"Seriously? That's the best you can come up with." She gives me a sardonic laugh, a brave act, but I catch each shiver. The way her shoulders hunch in. "Why don't you go feed that line to the whore sleeping at your parents' house."

"Your life being in danger is idiotic?" Now I'm angry, nearly snarling the words at her. "Anything but you being safe and happy is unacceptable to me. Don't you ever say that shit again."

"Bullshit." This time she jams a manicured finger into my chest, mimicking my defensive stance, eyes spitting fire. "You left me. You broke every late-night promise."

"To protect you."

"Stop with the lies." Tears spring to her eyes but Amberlyn looks away, blinking rapidly so they don't fall. "What have I ever done for you to continue hurting me like this?"

"Bebe, not everything is as it seems."

"Just, fuck you." I hate the defeat in her voice. "If you ever cared for me, at the very least as a friend, leave. Go on with your life, and I'll do the same with mine." Her high ponytail has come a little undone and a few wisps of hair curl around her cheek; I want nothing more than to sweep them back but grit my teeth instead. "All you do is force your presence on me. Make me think you want me—more—

but turn around and leave every single time. I'm done, Ivan. There's nothing more I can give you."

"You don't mean that."

"I do."

"Then you leave me no choice. I'm sorry." Whatever she sees in my eyes makes hers widen; there's a tinge of fear in them, and I hate it. This. Where we are. And I hold the blame, know that, but it doesn't stop me from advancing on her. "Run."

"What?" Voice shaky. Breathing choppy.

"You want me to chase you to the ends of the earth, then run. Just know that I will always follow."

"You're insane, Ivan. Just go. Stop this."

"Never, amorcito. I exist with you."

"Don't do this to me." This time a tear does fall, but when I try to wipe it away, she moves away. "I'm begging you."

"You are my heart, Amberlyn. Always have been, and always will be."

"I refuse to do this with you again, Ivan. You shouldn't have come here."

"So you expected me to sit back while the woman I love is taken? To let them have and abuse you?"

"Wait." The gun slips from her hand and goes off, breaking a large stone figure, but Sirenita just stares at me. She's trembling, hard. "What did you just say?"

"He's the nephew of President Rodriguez through marriage, sweetie. They were going to kidnap—"

"Not that." Heavy tears fall now. Lips trembling. "Please, I need you to repeat the first part."

My anger evaporates. Instead, what's left is a man splayed open and wanting to lay at the altar of his goddess to worship.

"I love you, Amberlyn. Always have, Mermaid."

"No. No." She's muttering something that sounds like *he's playing with me* right before making the biggest mistake she could at the moment. My girl ran. Literally took off as if her life depended on it, and I take a second to control my own emotions.

Her fear stings me as though she wielded a whip and cracked it across my chest. Yet there's also another emotion licking at my senses: pleasure.

I warned her I'd chase.

I'll prove my worth a thousand times over if it means she's mine.

Removing my shirt, I throw it over my shoulder and walk out of the restaurant. There's no doubt in my mind she's heading for the rented villa, but what she isn't aware of is a hidden pathway that connects those properties to this restaurant.

While she ran straight down the pier and toward the pools, I make a left and pick up the pace. Mermaid is quick, I'll give her that, and the last thing I want is to give her any inkling that I'm close or she'll veer off.

Through tropical foliage, I manage to keep ahead but once the main paths connect, I stop and wait. My girl's accommodations are on a private white sandy stretch of beach with an open-air jacuzzi and a lit pathway to the water.

Yet I never give her the chance to place a single foot on the smooth cobblestone, tackling her to the ground and twisting, landing on my back to take the brunt of the fall. Sand sweeps around us and settles, but the hellcat above me bucks and fights to stand while my teeth bite her neck.

"Get the hell off me, Ivan." Those fingernails dig into my chest while her lower half gyrates once, unconsciously, while trying to push herself up. It stings, but I don't complain. Not when she's in my arms again, scratching at my newest addition there: her name in my cursive handwriting surrounded by mariposa flowers in red ink. "This isn't funny. I'm no one's joke."

"No, but you are my world," I croon low, releasing her for the time being. "I love you, bebe."

"You don't." Like a scared rabbit, she fidgets and looks for an escape. "I know you don't."

"Now who's the liar." *Fuck, she's beautiful when angry.* Those warm eyes blaze at my words, spitting fire at me while her hands ball into tight fists. *That's right, sweet girl. Burn me.* "But then again, you've always been a little blind."

"What did you say to me?" Her tone is acerbic. Incredulous.

"I'm calling you out on your bullshit." Her hand flies toward my face, intent clear, but I counter her move and yank Amberlyn against me. She gasps at the move and shivers from our contact, but I don't let another word of denial fall from those plump lips.

Instead, I kiss her. Fucking take what's mine and breathe for what feels like the first time in days.

And for all her fighting, she's right there with me. Kissing me as if she'll never get the chance to do it again.

Our tongues fight for dominance while hands remove clothing, tossing everything in a manic rush to feel. She's nipping my chin while I'm roaming, squeezing her bare ass with both hands before picking her up—rubbing her slick core over my cock while walking us to a swing set beside two white hammocks.

The water here barely reaches my thighs but lines her up perfectly to take me. It's a wide seat, could be for two, but dwarfs her lithe forms. She looks like the perfect sinful doll, and I growl out a loud *fuck* when Mermaid leans forward—nearly folding herself in half—to take my dick in her mouth.

Son of a bitch, her mouth is velvet heat, so soft while applying the perfect amount of suction with each swallow around my girth. The bulbous tip touches the back of her throat on the next bob, and I grip the back of her head, forcing myself a little deeper until she gags.

"That's it, mami. *Fucking hell*…just like that." I can feel her smile at my eloquence, the cockiness that makes her pick up the pace and depth until her nose touches the base of my cock. My eyes close and balls draw up, the first electrical shocks of my impending release striking me, but I pull out. Her pout is adorable right after, too. "Next time I come, it's to fill your cunt. I want you dripping of me."

Lips glossy with my pre-come, she smiles. “That was all you are getting from me, De Leon.”

“You challenging me?”

“Just telling the truth.”

“Then let me rectify that.” A gentle tug by the back of her neck and she’s arching her chest while I squeeze between her thighs. Her hooded eyes watch me. They beg me to make the pain go away, and I place a gentle peck on her mouth—tasting myself—while lining up. She’s soaked. Tiny hole clenching in need as I rub my tip through soft folds. “I’m going to love you every day for the rest of our lives. There will never be another day where you doubt me, and if there is, then I’ve failed you.”

“I don’t need empty…*oh!*” That kills the stupidity she’s convinced herself of.

I’m buried to the hilt in one smooth stroke, biting back a curse as Mermaid’s walls grip me tight. They flutter around me, a pleasurable massage, but I pull out and thrust forward again. There’s no rush. I fuck her with sharp, measured snaps of my hips and slow, dragging withdrawals. Moreover, she lets me with furrowed brows and parted lips, those eyes watching me. They shift from my face to neck and lower, all the while meeting me thrust for thrust.

I feel the change in her the moment she sees it. Her body is flushed with her desire, nipples hard, but before I can take a tip between my teeth, my girl pushes my head back.

Slim fingers lightly trace the cursive there, and her bottom lip trembles. “Why?”

“Because I love you.” My own voice is hoarse, body wound tight, but I don’t pause my pace. If anything, I take her just a little harder. “Because my life is empty without you.”

“You hurt me, Ivan.” It’s a moan, a reproach, yet her thighs spread wider inside the swing. The momentum alone bounces her on my cock, an exquisite rhythm, and I grab her hip with one hand to slam in deeper. “How do I believe you?”

“Because you’re the only person in this world that truly knows me, mi amor. You know that I'd do anything to keep you safe, to remove any obstacle in our way, to then lay the world at your feet." I swallow hard and with my unoccupied hand, place hers right over where my heart beats. "You own this, bebe. That cadence has always been yours, and I'm sorry for not telling you before. I fucked up, and I own up to it."

"I don't—"

"Look at me. Look at me and tell me what you see." It doesn't take long for the fear and reproach to leave her expression, I'm baring my soul, and Amberlyn can read it. Tears begin to fall from her eyes while she tightens, those fingers dig into my chest as emotions overwhelm, bring her to the edge, and I love her through the discovery. "It was never about you being enough, Mermaid. I'm the one who lacked in this relationship, and I let my personal pursuit of that worth ruin us. For that, I'm so sorry. Don't leave me again."

A sob wracks her body, pussy spasming as her orgasm breaks us both, and I slam into the hilt. The way her walls suck me in deeper—massage—brings me to the edge and we fall over together. I fill her with my seed, overflowing her small passage and when it seeps from around my cock, I reach between us and spread the drops over the top of her thighs and mound.

Then, I slowly rock us to prolong the pleasure.

Shivers run through her naked form, and my heart settles when she seeks warmth in my hold. Amberlyn lets me wrap her in my arms, nestling against my chest and the tattoo of her name. There, she turns her head to place a kiss across the inked skin and I smile.

At peace.

We're not perfect. There's so much to still fix, but this is a start.

The chance I needed to right our story.

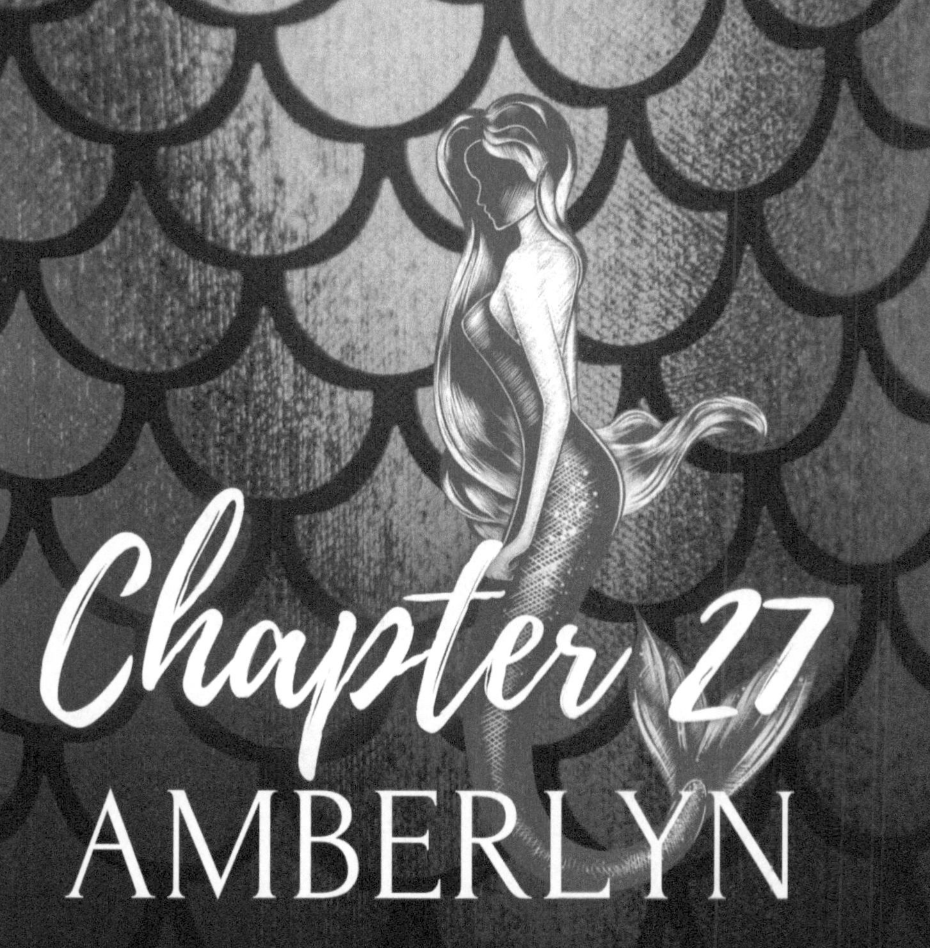

Chapter 27
AMBERLYN

THE NEXT TIME I open my eyes, I'm disoriented and a little afraid. It's clear to me that I'm on a plane, strapped into a very comfortable seat, but I'm alone. "What the—"

"I'm here, bebe." Ivan's voice calms me at once and I rub my eyes, trying to gain more of my equilibrium. We were up late into the night; mostly him talking, but I get it now.

The man I love is as idiotic as his brother, but it comes from a good place.

I told him this, too. Because had he been honest, we could've dealt with the brothers back home while they tried to fool me with the whole fake detainee disappearance. That earned him a smack to his shoulder, which led to him hissing, and my freaking out after I shot him.

In my defense, though, I was—am—under a lot of stress.

And for his good luck, my guilt made me cuddle him after we took a shower and I dressed the wound. It's not large, but I burned the skin there while also causing a four-stitch gash. The resort has a good medical staff with a lot of patience because this man is hard-headed as all get out.

The compromise was they close the wound, and I clean it. I'm responsible for dressing changes and kisses to his lips for the pain and suffering he endured.

"When did we leave the island?" A yawn escapes and I arch, popping my arms out hard enough to hear a crack. "Why didn't you wake me?'

"After everything I put you through, you needed the sleep." There's self-recrimination there along with his own guilt, and now that he's open to me, I can't look away. Not because I want to punish him—not at all. I too have my faults in this mess, but because of the beauty that is his soul.

For a killer, Ivan is sweet and caring when it comes to those he loves.

Not loyalty. Not respect.

But only those he truly loves, and it's now unhidden and open when it comes to me.

It's not pretty words or promises. No.

It's real and raw, and he's willing to sacrifice his happiness at any time to make sure I don't feel the pain of losing a loved one. It was putting his own desires aside so that he could eliminate every threat he felt was sent my way because of who he is.

Yet in his blind love, my papi forgot that I chose him. His life. His worries. Every part of who he is and what comes attached to his last name.

Ivan De Leon has one fault above all others, though, and it's that he carries the weight of what isn't his to shoulder. Not alone. Not without those who care for him just as strongly and would happily take the world on for him.

"I love you, too." Because it's my turn to give. To be vulnerable in this new us. Last night when he said the words, I froze. My mind and heart were at odds and confused, but today it's clear and undeniable, and he needs my truth just as much as his healed me.

We're not perfect, but we will be.

I won't hold this against him.

But I do demand swift justice to those who sought to break us. That's non-negotiable.

His seatbelt is unbuckled, and Ivan kneels at my feet seconds after my confession, his smile wide. "Are you sure you're ready to say it back? You don't—"

"I've loved you since we were kids, papi. That's never changed."

"I'm going to spend the rest of my life worshipping you, my little sirenita."

"Only if you let me spoil you, too. We're even in fuckups and celebrations." Cupping his face with both hands, I lean my forehead on his. My smile wide and eyes watery; I let him see me too. "A team, Ivan. Nothing and no one will break that again."

Chapter 28
IVAN

WE LANDED IN Cuba six hours ago with a quiet Jaime in tow and another body bag. This one belongs to Jasmin Davila after a quick encounter with Amberlyn where no words were exchanged between the two before the body slumped forward.

My mermaid hugged Mom like she hasn't seen her in years, both giggling a bit. They're wearing matching expressions, a mixture of relief and joy that my father basks in while her parents watch off to the side.

And when a second later my girl gives him the same embrace, I understand. He sees her and Luna as his flesh and blood, the Daddy's girl he never had, and thought she'd be upset with him over this.

"I'm sorry," they said in unison before wearing matching grins of relief.

"No, kid." The amusement dies for him then and my viejo kisses her forehead before pulling away, arms holding her at length. "You have nothing to apologize for. I know how stubborn that one is and should've surmised you didn't know. You are my child as much as he is, and I protect those I love. Never think differently, Amberlyn. We all adore you."

"Thank you."

"I also have a gift for you." Grabbing her by the hand, Dad walks my mermaid outside to where the Davila female kneels. "Her future is yours to decide."

"Dad, I don't—"

"A team, papi. Always." She also doesn't hesitate to grab my Glock and empty three shots into the woman's head without pause. Then she shrugs as if it's nothing. "Lesson learned, don't talk shit. Flies don't enter closed mouths."

"That's my girl." Her father and mine say in unison. Their smiles proud.

"He's going to kill you, De Leon. Mark my words." Jaime's trying to get under my skin. To play mind games, but in reality, is frustrating himself. My lack of engagement angers him. "We'll take turns using her holes, too. Right over your body."

"I'm sorry," my sirenita whispers and walks to where Israel walks with him. She smiles at my guard, all sweet, and asks that he breaks Jaime's teeth. Moreover, when Israel bashes the butt of his gun into the asshole's mouth repeatedly, Uriel cries, and I laugh. Hard. "What's so funny?"

"Not funny, love. I'm in awe of your ruthless tendencies."

She shrugs. "He's annoying."

"Agreed." I cut my eyes to Jaime once and what he sees quiets his sobs, leaving him a whimpering idiot while we continue to walk.

The city is awake and waiting. Demanding blood as retribution for what they've endured.

I hear the call. Embrace the darkness.

Many are waiting on my signal to approach the presidential palace, but I'll try to end this amicably and without any more casualties. Enough blood has been spilled on these lands, and while there's a part of me eliminating this man for personal reasons, there's another who's yearning for a better way of life for the people here.

I'm no hero. Will never claim to be, but sometimes justice comes under the guise of a monster.

Empty streets greet me all around, yet I can make out the ruffles sticking out from windows or holes in walls. Rodriguez has no idea how fine a line his future walks between my cruelty and total anarchy.

We walk up the stairs and into the large open lobby where Amberlyn's uncle and grandfather greet us with a nod. My girl smiles at them, so much love in her expression while controlled chaos ensues around us.

The newly appointed general stands proud with his men, all dressed in their military garbs, while traitors to the country kneel at their feet. He's one of those holding a gun to a member of the ruling party's head, his smile joyful.

Not at all the one of a man about to commit murder.

One by one, each gun goes off as I pass, and those bodies hit the floor, creating a haunting staccato to my entrance.

Each of these now dead citizens either killed, abused their power, or stole from those in a weaker position. A lesson for the next ruling class. I'll be watching.

"He's in the formal dining room. Placido has no idea what's going on."

"Thank you, General. Prepare for the elections."

"Gracias, Ivan."

"De nada. I'm not a saint."

"We know that, but you're fair. That's all we needed." He turns to start taking care of the clean-up process and then preparing for the future, while we walk straight into the private quarters of the Rodriguez family.

His wife is in Europe and knows to never return.

His extended family fled under threats of death.

Yet the man himself doesn't find anything strange in the mass fleeing of those he cares about.

"Buen provecho," I call out into the large room, and it echoes back to me, catching the president off guard. The coffee in his hand tumbles, burning him in the process to right it, and he hisses at the contact.

"What is the meaning of this! How did you get in?"

"And here I was simply just wishing you enjoy your meal."

"Guards!" he yells out, and nothing. "Guards!"

"No one is coming to save you, Rodriguez. Your time is up."

"Tio, do something," Jaime pleads through a busted mouth, his lip torn and hanging off to the side. Bruises litter his body, and the tank top and shorts combo we put him in show off each one. "You own the military! Call them to shoot these assholes!"

Junior locks the door, just in case there's a brave soul out there who still believes his propaganda, while I turn and kiss my girl. Just a sweet little peck to hold me over until later tonight.

She groans into my mouth, not caring who's present, and that makes me feel like a king. "End this, papi. I want to go home and start my life with you."

"I love you." A final taste, and then I place her beside Israel. The men with me know that she's to be untouched and will protect her with their lives. "Junior, open the bag in front of Jaime."

"Of course, boss." The large black bag has been kept away from him for a reason. We didn't want him to get suspicious, further stressed by the death of his lover. Jasmin Davila slept with both brothers, carried the same greed, and helped ruin a few lives in pursuit of a lifestyle she couldn't maintain on her own.

With the first few inches of the zipper open, her dark hair spills out and it's matted with blood. Her head follows, and Jaime gasps while Placido becomes shifty. Every room in this palace has a hidden escape, and he'll leave his nephew here to die without an ounce of remorse if it means he can escape.

"Try it, and I'll end it all now." That stills his movements while Jaime gags, violently vomiting what little is in his stomach at the disfigured sight of the woman who sucked his cock. Do I feel sorry for him? Not one bit. "Are there any words you'd like to say to her?"

"I'm going to kill her for this, you know. All of you, but I'll start with Amberlyn." His vows fall on deaf ears. It's as if he refuses to accept a reality where they have no power.

"No. You're not." Taking my place behind him, I kick the back of his knees and when he lands on them, I undo the ends of my bracelet and press the wire against his neck. The sharp metal embeds into the skin there, sliding through with ease as I pull left-to-right in a sawing motion. All the while, though, my eyes are on the president.

This is the by-product of his greed. Believing himself untouchable.

Jaime tries to fight off my hold, pushing back, but I dig my foot into his spine and use the imbalance as a counterweight. Within a minute I've torn open his neck, severing his jugular, and only let go, removing the wire when he spurts blood from the wound.

He'll choke on his blood, unable to breathe without blockage.

But before he takes his final bloodied breath, I lower to my haunches and speak loud enough that everyone hears. "Your brother died in a similar fashion, Jaime. I used the same wire that up until a few minutes ago only carried his blood. Dalian took his final breaths inside a gator's mouth, but I'd sentenced him to death before that. He died thinking you'd betrayed him."

"I'll step down and disappear. You won." Placido's voice is shaky, some might say stressed, but I know better than to believe an asshole like him has a heart. It's not grief he's facing, but self-preservation.

"No."

"I'll pay you to let me live."

"No."

"Then what can I do? Tell me, and I'll—" President Placido Rodriguez didn't get to finish begging for his life as Amberlyn raised the gun I'd given her from my collection and fired the first shot. Her decisiveness in stressful situations leaves me in awe of her. She did the same thing with Karen; Mermaid laid no blame on the woman who the Uriel brothers abused and forced an addiction upon.

Moreover, she offered to help them get settled after my guards retrieved her husband and reunited the pair shortly after we landed. And tomorrow, when they're back on American soil, I vowed to buy them the house this family promised and failed to deliver.

Following Mermaid's lead, I sank a bullet into his skull and then through his neck, as did those traveling with us. Every clip was emptied on a man worth shit, and who'd more than deserved the ending he got.

He ruined many lives and targeted my family, but his biggest mistake was threatening the safety of the woman intertwining her fingers with mine as we exit. She comes above all others, my biggest sacred rule, and I'd bring him back from the dead and do it all over again if I could.

Cheers ring out in the streets as we exit the palace. Many dance, some cry, and others drink to the end of an era not worth mentioning in the history books. No, it's time to remember what once was and what will be again: a culture of beauty and happiness.

Thriving people. A united community.

The devil lives among them now; I'll be relocating here with Amberlyn by my side to start our own dynasty. Thiago has Miami. I'll control Cuba. And who knows where the future generations will go.

Yet this place will always be home.

They'll live in peace, and I'll have my ports, and no one steps out of line.

I want a future here. With her, my sirenita.

In the back of the chauffeur's car, Amberlyn rests her head on my shoulder, still holding my hand. "Are you ready to start the next chapter with me, Ivan?"

A simple answer. No hesitation.

"Yes." What's more, I kiss her temple and nuzzle the soft skin there. "But I don't want one chapter, bebe." In my pocket, I've been carrying a ring since she disappeared. When I knew I couldn't let this treasure slip through my fingers again. "Today, tomorrow, and always. I want to own all the tomorrows we have left to share."

"Papi, that's so—"

"Marry me, Amberlyn Ibarra. Claim my future as I've already laid claim to yours."

"Yes."

Epilogue
IVAN

EIGHT MONTHS LATER…

"YOU'RE FREE TO go," I say, tapping the metal door keeping Kyle Montgomery trapped inside a small room in the basement of the private estate Amberlyn and I built in Cuba. He was smuggled in with Henry months ago, kept on the family compound, and then moved here when the accommodations were finished. I didn't kill him. Instead, I served as judge and jury while serving him with a one-year sentence that I'm ending today for good behavior. "My men will escort you home."

"I'm free?" He stands from the cot and walks to the metal bars of the door. This room isn't like the standard jail where my livestock roams and eats on the compound, but more refined. It's on the lower level of the main house; comes with basic human commodities and three meals a day. After all, I do plan to do business with the man.

He has connections. New routes to move merchandise.

Thiago also sees this now, and I plan to exploit every single one of them for my family's gain.

The U.S. needs him—the weapons he procures—and I want their money. For the name of every member of the Imperium to have legal immunity.

"You are."

"Thank—"

"Under one condition."

Apprehension dawns on his face. "What do you need?"

"Two things." Unlocking the door, I block the entrance and let him see the men standing behind me. Every member and their right-hand men are spread about the open area leading to this room. They watch him. Dare him to deny us. "You buy your weapons from the De Leons, and do what you're told and when. No questions asked. This is your opportunity to make a friend out of us, Montgomery. A friend helps and facilitates political advancements while an enemy will kill you, your son, and every male with your bloodline running through their veins." He's shaking, his eyes darting across each face before coming back to mine. "Do you agree?"

"Yes."

"Then welcome to South Florida. You'll be living here from now on." One of the guards from Miami comes forward and grabs Montgomery by the arm, leading him out and onto an awaiting plane that'll take him home. He'll be shadowed. So will his family. A single step out of line, and I won't hesitate to put a bullet between his eyes.

Just steps from the door leading upstairs, he pauses and looks back, brows furrowed. "What's the second condition?"

"You owe me quite the large amount of paperwork, beginning with the deal you had with Rodriguez and those prior. I want a legally binding trace to every weapon you've ever sold and the information on the buyers."

"I can do that."

"Then go and enjoy your freedom, Kyle. Your family misses you."

He's led out while the others begin to talk. We have plans.

Ambitions.

The Imperium is too large to contain, and many have taken notice.

We have a hand in every major industry except one: printing. However, acquiring Henry's machines have become the catalyst to change that as Malcolm will do more than just move and withhold money at his banks. The others approve as well. It transforms our plans a bit, but it'll be worth it to one day soon become the world bank and treasury. The Imperium's growth is what matters, as will our worldwide control over countries where it hurts them the most: money.

"You ready to get hitched the right way, bro?" Thiago asks, slapping my back while wearing a shit-eating grin. Singao. "It's about time, too."

"Fuck you." I know he knows, but I'll be damned if I admit it.

"Is that how you speak to my sister-in-law? No wonder I saw her flirting with—"

"Leave my son out of this, Thiago." Malcolm steps in beside us, just as amused. "Maximus is irresistible. Not his fault Amberlyn fell in love with his impeccable charm."

"This is where I leave you assholes. I have a bride to visit."

"You're not supposed to see her until after the wedding!" a British voice calls out, and I flip off Casper.

"So immature." That came from Javier. He's just as bad as the rest of them.

"Did any of you?" That quiets them all. Not a single peep. "Thought so."

Leaving them to talk, I quietly make my way up the stairs and onto our floor. Luna and Nat are with her, talking, but I bypass them and greet my mermaid with a passionate kiss.

Our wedding won't be a formal affair. Neither of us wanted it that way, and after going back and forth with our parents, they backed off. We live on the water and enjoy nothing more than cooking out, having a few drinks, and then taking a night swim when the weather allows it.

"You look beautiful, bebe." And she does. Amberlyn's wearing a floor-length white sundress with small sunflowers in the palest yellow, her feet bare. Her red hair is down, no more black chunks, and curly at the ends in a way that looks effortless. No makeup. No fuss. "You are simply perfect."

"As are you." I'm wearing an all-white guayabera and linen pants. Something I've discovered the woman currently biting her lips while eyeing my tattoos enjoys. Says they stand out more. "So handsome, papi."

"You ready to pretend this is our first time?"

"Our parents would literally kill us if they knew."

The day after I killed Placido Rodriguez, we wed on a beach in Varadero by the resort's Catholic father. We were lucky they had the service. Sometimes couples elope, and he performed the traditional vows with Israel and Junior as our witnesses.

After convincing Amberlyn to marry me today, she had one request: out on the water.

My mermaid wanted to feel the warm ocean lapping at our feet while the starry sky blessed this union. And I could never deny her. Not when she looks at me as if I'm her world.

She's wrong on that, though. I'm going to show her every day that I live and breathe for her.

I'll never take what we have for granted again. We do this together.

Tomorrow. Always.

"Do you, Ivan De Leon, take this woman to be your lawful wedded wife? Do you pledge this before God and man, to love and honor, through sunshine and dark times? Do you promise to love and hold, forsaking all others until death separates you? If so, answer "I do."

"I do. In this life and every single one that follows."

"Good." The Catholic priest looks over at Amberlyn, smiling while my mermaid sniffs. A few tears fell from her eyes, and I wipe them away gently. "And do you, Amberlyn Ibarra—"

"I do. All of it."

The priest chuckles. "I didn't ask."

"We both know it's the same question, sir." Her gaze turns to mine. So soft and full of love. "I do, Ivan. Always, will."

"Then I guess I have—"

Whatever he said after didn't matter. It all became background noise because a few seconds later, I was kissing my wife. The future mother of my children.

Best decision we ever made.

That was the blank page we needed after so much heartache, and I wouldn't change it for the world.

Yet, we knew we'd have to do something like this at one point to make those waiting downstairs happy. Her father deserved to walk her down the aisle, and the mothers needed something to fuss over.

That is, until we have a mini mermaid or killer of our own.

Reaching around her back, I fist the airy material and pull it up, exposing her to the mirror behind her. "Fuck, I'm a lucky man."

"Yes. You are." There's a teasing tone to her, a naughty gleam in her eyes, and I spread her wide. Saliva pools quickly in my mouth and I swallow hard, tightening my grip on her bottom as white lace teases me.

I'm hard at once. Throbbing at the sight of my baby in a pair of crotchless panties that exposes her pretty cunt and puckered hole on display, the latter of which is stretched full by a green jeweled plug that's my favorite. It's a little on the small side, but enough to prepare her for my girth.

Amberlyn likes to wear it for hours when wanting to play. Tempt me to lose control.

I also can't help it and touch the area, tapping the end where her hole clenches around the smooth metal.

She's wet, and it coats her inner thighs. Her pussy is bare and wanting.

"Hands on the mirror, bebe."

"Ivan, we need to—"

"Hands on the fucking mirror." Bending a bit more, she spreads her legs and complies. This gives me access to her pussy, so slick and pink. I can't fuck her how I want, but she'll be walking down the makeshift aisle slick with me.

I run the blunt head along her lips, coating the tip twice. "Fuck, you're soft and wet. So ready for me."

"Your fault," she whines when I don't slip inside. "The last few nights you've been talking shop late into the night."

"My apologies, sweetheart." I tap her toy next and rub our combined juices over the green emerald. Not fake, and I desecrate it just the same. "You'll have me at your disposal for a month. We're leaving for Greece tonight."

"Oh shit!" she cries. It's a little muffled behind my hand as I cover her mouth. Her parents should be up here soon to get her. "That's amazing, papi. Thank you."

"My pleasure," I grit out before slamming in, not able to take the torture of simply grazing her slit with the head anymore. "Knew you'd be excited."

"I am," she moans, gyrating against me as I pick up the pace. We won't last long. Not with the way she's gripping me—it's near painful, but I punch through it. My next few thrusts force her onto the tips of her toes, her wild eyes meeting mine in the mirror, but it's the pure look of bliss on her face when I slip two fingers to her front and pinch her clit that my girl lets go.

Amberlyn comes hard, milking me, and I follow shortly after. All it took is to feel her juices graze my balls while her walls quivered.

I fill her with my seed and then rub it against her slit and thighs in between a few lazy pumps.

The smile on her face afterward is sweet and satiated. Well worth the fact we are late to our own casual-style wedding, and many give us knowing looks.

Not that I care; I wear her ownership of me with pride.

"Better, bebe?"

"Much." Turning, she lets the dress fall as it may and then stands on the tips of her toes to kiss my chin. "You ready to make an honest woman of me for the second time, papi?"

"Every day."

"And all the tomorrows."

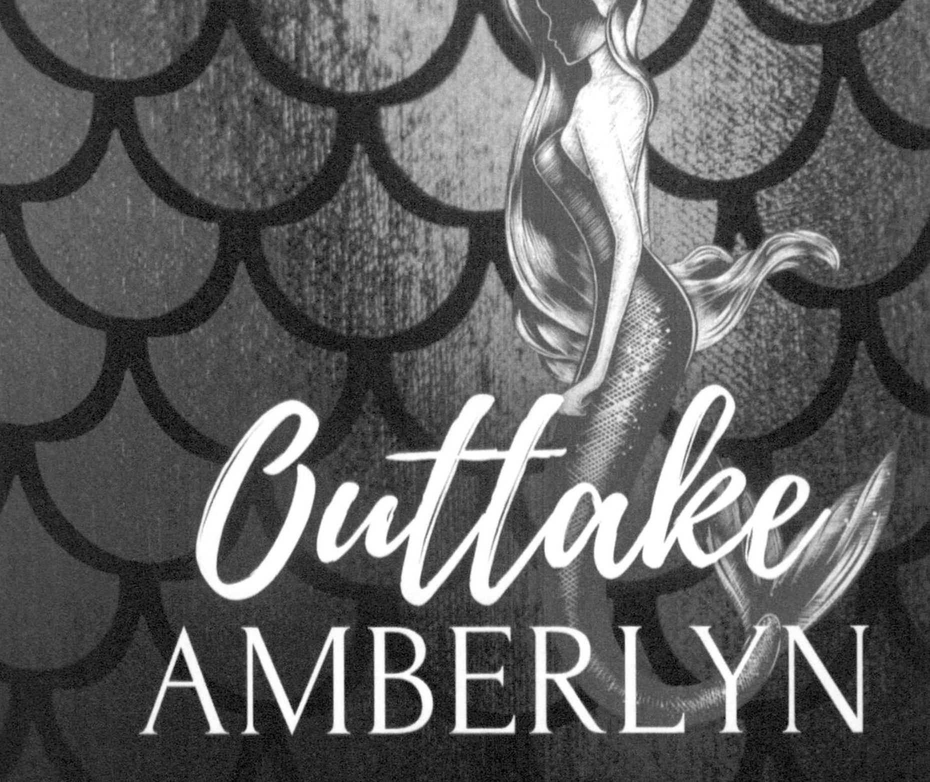

THE DAY WE MADE A COCK…

"HOW DO I let you talk me into these things," Ivan grumbles, giving me a glare when he's the one who bought the thing. "You owe me for this."

"Better yet, how do you figure it's my fault?" At my perplexed look, he only huff standing in the middle of my kitchen while holding his hard cock inside of a casting canister with the name *Clone-A-Willy* labeled on the front. "You're the one who got all upset because I was looking at a real-skin ten-inch toy. If anything, control the jealousy and you wouldn't be in this predicament."

"Are you really giving me lip as I clone my dick for you?'

"If the cast fits." His lips twitch at that response, and I lose it, doubling over while tears gather at the corners of my eyes. This—the ridiculousness of the situation—is us.

Ivan doesn't want to put a label on us, yet he can't stand the idea of me so much as looking at anyone, or any toy, sexually. Hence, he's naked in my kitchen and making me a silicone copy of his *willy.*

"You're enjoying this a little too much, bebe."

"Same as you watching my tits jiggle when I giggle."

"Touché." Scratching at his jaw, Ivan purses his lips. "And I'll also admit I'm a little overwhelming at times. It's part of the charm."

"If you say so." Walking to the fridge, I open it and bend a bit to reach the last can of Dr. Pepper in the back. "Do you want a Coke?"

"Yes."

"Diet or cherry?"

"Doesn't matter to me." The gruffness in his tone sweeps across my skin and goose bumps rise, my nipples tightening into stiff peaks that rub against the cotton of my shirt. I'm not wearing anything underneath. Never do when I'm at home. "Fuck, I think it's almost done. Should be ready to pour soon."

"Okay." What else can I say? His dick is occupied, and that tone never fails to turn me on.

Behave, Amberlyn. Don't come off as desperate.

"Yeah, it's getting tight. And warm, too."

"Wonderful." *Calm your breathing. You can get off later.*

"Perfect pocket pussy if I could lube it up and move."

"Hmm." That's my eloquent reply, which was no more than a squeak while shoving my head just a little bit deeper into the fridge, pretending to search for something before standing back up. That same fridge has its door slammed closed a second later when a strong chest presses against my back. "Did you need something?"

"Your pussy riding my tongue."

"I thought we were—"

"Or you could bounce a few times on my cock, Mermaid. For research purposes."

"Research?" I parrot, my body feeling flushed. Sweat is beading at my temple. "You want me to compare?"

"Yes." Ivan lifts the now-filled container with the silicone substance and places it in my hand. *When did he mix the solutions? How did I miss it?* "Hold tight, and don't spill. I'm going to test a theory."

"A theory?"

"For research purposes, I want to see what it takes for my mermaid to lose control. I want to hear her beg for my cock, cry for it, but I'm going to gradually test her. Tease her." Fisting the back of my shirt, he stretches the material tight against my chest. The friction feels so good. "Turnabout is fair play, don't you agree?"

"But I haven't—"

"So you walking around without a bra or shorts is normal? You spend your days in nothing but these barely-there shirts and cheekies?"

"I'm at home, and it's comfortable."

His audible groan makes me press my thighs together. "Keep talking. What else do you do when—"

He's cut off by a knock on my front door and the sound of my mother calling my name. Gone is the heat from a moment ago, the sensuality that comes freely when I'm with him. I toss the willy-goop and container in the freezer while rushing to my laundry room for a pair of sweats.

Not that Ivan is any better.

The boy is dressed, all contents of our experiment gone, and now drumming his fingers in my kitchenette while drinking my Dr. Pepper. The last one. All innocent-like, too.

"Mamita, are you home?" she calls through the door. "I got juicy gossip about your cousin, Yuli."

Christ. Please help me.

This is too much, and when I meet Ivan's eyes again, he's chuckling to himself.

"What now?"

"I'm pretty sure we're going to have to buy another kit and do this all over again."

Turn the page for some Beautiful Sinner News!!!!

BEAUTIFUL SINNER NEWS…

Wow. Just Wow.

I truly can't believe that we're here at the end of this series. Is it the end of my Beautiful Sinners? No. But this chapter has come to a close. When I started SIN, I always thought it to be a standalone, until certain characters made an appearance. Casper and Thiago made their presence known, and before I was halfway done writing SIN, I knew…

Knew it would be so much more.

But now it's time to meet the next generation.

Starting in early 2025, Beautiful Heir will be their kids' time to shine, fall in love, and kill a lot of people. My GOD, they are just as vicious, if not more, than their parents. LOL

And up first is Malcolm's son, *Maximus.*

He's been whispering to me.

Showing me things, and I already have a doc full of little notes for the future owner of Asher Holdings.

Now, I do have some spinoffs planned and a special standalone coming up first.

Kray and his girl: Met them in RISQUE
Kyle Bennett (Business Tycoon): Met them in YOURS

THE IMPERIUM (Special Project)

Follow me on social media to keep to date. I'll be posting more info soon.

Thank you so much for reading and loving these books.

I love you all to the moon and back,

Elena XoXo

BEAUTIFUL SINNER SERIES

<u>BEAUTIFUL SINNER SERIES</u>
<u>Each book is a standalone.</u>
<u>Now Live!</u>

SIN (#1)
COVET (#2)
MINE (#3)
YOURS (#4)
RISQUE #5
OWN #6

Beautiful Sinner Spin-Off
CORRUPT
MY SINFUL VALENTINE
SAVAGE KISS

ABOUT THE AUTHOR

Elena M. Reyes was born and raised in Miami, Florida. She is the epitome of a Floridian and if she could live in her beloved flip-flops, she would.

As a small child, she was always intrigued with all forms of art—whether it was dancing to island rhythms, or painting with any medium she could get her hands on. Her first taste of writing came to her during her fifth-grade year when her class was prompted to participate in the D. A. R. E. Program and write an essay on what they'd learned.

Her passion for reading over the years has amassed her with hours of pleasure. It wasn't until she stumbled upon fanfiction that her thirst to write overtook her world. She now resides in Central Florida with her husband and son, spending all her down time letting her creativity flow and characters grow.

Website: https://www.elenamreyes.com/

Find My Books Here:
https://www.bookbub.com/authors/elena-m-reyes

Email: Reyes139ff@gmail.com

FB Reader Group:
Elena's Marked Girls. Come join the naughty fun.
Link: https://www.facebook.com/groups/1710869452526025/

facebook.com/ElenaMReyesAuthor
x.com/ElenaMReyes
instagram.com/elenar139
bookbub.com/profile/elena-m-reyes
tiktok.com/@elenamreyes

ALSO BY ELENA M. REYES

FATE'S BITE SERIES

LITTLE LIES

LITTLE MATE

HALF TRUTHS DUET

HALF TRUTHS: THEN

HALF TRUTHS: NOW

OMISSION

TERO (TBD)

MARCIA (TBD)

BEAUTIFUL SINNER SERIES

Each book is a standalone.

Now Live!

SIN (#1)

COVET (#2)

MINE (#3)

YOURS (#4)

RISQUE #5

OWN #6

Beautiful Sinner Spin-Off

CORRUPT

MY SINFUL VALENTINE

SAVAGE KISS

ONE RULE

(BOOK #2 LIONEL TBD)

(Marked Series)

Marking Her #1

Marking Him #2

Scars #2.5

Marked #3

(I Saw You)

I Saw You

I Love You #1.5

Teasing Hands Duet

Teasing Hands #1

Taunting Lips #2

SAFE ROMANCE:

Taste Of You

Doctor's Orders

Back To You

STANDALONES:

Craving Sugar

Stolen Kisses